The Adventures Of Heine by Edgar Wallace

Richard Horatio Edgar Wallace was born on the 1st April 1875 in Greenwich, London. Leaving school at 12 because of truancy, by the age of fifteen he had experience; selling newspapers, as a worker in a rubber factory, as a shoe shop assistant, as a milk delivery boy and as a ship's cook.

By 1894 he was engaged but broke it off to join the Infantry being posted to South Africa. He also changed his name to Edgar Wallace which he took from Lew Wallace, the author of *Ben-Hur*.

In Cape Town in 1898 he met Rudyard Kipling and was inspired to begin writing. His first collection of ballads, *The Mission that Failed!* was enough of a success that in 1899 he paid his way out of the armed forces in order to turn to writing full time.

By 1904 he had completed his first thriller, *The Four Just Men*. Since nobody would publish it he resorted to setting up his own publishing company which he called Tallis Press.

In 1911 his Congolese stories were published in a collection called *Sanders of the River*, which became a bestseller. He also started his own racing papers, *Bibury's* and *R. E. Walton's Weekly*, eventually buying his own racehorses and losing thousands gambling. A life of exceptionally high income was also mirrored with exceptionally large spending and debts.

Wallace now began to take his career as a fiction writer more seriously, signing with Hodder and Stoughton in 1921. He was marketed as the 'King of Thrillers' and they gave him the trademark image of a trilby, a cigarette holder and a yellow Rolls Royce. He was truly prolific, capable not only of producing a 70,000 word novel in three days but of doing three novels in a row in such a manner. It was in, estimating that by 1928 one in four books being read was written by Wallace, for alongside his famous thrillers he wrote variously in other genres, including science fiction, non-fiction accounts of WWI which amounted to ten volumes and screen plays. Eventually he would reach the remarkable total of 170 novels, 18 stage plays and 957 short stories.

Wallace became chairman of the Press Club which to this day holds an annual Edgar Wallace Award, rewarding 'excellence in writing'.

Diagnosed with diabetes his health deteriorated and he soon entered a coma and died of his condition and double pneumonia on the 7th of February 1932 in North Maple Drive, Beverly Hills. He was buried near his home in England at Chalklands, Bourne End, in Buckinghamshire.

Index Of Contents

1 — ALEXANDER AND THE LADY

Secret Service work is a joke in peace time and it is paid on joke rates. People talk of the fabulous sums of money which our Government spend on this kind of work, and I have no doubt a very large sum was spent every year, but it had to go a long way. Even Herr Kressler, of the Bremen-America Line, who gave me my monthly cheque, used to nod and wink when he handed over my two hundred marks.

"Ah, my good Heine," he would say, stroking his stubbly beard, "they make a fool of me, the Government, but I suppose I mustn't ask who is your other paymaster?"

"Herr Kessler," said I earnestly, "I assure you that this is the whole sum I receive from the Government."

"So!" he would say and shake his head: "Ah, you are close fellows, and I mustn't ask questions!"

There was little to do save now and again to keep track of some of the bad men, the extreme Socialists, and the fellows who ran away from Germany to avoid military service. I often wished there were more, because it would have been possible to have made a little on one's expenses. Fortunately, two or three of the very big men in New York and Chicago knew the work I was doing, and credited me with a, much larger income than I possessed. The reputation of being well off is a very useful one, and in my case brought me all sorts of commissions and little tips which I could profitably exploit on Wall Street, and in one way or another I lived comfortably, had a nice apartment on Riverside Drive, backed horses, and enjoyed an occasional trip to Washington, at my Governments expense.

I first knew that war was likely to break out in July. I think we Germans understood the European situation much better than the English and certainly much better than the Americans, and we knew that the event at Sarajevo — by the way, poor Klein of our service and an old colleague of mine, was killed by the bomb which was intended for the Archduke, though nobody seems to have noticed the fact — would produce the war which Austria had been expecting or seeking an excuse to wage for two years.

If I remember aright, the assassination was committed on the Sunday morning. The New York papers published the story on that day, and on the Monday afternoon I was summoned to Washington, and saw the Secretary, who was in charge of our Department on the Tuesday evening after dinner.

The Secretary was very grave and told me that war was almost certain, and that Austria was determined to settle with Serbia for good, but that it was feared that Russia would come in and that the war could not be localised because, if Russia made war, Germany and France would also be involved.

Personally, I have never liked the French, and my French is not particularly good. I was hoping that he was going to tell us that England was concerned and I asked him if this was not the case. To my disappointment, he told me that England would certainly not fight, that she would remain neutral, and that strict orders had been issued that nothing was to be done which would in any way annoy the English.

"Their army," he said, "is beneath contempt, but their navy is the most powerful in the world and its employment might have very serious consequences."

It seemed very early to talk about war with the newspapers still full of long descriptions of the Sarajevo murder and the removal of the Archduke's body and I remembered after with what astounding assurance our Secretary had spoken.

I must confess I was disappointed, because I had spent a very long time in England Scotland, Ireland, and Wales, establishing touch with good friends who, I felt, would work with advantage for me in the event of war. I had prepared my way by founding The Chinese News Bureau, a little concern that had an office in Fleet Street and was ostensibly engaged in collecting items of news concerning China and distributing them to the London and provincial press, and in forwarding a London letter to certain journals in Pekin, Tientsien and Shanghai.

Of course, the money was found by the Department, and it was not a financial success, but it was a good start in case one ever had to operate in London, since I was registered as a naturalised Chilean and it was extremely unlikely that Chile would be at war with any European Power.

On the 3rd August, 1914, I received a message from Washington in the Departmental code, telling me that war with England was inevitable and that I was to sail on the first boat and take up my duties in London in full control of the British Department.

I was overjoyed with the news and I know that men like Stohwasser, Wesser, and other men of my Department, looked at me with envy. They did not think they had an easy task because the American Secret Service is a very competent one; but they thought I was a lucky pig — as indeed I was — to be operating in a country containing a population of forty millions, most of whom, as one of their writers said, were fools.

I landed at Liverpool on August 11th. My passport was in order and I immediately went forward to London. There was no trace of any excitement. I saw a lot of soldiers on their way to their depots; and arriving in London, I immediately received the reports of our innumerable agents.

With what pride did I contemplate the splendid smoothness of our system! When the Emperor pressed the button marked "Mobilise," he called, in addition to his soldiers, a thousand gallant hearts and brilliant minds in a score of countries all eager and happy to work for the aggrandisement of our beloved Fatherland.

Six of us met at a fashionable restaurant near Trafalgar Square. There were Emil Stein who called himself Robinson, Karl Besser — I need not give all their aliases — Heine von Wetzl, Fritz von Kahn and Alexander Koos.

Stein had arrived from Holland the night before and Fritz von Kahn had come down from Glasgow where he had been acting as a hotel porter. These men were, as I say, known to me, and to one another, but there were thousands of unknowns who had their secret instructions, which were only to be opened in case of war and with whom we had to get in touch.

I briefly explained the procedure and the method by which our agents would be identified. Every German agent would prove his bona fides by producing three used postage stamps of Nicaragua. It is a simple method of identification, for there is nothing treasonable or suspicious in a man carrying about in his pocket-book, a ten, twenty or a fifty centime stamp of a neutral country.

I sent Emil Stein away to Portsmouth and instructed him to make contact with sailors of the Fleet especially with officers. Besser was dispatched to a West Coast shipping centre to report on all the boats which left and entered. I sent Kahn and his family on a motor-car tour to the East Coast with instructions to find out what new coast defences were being instituted.

"You must exercise the greatest care," I said; "even though these English are very stupid, they may easily blunder into a discovery. Make the briefest notes on all you see and hear and only use the Number 3 code in case of urgent necessity." We finished our dinner and we drank to "The Day" and sang under our breath "Deutschland uber Alles" and separated, Koos coming with me.

Koos was a staff officer of the Imperial Service, and though he was not noble he was held in the greatest respect. He was a fine, handsome fellow, very popular with the girls, and typically British in appearance. His English was as good as mine, and that is saying a great deal. I sent him to Woolwich because in his character as an American inventor — he had spent four years in the States — he was admirably fitted to pick up such facts as were of the greatest interest to the Government.

I did not see Koos for a few days and in the meantime I was very busy arranging with my couriers who were to carry the result of our discoveries through a neutral country to Germany. The system I adopted was a very simple one. My notes, written in Indian ink, were separately photographed by means of a camera. When I had finished the twelve exposures, I opened the camera in a dark room, carefully re-rolled the spool and sealed it, so that it had the appearance of being an unexposed pellicle. I argued that whilst the English military authorities would confiscate photographs which had obviously been taken, they might pass films which were apparently unused.

I had arranged to meet Koos on the night of August 17th, and made my way to the rendezvous, engaging a table for two. I bad hardly seated myself when, to my surprise, Koos came in accompanied by a very pretty English girl. He walked past me, merely giving me the slightest side-glance, and, seated himself at the next table. I was amused. I knew the weakness of our good Koos for the ladies, but I knew also that he was an excellent investigator and that he was probably combining business with pleasure In this I was right. The meal finished — and tho innocent laughter of the girl made me smile again — and Koos walked out with the girl on his arm.

As he passed my table he dropped a slip of paper which I covered with my table- napkin. When I was sure I was not observed, I read the note.

"Making excellent progress. Meet me at a quarter to eleven outside Piccadilly Tube."

I met him at the appointed time and we strolled into Jermyn Street.

"What do you think of her?" was Koos' first question.

"Very pretty, my friend," said I. "You have excellent taste."

He chuckled.

"I have also excellent luck, my dear Heine. That lady is the daughter of one of the chief gun-constructors at Woolwich."

He looked at me to note the effect of his words, and I must confess I was startled.

"Splendid, my dear fellow!" said I, warmly. "How did you come to meet her?"

"A little act of gallantry," he said airily; "a lady walking on Blackheath twists her ankle, what more natural than that I should offer her assistance to the nearest seat? Quite a babbling little person — typically English. She is a mine of information. An only daughter and a little spoilt, I am afraid, she knows no doubt secrets of construction of which the technical experts of the Government are ignorant. Can you imagine a German talking over military affairs with his daughter?"

"What have you learnt from her?" I asked.

Koos did. not reply for a moment, then he said: "So far, very little I am naturally anxious not to alarm her or arouse her suspicions. She is willing to talk and she has access to her father's study and, from what I gather, she practically keeps all the keys of the house. At present I am educating her to the necessity of preserving secrecy about our friendship and to do her justice, she is just as anxious that our clandestine meetings should not come to the ears of her father as I am."

We walked along in silence.

"This may be a very big thing," I said.

"Bigger than you imagine," replied Alexander; "there is certain to be an exchange of confidential views about artillery between the Allies, and though we have nothing to learn from the English it is possible that the French may send orders to Woolwich for armament. In that case our little friend may be a mine of information. I am working with my eyes a few months ahead," he said, " and for that reason I am allowing our friendship to develop slowly."

I did not see Koos again for a week, except that I caught a glimpse of him in the Cafe Riche with his fair companion. He did not see me, however, and as it was desirable that I should not intrude, I made no attempt to make my presence apparent.

At the end of the week we met by appointment, which we arranged through the agony column of a certain London newspaper. I was feeling very cheerful, for Stein, Besser, and Kahn had sent in most excellent reports, and it only needed Alexander's encouraging news to complete my sum of happiness.

"You remember the gun-lathe I spoke to you about," he said. "My friend — you may regard the blue prints as in your hands."

"How has this come about?"

"I just casually mentioned to my little girl that I was interested in inventions and that I had just put a new lathe upon the market in America and she was quite excited about it It. She asked me if I heard about the lathe at Woolwich, and I said that I had heard rumours that there was such a lathe. She was quite overjoyed at the opportunity of giving me information and asked me whether in the event of her showing me the prints I would keep the fact a great secret because," he laughed softly, "she did not think her father would like the print to leave his office!"

"You must be careful of this girl," I said, "she may be detected."

"There is no danger, my dear fellow," said Alexander. "She is the shrewdest little woman in the world. I am getting quite to like her if one can like these abominable people — she is such a child!"

I told him to keep in communication with me and sent him off feeling what the English call in "good form." I dispatched a courier by the morning train to the Continent, giving details of the British Expeditionary Force. Only two brigades were in France — and that after three weeks of preparation! In Germany every man was mobilized and at his corps or army headquarters weeks ago — every regiment had moved up to its order of battle position. Two brigades! It would be amusing if it were not pathetic!

Besser came to me soon after lunch in a very excited state.

"The whole of the British Expeditionary Force of three Divisions is in France," he said, "and, what is more, it is in line."

I smiled at him.

"My poor dear fellow, who has been pulling your foot?" I asked.

"It is confidentially communicated to the Press, and will be public to- morrow," he said.

"Lies," said I calmly, "you are too credulous. The English are the most stupid liars in the world."

I was not so calm that night when I ran down in my car to Gorselton, where our very good friend, the Baron von Hertz-Missenger, had a nice little estate.

"Heine," he said, after he had taken me to his study and shut the door. "I have received a radio through my wireless from Kreigsministerium [The Prussian Ministry of War] to the effect that the whole of the British Expeditionary Force has landed and is in line."

"Impossible, Herr Baron," I said, but he shook his head.

"It is true — our Intelligence in Belgium is infallible. Now, I do not want to interfere with you, for I am but a humble volunteer in this great work, but I advise you to give a little more attention to the army. We may have underrated the military assistance which Britain can offer."

"The English Army, Herr Baron," said I firmly, "is almost as insignificant a factor as — as well — the American army, which only exists on paper! Nevertheless, I will take your advice."

I went back to town and dispatched another courier, for as yet the Torpington Varnish Factory (about which I will tell you later) had not been equipped with radio.

That night I again saw Alexander. It was at supper at the Fritz, and he looked a fine figure of a man. I felt proud of the country which could produce such a type. Where, I ask you, amongst the paunchy English and the scraggy Scotch, with their hairy knees and their sheep-shank legs, could you find a counterpart of that beau sabreur? Cower treacherous Albion, shiver in your kilt, hateful Scotch (it is not generally known that the Royal and High-Born Prince Rupprecht of Bavaria is rightful King of Scotland.), tremble, wild Wales, and unreliable Ireland, when you come in arms against a land which can produce such men as Alexander Koos!

I never saw a girl look more radiantly happy than did the young woman who was sitting vis-a-vis my friend. There was a light in her eye and a colour in her cheeks which were eloquent of her joy.

I saw Alexander afterwards. He came secretly to my room.

"Have you brought the blue print?" I asked. He shook his head smilingly. "Tomorrow, my friend, not only the blue print of the lathe, not only the new gun-mounting model, but the lady herself will come to me. I want your permission to leave the day after to-morrow for home. I cannot afford to wait for what the future may bring."

"Can you smuggle the plans past the English police?" I asked, a little relieved that he had volunteered to act as courier on so dangerous a mission.

"Nothing easier."

"And the girl — have you her passport?"

He nodded.

"How far shall you take her?"

"To Rotterdam," he said promptly.

In a way I was sorry. Yes, I am sentimental, I fear, and "sentiment does not live in an agent's pocket" as the saying goes. I wish it could have been done without. I shrugged my shoulders and steeled my soul with the thought that she was English and that it was all for the Fatherland.

"You must come to the Cafe Riche tonight and witness our going," said Alexander; "you will observe that she will carry a leather case such as schoolgirls use for their books and exercises. In that, case, my friend, will be enough material to keep our friends in Berlin busy for a month."

I took leave of him giving him certain instructions as to the course he was to take after reporting at Headquarters, and spent the rest of the night coding a message for our Alexander to carry with him. The hour at which Alexander was to meet the girl was eight o'clock in the evening.

His table (already booked) was No. 47, which is near the window facing Piccadilly. I telephoned through to the cafe and booked No. 46, for I was anxious to witness the comedy.

All was now moving like clockwork — and let me say that the smoothness of the arrangements was due largely to the very thorough and painstaking organisation- work which I had carried out in the piping days of peace. We Germans have a passion for detail and for thoroughness and for this reason (apart from the inherent qualities of simplicity and honesty, apart from the superiority of our kultur and our lofty idealism) we have been unconquerable throughout the ages.

You must remember that I was in London as the representative of a Chinese News Bureau. I was also an agent for a firm of importers in Shanghai. It was therefore only natural that I should be called up all hours of the day and night with offers of goods.

"I can let you have a hundred and twenty bales of Manchester goods at 125."

Now 120 and 125 added together make 245, and turning to my "simple code", to paragraph 245, I find the following:

"2nd Battalion of the Graniteshire Regiment entrained to-day for embarkation."

The minor agents carried this code (containing 1,400 simple sentences to covet all naval or military movements) in a small volume. The code is printed on one side of very thin paper leaves, and the leaves are as porous and absorbent as blotting paper.

One blot of ink dropped upon a sheet will obliterate a dozen — a fact which our careless agents have discovered. Clipped in. tho centre of the book (as a pencil is clipped in an ordinary book) is a tiny tube of the thinnest glass containing a quantity of black dye-stuff. The agent fearing detection has only to press the cover of the book sharply and the contents of the book are reduced to black sodden pulp. Need I say that this ingenious invention was German in its origin.

[As a matter of fact, it was invented by the American Secret Service— E.W.]

My days were therefore very full. There came reports from all quarters and some the most unlikely. How, you may ask, did our agents make these discoveries?

There are many ways by which information is conveyed. The relations of soldiers are always willing to talk about their men and will tell you, if they know, when they are leaving the ships they are leaving by, and will sometimes give you other important facts, but particularly about ports and dates of embarkations are they useful.

Also officers will occasionally talk at lunch and dinner and will tell their women folk military secrets which a waiter can mentally note and convey to the proper quarters. Our best agents, however, were barbers, tailors, chiropodists, and dentists. English people will always discuss matters with a barber or with the man who is fitting them with their clothes, and as almost every tailor was making military uniforms and a very large number of the tailors in London were either German or Austrian, I had quite a wealth of news.

Tailors are useful because they work to time. Clothes have to be delivered by a certain date and generally the man who has the suit made will tell the fitter the date he expects to leave England. Other useful investigators are Turkish- bath attendants and dentists. A man in a dentist's chair is always nervous and will try to make friends with the surgeon who is operating on him.

Of all agencies the waiter is in reality the least useful, because writers have been pointing out for so many years the fact that most waiters were German. But the truth is that most restaurant waiters are Italian, and it is amongst the bedroom waiters that you can find a preponderance of my fellow countrymen.

Prompt at eight o'clock, I took my place at the table and ordered an excellent dinner (my waiter was naturally a good German) and a bottle of Rhenish wine. A few minutes after I had given my order

Alexander and the girl arrived. She was dressed in a long travelling coat of tussore silk, and carried — as I was careful to note — a shiny brown leather portfolio. This she placed carefully on be lap when she sat down and raised her veil.

She looked a little pale, but smiled readily enough at Alexander's jests. I watched her as she slowly peeled off her gloves and unbuttoned her coat. Her eyes were fixed on vacancy. Doubtless her conscience was pricking her.

Is it the thought of thy home, little maid from whence thou hast fled never to return? Is it the anguished picture of thy broken-hearted and ruined father bemoaning his daughter and his honour? Have no fear, little one, thy treason shall enrich the chosen of the German God, those World Encirclers, Foreordained and Destined to Imperial Grandeur!

So I thought, watching her and listening.

"Are you sure that everything will be all right?" she asked anxiously.

"Please trust me," smiled Alexander. (Oh, the deceiving rogue — how I admired his sang-froid!)

"You are ready to go — you have packed?" she asked.

"As ready as you, my dear Elsie. Come — let me question you," he bantered; "have you all those wonderful plans which are going to make our fortunes after we are married?

So he had promised that — what would the gracious Frau Koos- Mettleheim have said to this perfidy on the part of her husband?

"I have all the plans," she began, but he hushed her with a warning glance.

I watched the dinner proceed but heard very little more. All the time she seemed to be plying him with anxious questions to which he returned reassuring answers. They had reached the sweets when she began to fumble at her pocket. I guessed (rightly) that she was seeking a handkerchief and (wrongly) that she was crying.

Her search was fruitless and she beckoned the waiter.

"I left a little bag in the ladies' room — it has my handkerchief; will you ask the attendant to send the bag?"

The waiter departed and presently returned with two men in the livery of the hotel. I was sitting side by side and could see the faces both of the girl and Alexander and I noticed the amusement in his face that two attendants must come to carry one small bag.

Then I heard the girl speak.

"Put your hands, palms upward, on the table," she said I was still looking at Alexander's face. First amazement and then anger showed — then I saw his face go grey and into is eyes crept the fear of death. The girl was holding an automatic pistol and the barrel was pointing at Alexander's breast. She half turned her head to the attendants.

"Here is your man, sergeant she said briskly. "Alexander Roos, alias Ralph Burton-Smith. I charge him with espionage."

They snapped the steel handcuffs upon Alexander's wrists and led him out, the girl following. I rose unsteadily and followed. In the vestibule was quite a small crowd which had gathered at the first rumour of so remarkable a sensation. Here, for the first time, Alexander spoke, and it was curious bow in his agitation his perfect English became broken and hoarse.

"Who are you? You have a mistake maken, my frient."

"I am an officer of the British Intelligence Department," said the girl.

"Himmel! Secret Service!" gasped Alexander, "I thought it was not!"

I saw them take him away and stole home.

They had trapped him. The girl with the sprained ankle had been waiting for him that day on Blackheath. She led him on by talking of the plans she could get until he had told her of the rough plans he already had. Whilst (as he thought) he was tightening the net about her, she was drawing the meshes tighter about him... Phew! It makes me hot to think of it!

Was there a secret service in England after all? For myself, my tracks were too well covered; for Alexander I could do nothing. He would not betray me. I was sure of that. Yet to be perfectly certain I left the next night for Dundee, and I was in Dundee when the news came that Alexander had been shot in the Tower of London.

2 — THE MAN WHO DWELT ON A HILL

When I left London hurriedly, after the arrest of Alexander Koos, I must confess that my mind was greatly disturbed. I sat half the night in my sleeper, turning over all the circumstances leading up to the arrest of my good friend. We Germans are the most logical people in the world. We argue with precision from known facts, and we deduce from those facts such subtle conclusions as naturally flow.

We do not indulge in frivolous speculations — we Germans are a serious people with a passion for accurate data.

Thus I argued: (1) if a secret police force bad been established it is a post- war creation. Otherwise our general staff would have known of its existence and have advised us. (2) Supposing a secret service had been initiated where would its agents be found? Naturally in the vicinity of the great arsenals and military camps. Under these circumstances it was not surprising that Koos, confining his investigations to Woolwich, had been brought into contact with a member this new organisation. (3) It was humanly impossible that the operations of an improvised secret service could be extended in a few days to areas other than military and arsenal areas. Therefore it behoved the investigator to avoid as far as possible arousing suspicion by pursuing his inquiries in the neighbourhood of arsenals and camps.

At eight o'clock in the morning I was taking my breakfast in the station- buffet at Edinburgh. Von Kahn was awaiting me, and over the meal, served by sleepy waitress, I had an opportunity of retailing the events which had I to my hasty departure from London. Von Kahn stroked his moustache thoughtfully.

"Koos was an impetuous man," he said. "I am not surprised that he has been detected. You must not forget, my dear Heine, that we Germans have only one thought, only one goal, the welfare of the Fatherland. Koos allowed his penchant for feminine society to overcome his judgment. That is a mistake which should never make."

I looked at our good Von Kahn, with his big red face and his short, well-fed body, and I could not help thinking that it would be indeed a remarkable circumstance if he allowed himself to be lured to destruction in such a manner.

He joined the train and went on with me to Dundee. We had not gone far from the station before the train stopped and an attendant came in and pulled down all the blinds, removing, in spite of our protest, all our baggage, which he locked in an empty compartment.

"What is the meaning of this?" I demanded.

"I am very sorry, sir," said the man "but those are my orders."

For a moment I had a cold feeling inside me that I was suspected, but his next words reassured me.

"We do it to everybody, sir, before we cross the — Bridge."

When he had gone I turned to von Kahn. "This is an extraordinary thing," I said. "I never suspected the English of taking such intelligent precautions."

Von Kahn laughed.

"The English here are Scots," he said, "and they are very cautious."

I should have dearly liked to peep out when the rumble of the wheels told we were passing the famous bridge, but in the corridor outside the carriage discovered, to my amazement, a Scottish soldier with fixed bayonet, and for some reason or other his eyes never left us.

It was not until we were a very long way past the bridge that the attendant returned my bag and suit-case and pulled up the blind, and not until we reached Dundee that I discussed the matter at with von Kahn.

"I have reason to believe he said, "that we have passed a portion of the British Fleet, and it will be my endeavour during the next few days to discover what units are at present in the region of Rosyth."

He told me this in the cab on the way to our hotel and he also gave me a great of deal of information about the East Coast defences which it had been his business to investigate.

"It is practically impossible to get near the important parts of the coast," he said, "and I think you must give up all idea of establishing light-signal stations at X and Q."

This was a sad disappointment to me, which I did not attempt to bide.

"My dear von Kahn," I said testily, "you are getting hypnotised by the English. You are giving them credit for gifts which are not theirs. You are imagining that these people, these Scots for example, have the same keen national sense of suspicion as we Germans possess."

We drove the rest of the journey to an hotel in silence. I registered here in the name by which I was known to the Chilean Legation. I had never been in Dundee before and I hope I may never see the town again, for reasons which will be sufficiently obvious to all the good friends who read my narrative.

My local agent here was a barber named Schmidt, and the first thing I did on my arrival at the hotel was to send for a barber! What was more natural than that a weary traveller should require shaving! Ah! do not smile, my friends! By such acts of forethought and detail was our great service built up and wonderfully established. Our good friend came with his little black bag and was admitted to my room. The honest fellow was almost overcome by the sight of one whom he regarded as being a veritable link between himself and his "Supreme War Lord".

"It is beautiful to be able to speak our noble German tongue again," he said; "think of it, Herr Heine! Here I am week in and week out talking Scotch — not even English."

He had much to tell me that I committed to memory. He even had had the good fortune to be called in professionally to an admiral who was passing through Dundee on the way to a certain town in the north.

"Naturally," said Schmidt "I was extremely tactful and suspicion-avoiding. But, Herr Heine, not even the high officers of State know discretion. Reticence is not!"

"I wish you'd take me with you, Sir Jones," I said; he was well-born and had been created a Sir for war knowledge."

"Come along," said Sir Jones, "but I'm afraid you will not be comfortable when our fleet goes into action next week against Heligoland."

"That is a strong fortress, Admiral, I said."

"We have been undermining it for a month," said Sir Jones.

"Herr Heine I nearly fainted with excitement. Consider the position. Here was I, a faithful servant of the Fatherland listening to one of the most important military secrets from an Excellency of the English Navy. I kept my blood cool and went on lathering without a tremble of hand. " 'That must have been terribly difficult Sir Jones,' I said. 'Not at all,' said Sir Jones; 'we have a new submarine on wheels that creeps along the bed of the ocean and fortunately there are beneath Heligoland several very large caves in which our divers can store explosives. I trust you will regard all I have told you as confidential!'"

By the time Schmidt had finished I was on my feet. I knew that there had been a secret vote or appropriation for the British Navy a year before. So this was the reason. "Send Herr von Kahn to me, you will find him in Room 84," I said; and long before my companion had arrived I was working at my codes.

"We must find a way to get this information to Germany," I said.

"The way is simple," said he; "the Sven Gustavus is in harbour waiting to clear for Bergen. She has wireless, and outside of the territorial waters she can get into touch with the Bremen wireless station."

The message I sent was a large code, and I have since learnt that it created something like a sensation at the Admiralty. All the warships in the vicinity of Heligoland were ordered away, the Corps of Divers came from Cuxhaven and the foundations of the island were thoroughly explored, although the Admiralty Marine Survey Department was emphatic on the point that no caverns existed under the island. As a matter of fact none were discovered, though a certain suspicious-looking hole was found in one of the rocks.

[This is not an extravagant story of German credulity but is based upon the fact. The more improbable a story was at the beginning of the war, particularly in regard to the British Navy, the more eagerly did the German Admiralty swallow it. — E.W.]

We stopped at the top of the hill and von Kahn pointed out the shooting-box which stood on the crest of the farther rise — a little white building.

"Our Mr. Brown is at home," he said and pointed to the flag, a yellow flag with a red lion in the centre, the same being the secret standard of Scotland, which is always flown in defiance of the English, whose banner is the Union Jack. We had discussed our plans thoroughly the night before because, obviously, nothing could be left to the last, and it would have been extremely dangerous to have talked in the presence of the chauffer of our hired car.

I have always made it a point to have no dealings with anybody outside our own service, and I had arranged with von Kahn to undertake all negotiations with this stranger. I said good-bye to my friend and wished him good luck, and I watched him as be descended a steep footpath and walked along the little road that led to the farther hill.

I sent the chauffeur back to the main road, telling him to rejoin me at noon, and profitably spent the time of waiting by exploring ground and coding a message on the Swiss incident, for transmission to Germany. Through my glasses I could watch from time to time the progress of my comrade. I saw him climb the hill and stand before the door of the cottage, and presently a man came out! They talked together for about ten minutes and then they both disappeared into the interior.

It was not until half ten that von Kahn made his appearance again. I saw him shake hands with his host and wave his hand cheerily and three-quarters of an hour later he rejoined me on the crest of the hill.

"Well ?" I asked. There was no need to ask von Kahn His eyes were gleaming with. triumph.

"I can only say," said he, "that our Mr. Brown is a remarkable man."

"In what way?"

"He speaks German, he reads German, and he is German," said von Kahn emphatically, "he has a library of all the German classics. I discovered that when he was out of the room. His flag-post obviously supports a, wireless aerial in the night-time, and although he is bland and uncommunicative, I have no doubt whatever about his character. He is one of the Higher Service."

I nodded.

"Did he give you any hint — ?" I began.

"Not a word," said von Kahn emphatically: "he speaks splendid English, is well acquainted with Australia, and pretends that he is a wealthy pleasure seeker with no other interest than fishing and shooting."

"I hope you were tactful," I said suddenly. Von Kahn smiled.

"My dear Heine," he said, "you need have no apprehension. I whistled a certain little tune you know, and he finished it without hesitation. He is not only in the Higher Service, but he stands very high in the Higher Service."

To make absolutely sure, we returned that night, and in company with von Kahn I crossed the valley and climbed the hill. I was half-way up the hill when I heard a familiar sound. If you can imagine the rattling of dried peas in a tin canister shaken at irregular intervals, you know the sound that wireless makes, and that a wireless message was being tapped from the cottage on the hill there was no doubt. More than this, the unknown Mr. Brown had taken elaborate precautions to avoid detection. We climbed the hill a little higher and suddenly my foot caught an obstruction. I flashed my electric lamp down and saw that I had snapped a tiny wire.

Instantly the "clickety-click" of the wireless ceased. There was a stealthy footstep at the top of the hill and I guessed that the aerial was being taken down, and that it would be stowed and hidden, together with the instruments, long before any intruder could reach the cottage.

"Go up now," I whispered to Kahn; "go quickly and reveal yourself."

I handed him the message I had coded and which I had brought with me.

"Give him your official number, show him your credentials and ask the illustrious gentleman to send this message through."

Kahn took the massage without a word and began the ascent. I watched him, lot moving from my position and presently I heard him challenged sharply.

"It is I," said von Kahn's voice and, like the bold fellow that he was, he spoke in German. Someone replied in the same language. There was a brief exchange of question and answer and the three — the Swiss valet was evidently present — disappeared into the cottage, and a few minutes later I saw the red glow of a light from the windows.

I was sorely tempted to creep up and listen. After all, there was no reason why von Kahn alone should have an opportunity of greeting this well-born gentleman who might, be in a position to speak a favourable word in the highest quarters regarding myself. Then again, I was not sure that von Kahn would fulfil his mission to my satisfaction.

I determined to risk it, and keeping as much in the shadow as possible, and feeling gingerly for other wire signals, I made my way to the little platform upon which the cottage stood. We had specially put on rubber-soled shoes for the night's work, and I moved noiselessly. The door was closed, but there was no difficulty in discovering the room to which von Kahn bad been taken. I crept nearer to the window. The two men were talking and laughing and, thank heaven their speech was in German.

"But how do I know," I heard Mr, Brown say, "that you are not a member of the British Secret Service?"

"For the matter of that," said von Kahn jovially, "how am I to know that your Excellency is not also of that phantom body?"

And they both laughed together. I heard the clink of a bottle on a glass and two hearty "Prosits," and then Mr, Brown spoke again.

"Now what can I do for you? I suppose you know that you ought not to have come anywhere near me? How did you find me out? Was it the ever-to-be-condemned tune I whistled?"

Von Kahn chuckled. "I have known about you for a long time," he said, "and as I am in need of help I thought I would take the bull by the horns and seek this interview."

"Are you alone?" asked Mr. Brown.

"Quite alone," said von Kahn promptly.

"I mean, were you alone in making the discovery?"

"Quite alone," said von Kahn again.

"Then you are a remarkably shrewd fellow," laughed Brown.

I can tell you it made my blood boil to bear this swine hound taking all the credit for this discovery. Little he know that I was standing outside the window listening to his immodest perfidy! Could he not have said, "No, Excellency, the credit is due entirely to my respected chief whose name I am forbidden to mention I am merely an instrument in a superior hand?" Oh, no! His vanity and deceit he must take full kudos to himself. Would he go any further?

Almost as I framed this question he spoke. "I would ask your Excellency," he said, "if you ever refer to this meeting to the illustrious Chief of Naval Intelligence that you will give him a testimonial."

I could hardly restrain myself. For one second it was in my mind to rap sharply at the window and denounce this underling. But, fortunately, I restrained myself, though I was boiling with rage. We Germans have a keen sense of justice and are inherently, almost transparently, honest, and nothing distresses us, so angers us, as duplicity and ingratitude.

"But surely," said Mr. Brown's voice, "you did not come alone to-night?"

I waited. Just as I had been anxious far von Kahn to give me full credit, so was I now anxious to hear him deny my presence. I do not know what it was that brought this revulsion of feeling, whether it was something in the tone of Mr Brown or some instinctive flash of knowledge that all was not well, but I sweated as I stood waiting for the answer which seemed an eternity in coming, though in reality it was only a second or so.

"No, I assure you, Herr Brown," said von Kahn, "I came alone."

"That makes matters simple," said Brown's voice, and as he spoke the light went out. I heard von Kahn shout, but his voice was instantly muffled There was a struggle, a thud that seemed to shake the little building, a groan and then silence.

I had my automatic pistol in my hand in a second.

Should I go to his rescue and take the risk of capture or should I leave him I his fate? It was a terrible decision I was called upon to make. We Germans do not shrink from our responsibilities nor are we governed by the foolish sentimentality which dictates the actions of the commoner tribes. I made n way down the hill with great rapidity You may say that I was leaving a comrade to his fate, but I answer that when one cog of a wheel breaks off do the other cogs disintegrate themselves in sympathy. We were part of a great machine von Kahn and I, and my action, if it needed such justification, was justified in the events which followed.

I was within fifty yards of the narrow road which winds along the base of the hill when I thought I heard a sound before me and I stopped, flattened myself on the ground between two bushes, and listened. There was no doubt that I had reason for my suspicions. I heard, not one stealthy footfall, but a dozen, and peering up, I saw against the artificial sky-line which I had created by lowering myself to the earth half a dozen shadowy figures. The nearest was ten yards away and my heart came to my throat when I saw a gleam of light upon the tunic of a policeman.

They were police, undoubtedly, and they were making their way up the hill such a manner as led me to believe that the hill itself was practically surrounded. I watched holding my breath. The first of the figures passed two yards away, the second on my right less than a yard. I waited until they were well up the hill before I moved, and then I wriggled forward with the utmost caution for I thought it was possible that they had left a guard on the road. This view proved to be correct as I had not got far before I saw a man pacing the roadway.

Fortunately his beat was long and I was able to gain the road and cross it.

I found myself in a field of cabbages Here again luck was with me, for running two sides of the field was a deep ditch. Into this I sank and with great labour reached the opposite hill, on the top of which, hidden in a small copse, were the two motor-bicycles which had brought us on our night adventure.

Here again German forethought saved me from what might have been destruction. Von Kahn had suggested we should have the chauffeur and the car we had in the morning, but as I pointed out, this would have aroused suspicion and so instead we bad hired two motor bicycles, not from the town in which we were staying, but one five miles farther along the line from whence we had set forth upon our quest.

Nearby by the copse, as I had seen earlier in the day, was a disused quarry overgrown with vegetation. Swiftly I wheeled Kahn's bicycle to the edge and flung it over. It would remain undiscovered for at least a few days, and possibly forever, unless a search was made.

To leap upon the other motor-cycle and to go flying down the road was the work of a, few minutes. I confess I was agitated and nervous. Who was the mysterious man who lived at the top of the hill ? How did he know we were coming that night and was so sure of the hour that be could surround his house with policemen to trap us? Why had be assaulted my friend when be and he servant could have overcome him or have held him at the point of a revolver until the police arrived?

My position was a precarious one. Von Kahn had been seen with me in Dundee and obviously my business was to make myself scarce. It was half past eleven that night when I rode up to the cycle dealer's in X —, and knocked at the door. The town was asleep and the street deserted, but the man had been expecting our return and was waiting up.

He looked surprised at my muddy appearance and more surprised at the absence of my companion. I apologized to him, and told him that my friend bad been called away to London and had ridden down to a station on the main line. I think he was most surprised when I offered to buy the cycle I was using and also to buy that of von Kahn. I told him that I had taken a liking to the machine and that von Kahn had similarly expressed a wish to retain his. The price he fixed was a fairly moderate one — we had already paid a large deposit — and I concluded the bargain there and then.

I was anxious, of course, to finish this business of the motor-cycles in order that I should not set on foot independent inquiries as to their whereabouts, inquiries which would certainly have identified me with von Kahn. Taking on a supply of petrol and trimming my lamp, I set out for Dundee, arriving at my hotel a little after four o'clock in the morning. After some difficulty I aroused the night porter, a sleepy old man whose name, I remembered, was Angus, and went to my room, packed my small valise and, awaiting my opportunity, stole out of the hotel, strapped my bag to the carrier of the bicycle, and rode through the drear, menacing streets of Dundee for the last time.

Twenty miles out of Dundee all trace of the mysterious person who had disappeared from big hotel leaving a £5 note to cover his bill and a polite request that his letters should be forwarded to the Majestic Hotel, London, vanished. A cool young Englishman joined an early morning train to Edinburgh at an intermediate station, and certainly that cool young Englishman in his grey tweeds and his eye-glass bore no resemblance to the muddy cyclist in soiled overalls who bad crossed the river at Perth and had excited the attention of a certain mounted constable.

That cool young Englishman, perfect in every detail, might have been seen leaving the Central Station at Glasgow that same afternoon not only accompanied by his valise but by a large portmanteau which he had taken from the cloak-room at the station and which with characteristic German foresight he had caused to forwarded to Glasgow on the night he left London for Dundee.

I had communicated with London by telephone. Nothing had been heard of von Kahn but the whole of my service in England was now on the qui vive. Posser, one of my assistants, was on his way to Glasgow to confer with me, and half a dozen agents in that town were busy investigating the mystery of the man on the hill.

I was sitting at dinner that night in one of the fashionable restaurants of Glasgow, a restaurant approached through a magnificent marble vestibule, searching the latest edition of the papers, hoping for two lines which would give me a clue to von Kahn's fate, when a staring headline met my eye and I gasped.

SWISS FORGERS
SENSATIONAL ARRESTS AT GLEN MACINTYRE

"The Sheriff's Court at Stirling was crowded to-day when Emil Zimmwald, alias Brown, a Swiss, Louis Swart, Swiss, and Heinrich Kahn, also described as a Swiss, were remanded on a charge of forging Swiss bank notes. Inspector Macguire, of the Stirling Constabulary, stated that the prisoner Zimmwald, who called himself Brown, rented a cottage at Glen Macintyre, Swart posing as his valet. The two men were well-known international forgers, and had been engaged in printing a very large number of Swiss banknotes. The attention of the police had first been attracted to the house owing to the noise of working of the small printing machine which the prisoners used for their nefarious purpose. On raiding the premises the prisoner Kahn was discovered in a dazed condition. There had evidently been a quarrel and. Kahn had been struck. The prisoner Zimmerwald made a rambling statement to the effect that Kahn was a detective who had been sent to arrest him, but this highly improbable story will be investigated by the sheriff at a later sitting. The man Kahn resolutely refuses to make any statement at all."

My poor von Kahn! Thou shalt go down in Scottish history as a confederate of forgers and shall spend many years in that grim penitentiary at Perth, pleading guilty to a crime abhorrent to thee, lest the confession of thy true crime lead thee to a firing party in the chilly dawn!

3 — THE LOVELY MISS LARRYMORE

In America, where the German and Austro-Hungarian population is so much larger than in any other foreign country, the work of my department is split up into three sections. There is a naval, a military, and a commercial branch, each under an expert controlling a distinct organization- which could, however be co-ordinated in the event of war. In the United Kingdom there was no separation of interests, and the root organization, that which I controlled covered, after the outbreak of the war, all three departments.

And let me say here for the information of my good friends who may perhaps imagine I am boasting, that when I describe myself as "controlling" the organization, I may inadvertently deceive. The exact position was that I had organized my department, dug the channels through which would flow the streams or rivulets of information; that I myself had been in the position of the central reservoir which collected and refined and transmitted the information so received. It does not necessarily mean that because I was the architect that I was necessarily the tenant of the fabric which I had created.

All the time in the first few months of the War there were great comings and goings. Men arrived from Germany, from America, from Switzerland, Sweden, and Holland, with forged passports, each charged with a distinct and separate mission. Lody, whose name you may have heard, came in the guise of a tourist agent, having certain definite discoveries to make and certain propaganda to forward. Other men came from America on similar missions. Some of these were gentlemen of the very highest character who were not associated with me in any way, but nevertheless sought me out in order to secure my assistance for the development of their plans. Of their adventures I know little. Whether they returned to Germany or not I am unable to say. Some got away and some were caught, but in what manner I never knew.

I was loth to believe, and, indeed, did not believe, that a Secret Service existed in Britain. There were, of course, detectives and plain clothes policemen, whose task it was to watch railway and steamship arrivals, but obviously it was impossible in the space of a few weeks to create such a bureau as exists in the Wilhelmstrasse, or that over which Captain von Treutchen presides with such distinguished success in the Admiralty Buildings.

In November 1914, I received orders direct from Berlin — the first I had ever received — telling me that I must devote myself entirely to industrial propaganda. I was informed that the sum of £12,000 had been placed to my credit in the West London and Birmingham Bank and I was told to make my headquarters at Manchester in the capacity of buyer for a well-known firm of Chilean importers with whom my chiefs had a working arrangement.

I arrived at Manchester late one misty afternoon and made my way to the best hotel, where rooms had been reserved for me. I went to the desk and registered, and upon seeing my name the clerk informed- me that two gentlemen were waiting for me in the palm court.

"I don't know whether you want to see them, sir," he said; "I think they are commercial travellers."

"I will see them in my room, if you will be good enough to send them up,"' said I, and five minutes later the "commercial travellers" were shown in to me, and introduced themse1ves as representatives of the Incorporated Carolina Cotton fields Company.

"I'm afraid I am rather tired tonight," said I," but as you seem in a hurry to do business I will compare your quotations."

When the door had shut upon the waiter who had shown them in we got to business. One, of course, was my friend Posser, and the other was young Klein, one of those brilliant children of the Fatherland who had been in the service of the department ever since he left Heidelberg.

"We are ordered to place ourselves at your disposal, Herr Heine," said Klein, "and we have been here two days investigating the conditions."

"Are they favourable?" I asked.

"Extremely so," said Posser; "but you will have an opportunity of judging for yourself."

We exchanged experiences, and half an hour later I rang the bell for the waiter and my visitors were shown out. After I had dined I left the hotel for the rendezvous I had made outside the post-office. It was now raining heavily, and I would like to have taken a taxi, but Klein suggested that we should make our way on foot to our destination, which proved to be a very small hall in some unsavoury part of Manchester. It was a dilapidated building, the entrance door being flush with the street and had the appearance of being a mission hall dedicated to one of those dour and unhappy sects which find a virtue in the very dreariness of their environment.

Two nights a week it was used for religious services, but on the other nights it was let out to whosoever cared to hire the place. On this occasion some sort of Labour meeting seemed to be in progress and a small bill attached to an inner baize door leading to the hall itself announced an address by Mr. William Craigmair on "Labour and the War."

The hall was sparsely filled and I do not suppose there were more than fifty people present when we walked in and took our seats. The man who was speaking was of the usual demagogic type, loud-mouthed, illogical, full of bitter jibes at Capitalism, which he said was the cause of the war and at the bottom of the whole European crisis. Klein nudged me.

"Imagine this in Berlin!" he whispered. I nodded. It was indeed pathetic, and only shows how wholly inefficient the English police service is that it allowed such men to be at large. I sat through the tirade, a little bored if the truth be told, because this was to be the least interesting part of the evening. After the meeting was over Klein told us to go over and wait for him, and presently he rejoined us accompanied by a man whom I recognized as the speaker, Mr Craigmair. He introduced us as sympathizers with the cause of Labour, and I congratulated this gaunt Englishman upon his "wonderful rhetoric," though worse balderdash I had never heard in my life.

The man's harsh arrogance melted under this well-directed stream of Teutonic flattery and he became almost human in the glow of our admiration.

"I am much obliged to you, gents," he said, grinning; "speakin' impartially, I can say it wasn't a bad speech for a self-taught man. Any Sunday afternoon you happen to be in Finsbury Park you will find me there addressing the proletariat."

"Finsbury Park?" said I.

"Do you come from London?"

"Yes," said the man. "Our comrade here," he nodded to Klein, "persuaded me to go round delivering a few addresses to the working classes. I've got a lot of friends in this part of the world," he went on," and you mustn't judge me on the audience I got to-night. I am addressin' the Junior Operatives' League to- morrow and then you will see an audience if you like."

I murmured my intention of being present, expressed my sympathy with the Labour movement, and invited him to meet me at lunch on the following day.

When we had parted Klein told me that he had first heard the man addressing meetings in London, either at Finsbury or in Hyde Park.

"He was such a fanatic, and he had, moreover, such a convincing way that I thought we might find him useful. I know you think what he says is nonsense," Klein went on, addressing me; "but what is illogical to us is sound sense to the common workman. To-morrow's meeting, for example, is of the greatest importance to us. The Junior Operatives have threatened to strike against the advice of their Trade Union, and as they have a working arrangement with Carters' Union, a strike would be of the utmost importance. Whilst I do not expect we can do very much in the early stages of the war to bring about a general stoppage of labour, we can embarrass the Government, and who knows how these little labour troubles may develop!"

I quite agreed with Klein, who is a psychologist of a very high order, in addition to being well born, his mother being a Frenheim-Hazebrucken, and his sister being married to Graf von Metzenheim, an illustrious gentleman with who I once had the honour of taking wine.

Mr. Craigmair came to lunch the next day. In order not to excite attention I arranged with him to meet me at Lytham, and there we spoke frankly and freely. I told him how intensely interested we all were in the Labour movement. I pointed out that this war might be brought to an end if some great leader arose from the people and seized his opportunity.

"For, Mr. Craigmair," said I, "what is war but a negation of all law? Is better that a few miserable capitalists and statesmen should be chagrined, or that thousands of human lives should be sacrificed in the red-hot pit of battle? Is not better that these money-grabbers should be ruined than that innocent people who have no concern in the war and have no hatred towards any nation should be compelled to walk into the shambles like dumb beasts? If they tell you that it is not patriotic to attempt to stop a war, even though you may acting contrary to the maddened sentiments of the majority of the people, you answer that there is no such thing as patriotism, that we owe our chief duty humanity which knows no frontier and no language. For what is there more precious in the soil of England than in the soil of Germany or of France? Do they not equally produce wheat and sustain life? Has anyone a more precious value than another? Does one handful of red earth contain a magic quality which is not possessed equally by a handful of any other kind of earth? Patriotism is the shibboleth of the capitalist and the ambitious statesman, my friend, and he who opposes his will to that hateful creed is doing magnificent work for mankind."

I spoke in this vein and I could see that Mr. Craigmair was impressed, made little notes with the stub of a pencil upon what looked like a laundry-book, interrupting my remarks with uncouth sounds of admiration and approval.

I gave him £50, as a mark of my interest in his work.

"And on the day you bring the people out on strike I will give you another £50," I said;

"not because I am anxious to promote industrial discord, but because war is against my principles as a hateful and an unnecessary evil."

I went back to my hotel fee1ing that I had done a good day's work. I did not attend the meeting of the Junior Operatives, but I am told that it was very enthusiastic and that by an overwhelming majority the men and the women members had decided to strike, and had received a promise of support from the transport workers.

My interest in the Labour movement was momentarily diverted that same day by the receipt of a message from. London — it was brought by courier on the afternoon train. The message was an important one, and it had been received by radio direct from Potsdam, and had been decoded in London and transmitted to me for report.

News had reached Berlin that the firm of Pollygay & Moxon, a chemical firm on the outskirts of Manchester, were engaged in conducting secret experiments with a new bomb. The news had reached Berlin from a very reliable source. I believe that it had been mentioned after dinner at a well-known Bohemian club in London by an under-secretary in a certain Government department. He had spoken rather boastfully of "something" very deadly which the Government were experimenting with, and our agent, who was one of the party to whom this was told, discovered, by a well-timed display of scepticism that the experiments were being conducted by Pollygay & Moxon, and had sent forward the information which, had I been in London, must have gone through me.

I put Klein on to the job immediately, and he called in the assistance of Craigmair who apparently was in touch with workmen in most of the big factories, and fortunately numbered among his acquaintances a wretched German named Bluer, who was employed in the laboratories of the firm. As a matter of fact, we did not know of the existence of Bluer, a dour, taciturn man of the hateful socialistic type who had no patriotism, no love for his Fatherland, and was tainted with poisonous internationalism.

This renegade, living in England, with excellent opportunity for serving the Fatherland, had never put himself into touch with the superior authorities, nor had he offered the slightest assistance to the officers of State, and it was only by accident that we discovered his existence. However, his internationalism served one good purpose. Though he might earn his livelihood by preparing deadly weapons for the destruction of his fellow-countrymen, he was in theory an opponent of war, and Mr. Craigmair, after a while, enlisted his sympathies and introduced him to Klein, who said he was an author engaged in writing a book painting war in its most horrible aspects. He also told him that he was compiling as long and as formidable a list of deadly weapons as he could secure.

"And when I have finished, my friend," said Klein, "we shall have the most damning indictment of warfare that the world has ever seen."

This interested Bluer and it was not long before he told of the secret experiments which had been conducted on the firm's private range with the new hand grenade.

"I don't know how it is made," said Bluer, "because that is not in my department, and all the chemical experiments have been in the bands of the head chemist, but my brother-in-law is a night watchman and has the entry to the records office and I daresay I could give you a rough idea of what it's like."

I was overjoyed to hear this news, the more so since I bad received another, and even more urgent, message from Headquarters, telling me to spare no expense or pains to secure a specification. I now come to the remarkable part of this narrative, one which I cannot tell without a little shudder.

Bluer and his relative certainly made an attempt to locate the specifications and drawings. I will do this un-German Teuton (to whom Klein was eventually compelled to reveal something of his designs) the credit of saying that he tried his best — but for a week he and his relative were unsuccessful.

The manager was a gentleman named Tyson, or Tynson, a good-looking man of about twenty-eight. Naturally, I had set my people to work to find out all the particulars about every member of the firm, and it was reported to me that Tyson had been frequently seen in the company of a very beautiful lady, named Miss Harrymore.

I put my own men on to discover something about Miss Harrymore, and found that she was a stranger to Manchester, that she had only arrived a month previous to my appearance on the scene; and that she occupied a small house which she bad taken furnished in the most fashionable suburb of the Lancashire city.

She had come from London and almost immediately had made friends with the manager. They used to dine occasionally and they went to the theatre together once a week, but there was no evidence that the friendship was a very warm one. Miss Harrymore had been a dancer; but apparently had retired from the stage — at least that was the story which her maid told Posser, who investigated the matter.

I smoked many cigars over this friendship and formed certain conclusions, especially after I had learnt that on the nights Mr. Tyson was working late this lady had driven down to the factory in her car, had spent some little time in the manager's office, and had driven that gentleman to supper.

I have already told you of my disbelief in the existence of a secret service in England, but I had modified that view after the experience of my poor friend Koos, who was brought to an untimely end through the artfulness of a chit of a girl.

Naturally I was suspicious of beautiful ladies who were on terms of furtive friendship with Government officials — and to all intents and purposes Tyson was a Government official — and I kept my eyes "skinned," as they say in England.

The business of the bomb was worrying me more than I cared to confess to my assistants. A third message had come through from Berlin, even more urgent than the last, and one paragraph of that message considerably disturbed me. It ran: "Whilst we expect you to secure these plans we are leaving nothing to chance. We hope, however, that the credit for securing them will fall to you."

I understood this significant passage. It meant that Berlin was sending independent agents to England to try their luck, and I was determined to justify myself in the eyes of the Fatherland. I sent for Posser and Klein to come to my room and I outlined my views and gave my final instructions. Posser gave me encouraging news. He told me that Bluer had secured some information of the greatest importance. It appears that the Government had sent in a rough drawing of the bomb, and that one of the engineers was coming next night to make the drawing and a copy of the secret specification, and that the original was kept in a safe in the records office.

The combination safe opened to the word "Track" and the specification would be found in No. 3 drawer, the lock of which could be picked. So far, so good, but the situation was still desperate. It was as clear as daylight; that my chief difficulty was going to be, not to circumvent the manager, but to get past the guard which the secret service had set up. It was then a struggle between Miss Harrymore and Heine. Very well, Heine picks up the gauntlet with a clear mind and a high confidence in his German genius.

Klein saw Bluer on the following afternoon and an unexpected difficulty arose. Bluer, if you please, had discovered a conscience! This renegade, this traitor to the Fatherland, this dirty Swabian refused to go any further in the matter!

"The English have always treated me well," he told Klein; "My children have been born in the country and I have friends here. I cannot help you any more, Herr Klein. I should not only be a traitor to the English, but a traitor to the Internationale, if I betrayed my employers. You have the combination word — I can do no more."

"If you refuse your help," said Klein, who was by now filled with holy annoyance, "you are a traitor to your Kaiser and to your Fatherland." Klein threatened and argued, pleaded and raved, but all to no purpose.

"I have told you where you will find the specifications," said Bluer doggedly; "you have a plan of the factory — which is not guarded — and you know the way to the records room. In telling you this I have done more than I ought to have done. If you threaten me any more I will go for the police and tell them all) I know."

Ingrate! Rascal! Black swine of Württemberg! I paced my room cursing the villain, and Klein stood by in respectful silence, as I "let off steam," as the British say. However, I soon mastered my rage and sat down to evolve a plan. We Germans can meet all contingencies and adapt our minds to any difficulty which may arise. I drew out the plan of the factory and soon Klein and I were deep in the discussion of the alternative scheme.

The factory was a straggling collection of buildings, enclosed on three sides by high walls and on the fourth by a canal, alongside of which ran a double- track railway siding. There were three gates and two small wickets, none of which were practical for our purpose, since there would be a night watchman at each, and, moreover, the records office was a fairly long distance from all. This squat building adjoined the main warehouse near the canal-siding and obviously it was from the canal that we must make our entrance. We had learnt that the wharf was patrolled by a watchman who had a little hut at the northern end of the quay, to which it was his habit to retire between eleven and twelve at night to make his coffee or tea, or whatever refreshment he favoured, and we decided that this should be the hour for our attempt.

Our plan was to paddle down the canal in a small collapsible canoe (an advertisement of which Klein had seen), wait our opportunity and land. With Klein's equipment of keys and instruments we should have no difficulty in forcing an entrance, and the rest would be easy.

When we had agreed upon our scheme, Klein went off to Chester to purchase the boat, whilst I elaborated my plan for conveying the specifications to Germany.

I was working away at this all the afternoon, telephoning to certain garages, arranging routes and rendezvous, and reporting points, newspaper advertisement codes, etc., and had almost finished my organization work when the waiter brought me a card. I took the paste-board from the salver and as I read the name I felt myself grow pale. It was —

MISS ANGELA HARRYMORE.

"Show the lady up," I said. As soon as the waiter was gone, I took my Browning from my pocket, examined it and slipped its bank barrel under my left armpit, the butt concealed by the fold of my coat. Only thus can a danger-waiting man be sure that he has his pistol ready for use.

The door opened and I rose to meet the lady. She was, as far as I could judge, about twenty-six years of age. She was tall and willowy, and perfectly gowned in some blue stuff which admirably suited her fair complexion. About her neck and shoulders was a Chinchilla wrap which I valued at £250, and beneath the white kid gloves of one hand I saw the bulge of many rings. Her features were regular and aristocratic, her eyes blue and steadfast, her hair of pale gold. She was a type one meets as frequently in England as in Northern Germany or Denmark. In time, the first impression I had was that she was of my own race, an impression helped very cleverly by her greeting.

"Good day, Herr Cannelli," she said (Cannelli being the name I traded under) and she spoke in faultless German.

But, O gracious lady, Heine was on guard!

At all times, I think, I am clever and alert; at some times I may be a little too clever, but never am I caught napping. I frowned, smiled, and shook my head.

"You are speaking German, are you not?" I asked in English, "I am afraid I do not speak that language."

It was her turn to smile. "Come, come!" she rallied me, you are not going to pretend with me," and she laid two slim fingers on her chin, the old sign — the pre-war sign — by which one recognizes a member of the Admiralty Secret Service.

Aha! Gracious lady, thought, would you try an old trick upon an old wolf! Do you not know that all the spy-revealing signs and make-knowing signs had been changed on the outbreak of war? On me, on Heine will you try these subterfuges!

"I do not speak your language madam," I said, shaking my head; "Harla usted Espanol."

I saw a shade of disappointment dim for a moment the brightness of her eyes, then she laughed.

"I don't know why I thought you spoke German," she said coolly and speaking in perfect English; "but somehow you reminded me of a man I once knew in New York — a gentleman called by his friends 'Heine.'"

She was watching me closely, but I never so much as blinked.

"I am indeed fortunate, madame, even to resemble one whom you have remembered," I said; "but I have never been to New York except on one occasion, and then only for a few hours."

"Then I'm sorry to have bothered you," she smiled, and her smile was a radiance.

"I saw you at dinner the other night and I was almost sure that you were the friend of other days who had sung 'Es stehen unbeweglich.'"

I could have laughed! Again the old song and the old "code of recognition" — a code which had been changed for six months.

"My dear lady," I said gently, " I have never sung in my life." She was baffled and showed signs of distress. She stood biting her lips and frowning into the fire until, recovering her self-possession, she smiled, shrugged her shoulders and offered me her hand.

"I am afraid you must think I am very stupid," she said frankly, "but I could have sworn I knew you."

I took her hand and conducted her to the corridor and to the lift, and summoned Posser. Briefly I retailed all that had happened.

"There is no doubt about it at all," said Posser; "she came to trap you. We must get out of Manchester to-night, and we must take with us the specifications."

At eleven o'clock that night we slipped down the canal, Klein at the bow and myself at the stern. Fortunately it was a dark night, with a thin fog, and we moved silently and unchallenged to our destination.

Klein had made a very careful survey of the wharf and he guided the canoe to one of the big supporting piles up which ran a steel-runged ladder.

Klein made a reconnaissance. Looking along the wharf, we could see the little glass-windowed hut and the night-watchman standing before a small fire evidently boiling his kettle. We tied the canoe to the ladder and moved noiselessly across the wharf.

The factory was in darkness, but we had no difficulty in discovering the record office, a small, dark building thrown out as an annexe to the main machinery warehouse. To open the outer door was the work of a few seconds. We entered, closed the door, and us and found ourselves in a little wooden vestibule from which opened yet another door. To my surprise the inner door was not locked but still ajar.

Down the centre of the building ran a corridor and from this various doors led to offices. Our objective was the last on the left and quietly we crept forward and reached the door. I gently turned the handle in order to secure a grip and was inserting my skeleton key when I felt the door give. All my nerves were or edge. Things were going much too easy and I pulled my gun and slipped down the safety catch. Now, as I pushed the door gently open I could have sworn I saw the faint reflection of a light, such a reflection as you would expect from the varnished matchboard-lining to the office, if some person had incautiously shown a light for a second. I hesitated on the threshold. The office was in darkness. There was no sound, no sign, and I thought that the light I saw must have been reflection from one of the street lamps on the other side of the canal, until remembered that the fog was quite thick enough to veil any of the outside lights. I stepped forward cautiously towards the safe, felt for it and found the handle, and had replaced my pistol in my jacket pocket and was feeling for my electric lamp, when Klein whispered fiercely in my ear:

"There's someone in the room."

Almost as he spoke, we beard a quick rustle and swish, and a figure dimly seen flashed across the room and through the door. At that moment I felt the safe door swing back in my grasp, and I realized that we had come too late.

I was out of the office in a trice, flashed my lamp along the corridor, and caught just a glimpse of a woman's figure as it disappeared through the other end. She sped across the yard, we behind her, and disappeared in the gloom. There was no time to search for her. We had to consider ourselves. We scurried down the ladder and I heard the hoarse challenge of the watchman. By this time we were in mid-stream and paddling furiously. It was too dangerous to keep to the canal and at the first opportunity we found a landing place and reached a street, an ill-favoured, dingy slum, which suited our purpose very well.

Ten minutes rapid walking brought us to one of the main thoroughfares where we found a taxi-cab, and in the brief space of time between this discovery an our arrival at the hotel, I gave my instructions to Klein.

"She is evidently a member of the secret police," I said, "and she got to know that we were after the specifications to-night and forestalled us. I think Manchester is a little too hot for you and me, Klein, and we will fade away."

We dismissed the cab at the hotel and walked into the brightly-lighted vestibule, and came face to face with Miss Harrymore! There was no doubt in my mind. There she stood, her face flushed with triumph. I could see the mud on her shoes, I recognized the fur-edged coat, and I realized my danger: She probably had a motor-boat waiting for her and had taken the short-cut back to the hotel in time to confront and denounce us.

In that moment all the latent genius of our race came to the surface. We Germans make our decisions quickly, boldly. With such rapidity did I act that I even surprised myself. Extending my forefinger I pointed at Miss Harrymore, "This woman," I said; "is a German spy. She has in her possession certain specifications and plans of a new and secret weapon."

I said this in a loud voice and a quiet-looking man who had been sitting reading dropped his paper and springing up edged his way through the little crowd which had collected about us. I saw the girl go pale. I knew that she could not betray herself as a secret gent and that, found in possession of the plans, she would not be able to explain how she came by them.

The quiet-looking man moved to her side and caught her arm.

"I am Inspector Lovell, of the Manchester Detective Department," he said, "and on this gentleman's accusation I shall take you to the Central Police Station."

He told us to follow, and led Miss Harrymore out of the hotel. I gave a sign to Klein, and we followed, but not to the station. Our big Mercedes was waiting round the corner and dawn found me in London, so changed in appearance that I doubt if the admirable Inspector Lovell would have recognized the man who had trapped Miss Harrymore.

So far this comedy goes and now comes the tragedy. I found in London, waiting for me, a code message from Berlin.

"Reference Pollygay bomb. Fraulein von Liebman of the Secret Service is in Manchester under the name of Miss Harrymore. She has love affair with manager and reports she can secure specifications. Assist her all you can. Instruct her in new code."

It was signed by the High Chief of the Admiralty Intelligence. For an hour I was prostrate and then I coded my reply to Admiralty, Potsdam.

"In spite of my efforts, Fraulein von Liebmann arrested in possession of specifications, which she carried against my wishes."

I think it was an admirable explanation. As for the fraulein, it will be many years before she will be able to supply her personal narrative!

4 — THE AFFAIR OF MISTER HAYNES

In February, 1915, there occurred an event which I cannot pretend did not give me a certain amount of satisfaction, tragic and ever-to-be regretted as that event proved. I had constantly urged both upon the naval and military Intelligence Departments in Berlin that the work in England should be left entirely in my hands, and that I should not be badgered or embarrassed by amateurs being sent to operate in my territory, independent of my control and very often without my being acquainted with their presence or purpose.

The event I refer to was the arrest of Herr Blaumberg, who was sent from America without my knowledge to secure an accurate list — "accurate"— mark you! — of the warships which the British were laying down, especially in reference to the super-X battleships which were destined to prove Mr. Churchill's happiest experiment.

Herr Blaumberg had no sooner landed than he was arrested. I received an inquiry from Wilhelmstrasse which was the first information I had of Herr Blaumberg's foolish attempt to meddle in matters which be obviously did not understand. The second intimation was the official notice in the English papers: "This morning a man tried and convicted of espionage at the Central Criminal Court, was executed in the Tower of London."

I was in London when the news came, firmly established in my role of Chilean importer and was so well did I play my part that I had secured certain little Government orders and was even assisted by Government officials, all unknowing, you may be sure, to the pursuit of my investigations.

It was on the very day that I read this doleful news of Herr Blaumberg's sad end that I made the acquaintance of Mister Haynes. I saw him standing on the corner of Bouverie and Fleet streets — a, tall, young, unshaven man, wearing pince-nez, and a very shabby suit. With one quick, comprehensive glance I sized him up. The bundle of various coloured pencils and the fountain-pen in his left- hand waistcoat pocket, the absence of watch and chain, the hat carelessly balanced on the back of his head, the hands thrust into his trousers pockets, the drooping cigarette, and the listless eyes which watched the traffic passing up and down, told me as plainly as though his biography had been handed to me, all the history I wished to know. His linen was not clean, his collar was two or three days old, his boots were down at heel. With that decision which has always marked my actions I walked up to him with a smile.

"I think I have met you before, have I not?" I said.

He turned his head and looked at me from the crown of my hat to the soles of my boots.

"I daresay," he said.

"Come on and have a drink," said I briskly, and he obeyed with alacrity.

We turned into the private bar of a public-house, ordered our drinks and withdrew to a little round table and a couple of chairs in a corner of the saloon bar.

"I don't remember your name," said I, "but I know you are a newspaper man and if I remember rightly you have not had a great deal of luck lately?"

"You have a good memory," he said, "and if mine was as good I could tell you your name, your age, the place of your birth and the state of your banking account, but, unfortunately, my memory is a little groggy."

He lifted his drink with a shaking hand. I saw the whole story.

He was what is commonly called in England, a "liner," or a free-lance a man not attached to any newspaper but contributing whatever stories, interviews or articles that come his way. They are not so common in Fleet Street as they used to be when I first came to London. The great news agencies have killed them. The new system of journalism has passed them by. But occasionally you meet a man with that hungry, hard-up look, with a grievance against the world, and a pretty taste in whisky-and-soda, and this was such a one.

Under the genial influence of a second drink he confirmed my diagnosis. He had a grievance against all the papers and admitted that he was on the black-list of three or four for sending in contributions which were not exactly true. I asked him why he had not enlisted and his lips curved in a sneer. He said he was an Irishman, and that he hated England anyway, and that be hated the army more poisonously than anything else. He hated the war, he hated the Northworths and a long string of other newspaper proprietors, but most of all he hated Fleet Street, its editors, sub-editors, reporters, advertisement managers in fact, his hatred extended to the very boys on the streets.

This was the man for my money. I explained to him that in addition to being a Chilean importer I was running a Chinese news agency to collect and distribute news pertaining or of interest to Europeans in China, and when I told him that I was short of a reporter for news collection and offered him £6 a week, he nearly jumped into the air with delight. In engaging him I was putting into practice a plan which I bad long formed. Here was an opportunity for collecting news without arousing suspicion.

A newspaper reporter can ask questions which none of my agents would dare to frame. He can go up and down the country without exciting suspicion, and the mere fact that he is a reporter, is sufficient to give him an entree into circles, admission to which we could only risk at grave danger to ourselves. An ordinary reporter might have been valueless, but a man with a grievance, a man who was "broke to the wide," to use Mister Haynes' own expressive idiom, was especially valuable. I took him down to the news agency office, and there he had tangible proof of the solidity and bona-fides of the agency. The two rooms in Fleet Street, which I had fitted up, were well furnished. The name of the agency was painted on the windows and on the glass panels of the office door, the files of the news- papers were carefully kept by the boy I employed. There were telephones and a "tape machine"— in fact, it was the most convincing environment that German forethought could design. I never saw a man so content as he was when I sat him down at a new desk within reach of the telephone, handed him £5 note on account of expenses, and outlined the plan of inquiry.

"Do you speak any foreign language?" I asked. He said he spoke French indifferently and German not at all which was excellent news.

"My principals," I explained, "are very anxious, of course to receive news of the war. The London hospitals are filled with wounded, and I have no doubt that you would be able to obtain admission to the wards and collect the personal narratives of the men as they come home."

"I get you, Steve," he said.

"You want stories of heroism in battle?"

"Exactly," I said, "but don't dwell so much upon the romantical side of the war. Encourage the men to speak not of their own battalions but of the gallant fellows who were fighting on their left and on their right. Find out what other regiments are in their divisions. Learn something about their officers. Who are the most popular and who are the most unpopular. What sort of men are their colonels; We want to see the war at a new angle," I went on hurriedly, for be looked a little dubious and disappointed, "and we can only do that if we get off the beaten track. When you have written your matter you will hand it to me and I will embody it in my weekly letter to — er — China."

From the very first my scheme was a success. Not a day passed but Mister Haynes brought into me precisely the information which Headquarters required.

You must understand that until you take prisoners it is almost impossible to discover what is your enemy's order of battle. Once you have discovered where certain divisions fit in and what places particular battalions take, you will no longer be in the dark in any subsequent actions in which those divisions take part. For instance, if the Wessex are on the right of the 99th Division and the Royal Hertfordshires are in the centre, and you know the positions of every other battalion, you have only to pick up one prisoner from one battalion at any point of the line to know exactly the disposition of the others.

Mister Haynes brought information of the first class, but nothing so enthralling as that which he brought one afternoon about three weeks after he bad started working. I remember the occasion so well. I can see him almost as tangibly as though he stood before me leaning against the desk his rusty hat on the back of his head, his hands as usual in his pockets.

"I got a queer story from one of those chaps at the London Hospital," he said. "I don't know whether I can use it."

"What is it?" I asked carelessly.

"This man said that every night our front line near Bois Grenier is evacuated to save the men from the effect of the German shelling. As soon as it gets dark the whole line on a front of six miles is withdrawn to the support trenches, and he said he was wounded through being ordered back to the front line before the German artillery strafe had finished."

"That is very interesting," said I, "on a front of six miles you say?"

"That's right," he said, "from Bois Grenier down to Festubert. Do you think I had better use the story?"

"I think not," I said shaking my head, "I don't think it would be patriotic. Those horrid Germans might get hold of the information and use it to destroy our brave soldiers."

You may be sure that I was not very long in coding this news, though it was some time before I could get my telegram to Stockholm. Apparently the British Government were holding up all messages for forty-eight hours, but this did not worry me so long as it reached its destination eventually. Naturally I received a reply in a much shorter space of time. In fact, Berlin acknowledged my message within twelve hours of its receipt.

You may remember that in the first week of February we Germans delivered a sudden and fierce attack upon the British front line positions between Festubert and Bois Grenier. Owing to some unhappy and unfortunate change of plan the front line of the British positions were filled with soldiers, but this was probably due to the carelessness of General von Klaus who had assembled his troops for the offensive in broad daylight under the eyes of the British airmen. Von Klaus himself denied this, but that is the theory which I have formed because Mister Haynes afterwards told me that he had had his story confirmed from three independent sources, and gave me the names of his informants, He even showed me the photograph of one of them.

Klein, who was up on a brief visit to London — he was very busy in South Wales on propaganda, work with his friend Mr Craigmair — was anxious that should send Mister Haynes to the West of England where certain experiments were being made with a new kind of armoured car. He had attempted to go into the camp which was guarded as carefully as any prison, and bad narrowly escaped being arrested.

It is a well-known fact that long before the famous Tank — that atrocious and unfair weapon which the English used, contrary to the laws of the Hague Convention — came upon the scene secret experiments were being made. Potsdam had heard of these, and I had received instructions to prosecute my investigations with the greatest vigour. Naturally rumours were rife, and there were many mares' nests before, by, lucky chance, our good friend Klein heard of this experimental camp.

I had no difficulty in concocting a story for Mister Haynes. My suggestion was that he should write an article on the marvellous mechanical contrivances which the genius of Britain had brought into being and I dispatched him, with Klein hot upon the scent to investigate and report. They left by the night train from Paddington and I saw them off. Klein was very decorous, the picture of an English gentleman in his check cap and his long travelling coat, his neatly- gloved hands and his English magazine, and Mister Haynes was untidy as ever, curled up in the corner of the carriage and, I should imagine, asleep before he left the station.

What happened was told me by Klein on the telephone. It was a happening so disconcerting, so mysterious, that I must confess that I regarded the unlooked for outcome of this adventure with more than ordinary disquietude, even had there not been the more terrible sequel.

They reached their destination, a small West Country town, in the early hours of the morning and went to their hotel where they were joined by Posser, who was working with Klein, and who, deeply conscious of the importance of finding out details of this particular machine, had been spending that day in making judicious inquiries.

They had breakfasted together the next morning, when, of course no mention was made of the camp or the new armoured car, Klein introducing Posser as his secretary. I might explain that Klein was posing as a Swedish mining engineer who had a patent for sale connected with coal haulage.

I had sent Mister Haynes on the same train and in company with Klein, on the pretext that, as Mr. Klein was a friend and was going to the same town, they might travel together and that Mr. Klein might possibly give my reporter certain introductions which would be useful. Mister Haynes spoke about his mission quite openly, though Klein advised him, laughingly, not to mention his business if he wanted to secure the information he required.

Apparently Mister Haynes met with little success, and came back to the hotel to dinner and said that all his efforts to induce any of the soldiers attached to the camp to give him information or to secure admission had been fruitless.

Klein was not greatly perturbed. In fact, he was very much elated because Posser had told him secretly that he intended making his way into the camp that night in the guise of one of the waiters at the officers' mess. They all ostensibly went to bed soon after ten o'clock. Mister Haynes went to his room and Klein went to his though not to sleep.

He made himself comfortable and took up a book and began reading. Presently be heard a scraping on his door, and smiled, for it was the agreed-on signal that Posser was stealing out into the night to secure his information.

The house was wrapt in sleep at eleven o'clock, and Klein read on. At one o'clock he heard a tap on the door. His room was next to Mister Haynes, and thinking that Posser could not have returned at so early an hour and that it was Haynes who was knocking, he opened the door. And to his amazement and delight, for he saw success shining on his comrade's honest face, he admitted Posser.

"I've got it!" whispered our good Posser.

"Wait," said Klein in the same tone, and kicking off his slippers he went into the corridor, softly opened Haynes's door and listened. He heard the regular breathing of the reporter, closed the door as softly and came back.

"Now tell me," he said quickly.

Posser explained how he had walked boldly into the camp in the darkness, and how he had reached the shed, crawling through the sentries, and had seen the most remarkable machine that the war has produced.

"It is a triumph my dear Klein," he said, his eyes shining, "I have in my head," he tapped tho good, broad German forehead "the whole construction of this engine. In twelve hours I will give you a drawing and notes which —"

"Hush, hush," said Klein for in his natural excitement, Posser's voice had risen.

"Here is the rough idea." Posser rapidly sketched a now familiar shape briefly outlined with rough squares and oblongs the position of the engine and the guns.

"I will keep this," said Klein. "You must get to work at once, my dear fellow, and give us a more detailed drawing. But first we will drink mutual congratulations."

Klein got out a bottle of champagne, pulled out the cork, and these two fine fellows, true and loyal sons of the Fatherland, drank in a whisper to the destruction of civilization's enemy — England!

Klein accompanied Posser to his room. They pulled down the blinds before they switched on the light. Quickly the drawing pads, the rulers, the T-squares and the compasses were taken out of Posser's suit-case and arrayed on the table.

"Now I will leave you," said Klein, shook hands heartily with the hero of that night's adventure and left the room, as he said, without a sound. He had scarcely got into his own room and shut the door when be heard the click of the lock on Posser's door and smiled his approval.

It was as at a quarter to two when he went to bed and at half-past seven the maid brought him a cup of coffee and some biscuits. He drank his coffee and rose, slipped into his dressing-gown and went over to Posser's room anxious to know what was the result of the night's work.

He tapped at the door. There was no answer. He tapped again. There was still no answer.

He tried the handle, remembering at the same time that Herr Posser had locked the door. He was a little surprised to find that the door yielded. The room was in semi-darkness, the blinds were still drawn and be walked to the window and let the blinds up with a sash. What he saw, or rather what he did not see, struck him with amazement. The bed had not been slept in. All the drawing materials had been cleared, Posser's trunks were still in the position where he had left them, but there no sign of Posser.

He went back to his room and rang the bell. The night porter was summoned but neither he nor any of the servants had seen Posser, who from that moment vanished from the earth as completely as though the ground had opened swallowed him, and not only vanished but had taken with him what drawings he had made.

In his perturbation Klein went to the room of Mister Haynes, who was in bed and sleeping soundly.

"Get up!" said Klein testily; "have you seen Mr.—, my secretary?"

Mister Haynes sat up, rubbing his eyes and yawning.

"What's the time?" he asked.

"Confound it," said Klein angrily," what does it matter what the time is? Have you seen my friend?"

"Why should I have seen your friend?" growled Haynes. "What happened to him?"

"He has disappeared," said Klein.

"Gone out for a walk, I expect; it is a beautifn1 morning."

"On the contrary, it is raining and blowing," said Klein angrily; "Why should he go out on a morning like this?"

Haynes rose and dressed himself leisurely, spending an unconscionable time in the bathroom for a man whom I never suspected of washing, and turning up at breakfast wholly unconcerned in his callous English fashion as to what happened to poor Posser.

Klein, who was all nerves, could eat nothing. He had questioned everybody in the hotel, but nobody had heard a sound in the night and the night-porter supplemented his previous statement, declaring that it was impossible for Posser to leave the house except with his knowledge.

Klein was not satisfied and made an examination of the outside of the hotel, hoping to pick up some trace of his comrade.

Outside Posser's window he made a discovery. A line of bushes grew within a foot of the house-wall, and beneath Posser's window these had been broken as though by some heavy body having jumped or fallen upon them. Moreover he discovered a small pair of dividers which he recognized as Posser's.

Pursuing his investigations beyond the grounds of the hotel, he came upon the tracks of motor-car wheels which he followed to the outskirts of the town where he made another discovery. The road here was undergoing repair; owing to the wetness of the morning the night watchman was still on duty, not having been relieved as usually is the case at the hour when the men started work.

This old man Klein questioned.

"Yes," said the watchman, "I saw a motor-car. It was an ambulance with green lights. It went past here a little after one this morning and came by a little after two. It stopped very near the hotel, because I could see its tail lights and I saw it turn round."

Klein went back to the hotel with his nerves shaken and his usually well ordered mind in a condition of chaos.

"I am going back to town by the ten o'clock train," he told Mister Haynes. 'I suppose you will be staying?"

"No," said Mister Haynes with another yawn. "I shall go back, too. There is nothing to be got out of this place."

And so, much to the disgust of Klein, who in his state of mind would have preferred to have been alone, they went back together. They had to change at Basingstoke, and there finding that he would have half an hour to wait Klein crossed to the nearest hotel and got me on the 'phone. It was in this way that he related to me as far as he could with safety the extraordinary happenings of the previous night.

"It is inexplicable, my dear Heine," he said, speaking in Spanish. "I am bewildered, stunned."

I no less was agitated.

"Did he not communicate anything to you?" I asked.

"Yes, thank our good Gott!" said Klein's voice; "he gave me a rough sketch which may be sufficient. Whatever has happened to him the good fellow's work is not fruitless." Then suddenly his voice sank and he spoke hurriedly.

"I cannot say more," he said, "that infernal reporter of yours is outside the box. Does he understand Spanish?"

"He understands no language except bad French," I replied, and heard the click of the telephone receiver being hung up.

So distressed and puzzled was I that I went down to the station to meet my friend. I walked along the platform as the train came to a slow standstill, and the first person I met was Mister Haynes looking more untidy than ever.

"Where is my friend?" I asked.

"I don't know," said Haynes, yawning; "he went over to the hotel to telephone to somebody at Basingstoke and left before I did. In fact, I had to run to catch the train," he explained. "He is here somewhere."

"But here was no Klein. If he had been left behind he would have telephoned me. I made inquiries of the guard.

"A gentleman in a check cap and a long ulster?" said that official. "Yes, I remember him. He got on to the train at Basingstoke, first-class passenger, wasn't he? I particularly noticed he was in a carriage by himself and was reading. This is the carriage," he said, pulling the door open, "here is his magazine."

On the rack above was Klein's suit-case. It was evident that it had been rifled because the collars and night-shirt, brushes and combs, were all mixed together in confusion. I stared at Haynes and Haynes looked at me.

"How extraordinary!" said Mister Haynes.

It was not until that night that Klein's body was recovered, lying in a ditch by the side of the railway shot through the heart, with every pocket turned inside out, and yet, curiously enough, with all his money, his watch and rings left intact. Of the rough drawing which he had promised to deliver to me there was no sign. Close at hand was his revolver with one chamber discharged.

Mister Haynes was in the office when the news came. He had been out all the afternoon and had, he said, met with an accident, for his arm was bandaged and in a sling. I was so upset by my anxiety over Klein that I had barely noticed Mister Haynes's injury, but now I looked at him narrowly.

"What is the nature of your injury?" I asked. He laughed.

"Mr. Cannelli," he said, "I don't know very much about you. You may be a very honest man, the tool of very dishonest men."

"What do you mean?" I asked.

"It may be," he went on, without taking any notice of my question, "that you are being duped and that it is only coincidence that you have friends who pursue extraordinary inquiries. All the records we have of you," my heart gave a throb and I could feel my bands trembling, " all the records we have of you," he repeated, "seem to be in good order. I will give you two pieces of advice. The first is to be careful in your choice of acquaintances. The second is to refrain from allowing your very natural anxieties to lead you into further inquiries as to the fate of Mr. Adolph Klein, alias Simpson, and if I would add a third," he said, looking out of the window and speaking in his slow drawl, "it is to advise your friends in communicating with you to avoid both the telephone and the Spanish language. Good afternoon."

He picked up his hat and went out, the picture of a broken-down journalist, and I did not see him again until one day in Whitehall I passed an officer, wearing the badge of the Intelligence Department, who smiled and waved his hand to me.

It was my reporter.

5 — THE MAN FROM THE STARS

In the summer of 1915, I received a request from Berlin which somewhat surprised me. I was instructed to send to Holland as many good maps of London as I could buy, and I was told also to prepare one special map, marking the areas which the street-lamps had been darkened. This was followed (or it may have come I the same dispatch, I forget) by a request that I should instruct my men to discover how it was that the British Government knew we contemplated an air-raid on London.

I myself wondered what information the British Government had secured and how they had secured it. For months the streets had been lit as gaily as pre-war days. The theatre signs glowed and flashed, the West End streets were bathed in radiance and then, almost by a touch of the magician's wand London "went dark." Street lamps were shaded, the light signs outside the theatres were extinguished and it was almost impossible to pick your way through the streets.

I suppose my excellent friend, the High-Born Baron von Hertz-Missenger would have said, "English Secret Service." He reminds me of a character Charles Dickens the great English poet, who invariably thought that his head was the head of King Charles II!

The explanation I offered was, that some of our too impetuous airmen must have betrayed the fact by shouting with haughty insolence to the English airmen they met in the air. As this has never been denied, it is probably true.

At any rate I set myself to work upon a map. It was a long business, and very unsatisfactory, because the whole of London was dark, and no place was more light than another. This I reported, forwarding the maps by special courier.

And then I received a request from our Headquarters that I should arrange light-signals which should be seen by Zeppelins. The idea was to post three lights so that they formed a triangle, one near Albany Park, one near Maidstone Road, and a third in the east, near Shepherd's Junction. The triangle thus made would contain all the valuable city area which it was our Zeppelins' intention to utterly destroy.

Of the first raid in September, it is not necessary for me to tell. Of how the cowardly Englishmen trembled beneath the midnight hail of bombs, you have read. I myself did not witness the raid, because, on receiving information on the afternoon Zeppelins were due, I had left London for Cornwall. Since it was impossible for the brave fellows who piloted our good Zeppelins to distinguish between a patriot and a hateful enemy, I thought that in the interest of the Fatherland, it was necessary that I should be as far away as possible when the dread visitation came.

I returned to London the next morning and arrived at eleven o'clock. Oh what consternation there was. Oh what vile language these unkultured Londoners used, what epithets, what adjectives, the A's, and B's, and C's, and D's, they called us — but of that anon!

I was in some anxiety before my journey's end was reached as to whether I should have to walk a part of the journey, and I was greatly relieved on questioning the conductor to learn that Paddington Station had escaped the holocaust. When I arrived at Paddington everything was going on as usual. To my amazement buses were running and cabs were plying for hire.

"Where was the raid?" I asked.

"In the East End and the City," was the reply. So, I thought, my triangle had proved efficacious, and calling a cab, I said: "Will you please drive me to the ruined area?"

The poor, ignorant fellow thought at first that it was the name of a public- house, and I bad to enlighten him.

"Where the bombs struck," I said.

"Oh, yes," he said, brightening up, "I will ask a policeman where they fell."

"Do you mean to tell me," I inquired, "that you don't know? Perhaps you haven't been to the City?"

"Yes sir," he replied in the true boorish cabman spirit. "I've been to the city three times but I ain't seen no place where the bombs fell."

This of course was "eye-wash." For my part I had removed all my archives from my office, and as that was on the edge of the City, I drove there first and as pleased to find that my office had not been touched. I drove up Ludgate Hill and apparently everything was as usual, and it was not until he had driven farther on and. had penetrated a side street that I saw the wreckage of a house. It was pleasing and yet disappointing. A number of windows had been smashed, one house was in ruins and there was a big hole in a court-yard, but the damage was as such as might have been caused by an explosion of gas.

It took me a long time before I found the second place where a bomb had fallen, and there again the results were not as I expected. I spent the whole of that day wandering about looking for devastation. I went east and south, and north, and although I saw some damaged houses, the results of our gallant Zeppelins' visit left much to be desired.

Returning to my office I was called on the phone and a code message was sent through to me. As I expected, it was from Berlin asking for full particulars of the damage done, and very faithfully I described what I had seen, coded it and passed it on to the proper quarters.

To my wrath and humiliation, the next evening brought a peremptory demand from Berlin. It had been sent by radio, picked up off the coast by a little steamer plying the flag of —, and was brought to me from an East Coast port by one of the couriers we employed for that purpose. The message was, as I say, peremptory, and there were tears in my eyes, tears of sorrow and injury as I read it.

"Cannot understand your message. Our pilots report Westminster Abbey as bombed. Whole streets of the City are in flames, Houses of Parliament partly destroyed, also London Bridge and Tower of London. Several ships in docks hit and sunk. Please personally investigate and report."

Of course there was a chance that these cunning English had, by means of scene painters and workmen labouring through the night, removed all sign of the destruction, but I walked over London Bridge without any difficulty, and as far as I could see the Tower of London was uninjured.

I reported the same, and three days later, had this message back:

"Be on south side of Three Mile Wood, north-north-east Saffron Walden, at eleven o'clock on the night of October 7th."

I could not understand this message, and my new assistant, who had arrived from America, Herr Wilhelm Peters, was as much puzzled as I. However, on the 7th of October, I journeyed to Saffron Walden, which is a little town in Essex, and by studying a map I discovered that Three Mile Wood was inaccurately named because it was about seven miles from the town. I decided to walk, and arrived in the neighbourhood of the wood at about ten o'clock at night. Having ascertained by consulting my compass which was the south side, I made my way across fields and muddy ditches to a big meadow which was exactly placed to the south of the sparsely-wooded little forest.

It was a clear night with a thin ground haze and was rather cold. I had brought one of those walking-sticks, the top of which forms a seat, and this found very comfortable; for the inner man I had a flask of brandy and some liver sandwiches, and I settled myself down to my vigil, wondering what on earth ad induced Headquarters to send me upon this wild adventure.

Then suddenly my heart began beating at a tremendous rate as I divined the reason ! It was intended this night for our airships to reach London, and they desired that I should be a witness. What folly! What folly! What incomparable insanity to risk the life of a high Officer of Intelligence, to place him in such horrible jeopardy. I felt myself grow pale, but then with an effort I braced up. I was a German!

We Germans fear God and nothing else, and, besides, I thought there might not be an air-raid after all.

But what satisfaction I got out of that thought was quickly dissipated. Suddenly an ominous sound came to me. A double "boom!" far away in the east, was followed by three staccato explosions. Another bomb fell, suddenly the whole of the eastern sky was illuminated by the tracing fingers of searchlights.

"Boom!" The sound was growing nearer and my mouth was dry. I was choking. I loosened my collar and mopped the sweat from my forehead and stood up, my knees trembling.

I have thought the matter over since and I have come to the conclusion that my agitation might be explained in this way, that I was trembling with pride in the fearless exploits of our gallant airmen, those intrepid messengers of death who sailed the midnight skies fearless of foe; that I perspired because the liver sandwich was perhaps a little too highly flavoured. Anyway, the cursed things were corning closer and who knows what mistakes a blundering fool of a pilot might make. The searchlights were suddenly extinguished, the guns were silent and for ten minutes I heard no sound save a faint but ever-growing- nearer hum of an engine in the sky. Then there was a shrieking whistle, a crash that seemed to shake the very earth, a blinding fan of flame and, then silence.

In my rage I shook my fist at the sky.

"Stupid jackasses, miserable, bat-eyed swine-hound!" I cried. "Have you not the highest instructions in your pockets to avoid bombing an Intelligence Officer?"

The cursed thing passed overhead. It was roaring like a railway train passing through a tunnel. I saw the bulk of it outlined against the stars and then I saw something else, a little black dot that moved and swayed against the sky. I thought it might be some infernal machine and I nearly fainted.

Understand that my chief thought was of Germany. I had no fear for myself, I was merely a cog in the wheel of the great machine and stood ready at any hour and all days to sacrifice myself for our dear Deutschland. Fortunately, there was a fallen tree in my neighbourhood, and under this I crept, looking out from time to time to see what had happened to the strange thing in the air.

Then I heard a thud, a rustle, and an oath, and I jumped up, bruising the back of my head against the tree-trunk, and ran towards the sound, for that oath was in good German.

"Wer da?" called a sharp voice. "It is I, Heine," I replied.

"Oh, good," said the voice in German. "You are on the spot, I see. Help free me from this doubly rotten parachute."

I made my way to him and helped unbuckle some of the straps that fastened him, and presently he was free.

"Have you got a pocket lamp?" he asked. "No, perhaps you had better not use it. Where can I put the parachute?"

I suggested the tree under which I had been — I won't say hiding, let me rather say taking cover.

"Have you a car?" he asked.

"No," I replied.

"You are an ass," said he; "why haven't you a car?"

I knew by the imperiousness of his tone that he was a true German gentleman probably highly born and connected by many social ties with an old family of Prussia.

"I am the Baron von Treutzer," he said, as though answering my thoughts "and I have been sent here to survey the damage that was done in the last raid."

"Your Excellency will discover that I have spoken nothing but the truth," I said humbly. The sound of the Zeppelin's engines, which had diminished, was now increasing in volume.

"Is the airship returning?" I asked.

"Yes, yes," he said testily. He took from his pocket a small electric lamp and flashed it three times in the air and immediately after three tiny sparks of light showed in the sky.

"They won't be dropping any more bombs, Herr Baron?" I asked carelessly.

"Good heavens! What does it matter if they do? " he boomed — he was a booming kind of man, born to command, typical of our virile aristocracy which has placed Germany in the forefront of world-nations.

"I only asked," I said. "I am a mere observer."

"We only dropped a few bombs," he said, "just to explain our presence. The real business of our visit is here." I heard him slap his chest in the darkness.

"I did not know where the raid was intended," I said, "or I would have arranged for a leader."

"A leader?" he asked. "What the devil do you mean?"

"Evidently Herr Baron is not a member of the Zeppelin crew," I said humbly, "or he would know that the Zeppelins are 'led' to their destination by motor- cars with strong head-lamps."

"Of course I am not a member of the Zeppelin crew," he said in deep disgust, "I am a Royal Lieutenant of the 31st Regiment of the Prussian Guard."

"Does your Excellency intend staying here very long?" I asked, as we trudged along the country road.

"For a week," he replied, "after that I return —"

"By—?"

"That is my business," he replied, "if a Zeppelin can bring me here, a Zeppelin can take me away."

Though I had never heard of parachutes that go up, I know all things are possible owing to the inventive genius of our nation, so I questioned him no further. Outside Saffron Walden we stopped while I went to the hotel to collect the handbag which I had left there.

Needless to say the people in the hotel were in that condition of cowardly funk which our Zeppelin always inspires. The children were crying because they had not seen the airship, and again I heard in the common bar of the hotel those terrible words which my modesty would only allow me to designate by using certain letters of thee alphabet.

I rejoined the Baron and we made our way to the railway station, which was in darkness. Fortunately the train which came in was also darkened and remained that way until we reached London and I was able to bring the Baron to my flat without observation. He was a tall, handsome gentleman, dressed in civilian clothes of a noble cut and rich texture, and over a glass of whisky he graciously unbent and told me that he had come to England by this curious method to discover the extent of the damage, not only of the first raid, but of a raid which was projected and by which it was hoped to lay London entirely in ruins.

"On what day will that occur?" I asked.

"You will be notified in due time. It may be to-morrow, and it may be the next day," he replied.

"I only asked," I said carelessly, "because it is necessary for me to see one of my agents in North Devon one day this week, and I should not like to miss the raid."

"You will stay here until I go. That is an order. Why are you looking so pale?"

"It is the pressure of work, your Excellency," I replied. "I am afraid I have rather taxed my strength. My doctor suggested that I ought to go away at once to Cornwall or perhaps Scotland."

"We hope to bomb Scotland," said the Baron thoughtfully. "It would not be a bad idea if you were there."

"When I said Scotland," I said hastily, "I should have said that my doctor suggested I should go to Scotland in the spring. This of course is the very worst weather. Are you likely to bomb Wales?"

"We cannot reach there. It is beyond our reach," said the Baron.

"I only ask," I said, "because he also suggested that I should go there."

"When the raids are over you can go to the devil. I only want your assistance when they are on."

"Did you say raids or raid?" I asked.

"There may be two," he replied callously.

The next morning he expressed his intention of going through the City and the East End to photograph the worst of the damage. I did not offer to accompany him, and indeed, had he suggested that I should do so, I should have firmly declined. Fortunately, he knew London very well, for he had been an attaché the German Embassy a few years before the war broke out, so ha had no need my assistance or guidance.

He left the flat at eleven o'clock and I arranged to meet him at a restaurant in Piccadilly for lunch. I need hardly say that he was armed with a passport not only very completely filled in, but endorsed with an exact imitation of rubber stamps which were used in those days by examining officers at Folkestone when passengers landed.

I was waiting for him at one o'clock, but he did not arrive. Half-past one came, a quarter to two, two o'clock, and I began to feel seriously alarmed, and was thinking what an excellent text his arrest would provide for a letter Potsdam on the futility of sending amateurs, when he came through the swing doors.

He uttered no word till we were sitting at the table, and the waiter had served the soup.

"These English people are very clever," he said at last.

"In a way they are clever," I said, "but by the side of the German—"

"Don't talk nonsense. Our German people are merely slavish imitators of everybody else in the world. If Germany was not a nation of slaves we should never have an army."

This put an end to the easy flow of conversation, but presently I ventured ask: "Why does your Excellency think the English are clever?"

"I am referring to the way they have cleared up the mess we made and have run up new buildings." He looked up at me curiously as he spoke.

"Don't you agree?"

"Naturally," I said heartily, "I have reason to believe that hundreds thousands of workmen have been working day and night to restore tube damage.'

He laughed.

"In addition to being a fool, you are a liar," he said, and I could only smile the good humour and buoyant frankness of this high-born officer who was in a probability in the entourage of the All-highest himself and, at any rate, as I have since learnt, had frequently dined with that exalted Prince whom we call the Hope of Germany.

"No," Baron von Treutzer went on, "the Zeppelin did little or no damage. It caused nothing of the smash that we expected it would. We will see what tonight's raid brings out."

"To-night?" I said, half-rising from my seat.

"Did I say to-night?" he said in an off-band way. "Well, whenever it happens."

But I knew that in a moment of incaution be had spoken the truth.

"By the way, I shall want you with me to-night," he said.

"To-night?" I repeated. "I am very sorry but this is the one night I cannot be with your Excellency. I have an important messenger coming from Ireland with particulars of a rising, and the Foreign Office has particularly asked me—"

"I shall want you to-night," repeated the Herr Baron, "and you will meet me at ten o'clock, let us say, in St. Paul's Churchyard."

"Himmel! Herr Baron!" I exploded, "that would be in the very centre the raid!"

"Did I ever say that it would not?" he asked coolly, "Of course it will be in the centre of the raid. You understand, at ten o'clock. The War Office require a detailed account by eye-witnesses of the damage which is done,"

"But my messenger arrives at Fishguard to-night," I said with a tremor in my voice, "Forgive me if I am agitated, Herr Baron, but I realize the terrible importance, the absolute necessity, of meeting that boat."

"At ten o'clock you will be in St. Paul's Churchyard," said the Baron.

How I loathed and hated this tyrant. We Germans are naturally lovers of freedom. We despise the sycophant and the toady. Tyranny to us is a pestilential disease to be stamped out with an iron heel. Woe to those who endeavour to enslave the Germans, for they are biting on granite!

I told the Baron that I would meet him at the appointed time.

"Don't come before ten," he said. "We will remain until the raid is over."

I lifted my hat and bowed as I parted from him in Piccadilly, and I prayed most fervently, that the earth would open and swallow this pig, whose abominable manners and low attitude to men not so well born as himself (though of that I am not sure, for there were many stories about my mother's friendship for the Graf von Maldesee, which I sometimes reflect upon with a certain amount of satisfaction) aroused in me the deepest scorn.

I could eat no dinner that night, I could do no work that afternoon. I sat in my office until a quarter to ten, suffering, I think, from a touch of malaria and ague which I contracted in America. I arrived in St. Paul's Churchyard, dark and gloomy and silent, on the stroke of ten. I had arranged to meet the Baron at the corner of one of the lanes which slope down to Upper Thames Street, and here I took my station.

At a quarter past ten he had not arrived. At twenty minutes past ten a hundred searchlights flashed into the sky and the first gun-shot woke the sleeping city. The Zeppelin was coming straight to the City, but was west of where I stood. I heard the thud of its bombs and the devil's chorus of the guns. I saw the skies speckled with shrapnel bursts, but much of what happened in that brief space of time between its appearance and its disappearance is blotted from my memory.

I could only stand crouched in a friendly doorway, my hands before my eyes, thinking of my dear friends, and particularly of a certain girl in Chicago with whom I had exchanged photographs, of my dear home, my little brothers, in fact all my life passed before me. I dare not go out to look for the Herr Baron.

How I envied him, that hardened man of war to whom this terrible concatenation of sound was as the gentle zephyrs; who could stand uncowed and watch with his stern military eye the destruction that was going on about him, uncaring, unafraid, contemptuous of danger, seeking only the information he required for his superiors!

In that moment I almost loved the man, even though I hated to meet him lest be mistook my ague for a more ignoble emotion, but presently I plucked up courage and went out to look for him. He was not at the corner of the lane nor was he on the pavement at all.

I made a circuit of the Cathedral without meeting him and then I realized that the Zeppelins had not been near St. Paul's but had passed westward. Naturally he would have been informed at the last moment and would have been on a spot where they would pass.

I did not attempt to join the throngs that gathered about the places where the bombs had fallen, but made my way homeward. At one o'clock he had not returned; two, three, and four passed. I still listened and then the horror of the possibility seized me. This gallant man had perhaps paid for his temerity with his life and I bought an early morning paper as soon as one was procurable and searched in vain for some indication of his fate.

Such a man could not be stricken down without attracting attention, but there was no reference whatever to such a one as he. In a fever of anxiety I paced my room. I called up my various agents but they could give me no information and I had almost abandoned hope when, at half-past eleven, the Baron came, debonair and calm, into my office.

"You had a good view," were the first words he said.

"Oh, Herr Baron," I said. I grasped his hand and shook it (a most presumptuous thing to do); "I am so glad to see you back! If you missed me I was on the spot."

"I didn't miss you," he said.

"Where were you?"

"I was at Fishguard, meeting your man, but apparently without success, for he did not come."

"You were at Fishguard?" I gasped.

"Naturally," he said, "you don't suppose I am such a silly fool that I am going to stand under a bomb to see it burst, do you?"

Such a man was this mean-souled dog, von Treutzer!

Thank heaven! He disappeared in a week. He may have been picked up by a descending Zeppelin. He may have been taken off by a near-approaching submarine. I have had no news, but if I hear he got back to Germany alive, I, Heine, will be sorry.

6 — THE AFFAIR OF THE ALLIES' CONFERENCE

I think it must have been my association with the spurious journalist, Haynes that not only awoke a certain uneasiness in my breast, and shook my confidence in my judgment as to tho existence of a British secret service, but it also showed me a way to dispel any suspicion which I might have created in the bosom of the police, and also to advertise my innocence to the great public.

I began systematically to write letters to the newspapers. You may remember my long letter in the Evening Post on the necessity for limiting the supplies to neutrals. You may recall the letter which was given due prominence in the Post Telegraph on the urgent necessity for a South American Federation to show a united front against German "cruelties" — I felt a foul traitor to Deutschstum when I wrote this! — you may have clipped from numerous papers, both in London and in the provinces, innumerable epistles signed Francisco Cannelli, on the heroism of France, on the splendour of Belgium on the necessity for learning Spanish, so that, the good English could come to South America and take away the wicked German's trade, and you would certainly have found my name against respectable amounts in the subscription lists which were opened by various newspapers in the early days of the war.

It was a scheme of colossal daring and how well I succeeded! No less than seven newspapers published my photograph. I was interviewed for the Times Herald. I was referred to in other letters to the editor, and my frankness and geniality were praised in the highest measure.

For, in the course of these letters I admitted frankly that, quite unwittingly — because of my foreign origin — I had been acquainted with many notorious spies in England and I even suggested methods by which the spy could be traced and brought to justice (this was in one of the four letters I wrote on "The Unseen Hand")

I took up "The Unseen Hand" idea with enthusiasm. It was a popular cry and who was I, that I should not take advantage of the onrushing wave and ride to popularity upon its crest?

To the everlasting honour of the illustrious and excellent chiefs of my Department in Berlin, they recognized the object of my scheme, and I could show you now, if the codes bad not been destroyed, messages of congratulation couched in the most gracious terms and signed by names which indicated personages of the most exalted character.

There was living in England (in Kent to be exact) at this time, the Baron von Hertz-Missenger, who was what was termed a naturalized German, and as I have remarked on many occasions (and have been complimented on my delicate wit, a naturalized German is a German in his natural state.

The Herr Baron had a beautiful house and was in a position to secure news, both from the Fatherland and from certain exclusive circles in London. From that high flagstaff of his, many a message has leapt into the night and been caught by our vigilant radio operators at Wilhelmshaven. From that closed study, with its rows upon rows of books, its gorgeous Persian carpets and its shaded lamps, many a British secret has been coded into a few meaningless words. Herr Baron and I were good friends, though we seldom met. I think he pleased with me because I never forgot the homage which is due to the high- born, and he was certainly popular with me because he had the ear of Potsdam and the All-Highest Confidence of He Whose Name we will not mention. My reputation as a writer of letters had been firmly established when I received a note asking me to meet the Baron at a certain hotel in a south coast watering place. Precisely on the day, at the hour, and to the minute of my appointment I presented myself in the private suite of his Excellency, who always received me with the most gracious condescension.

"Heine," he said, when he bad closed the door, "I am very troubled about you."

"About me, your Excellency," I said in surprise.

"Yes, about you," he repeated. "It is clear to me that you are suspect. I have heard all about the things which have happened in the past, and knowing he British Secret Service as I do, I cannot imagine that you have, as the Americans say, got away with it."

"Secret service, your Excellency?" I smiled; "surely you do not believe in a widely organized—?"

"Don't be a fool, Heine," said the Herr Baron sharply; even to be called a fool by a man of his position and rank is a compliment, implying as it does a friendliness and an intimacy which few of us attain with our superiors.

"Of course there is a Secret Police. The whole country is over-run with them. It is the most deadly Secret Police in the world, with the exception of the American, because it doesn't boast and it doesn't talk. Its very silence is its strength."

For my part, though I was not feeling strong, I was silent. One cannot argue the point with an amateur, even a distinguished amateur, and whilst I was always willing to admit that the police of

England were undoubtedly brilliant and extraordinarily lucky, I could not admit the existence of an organization on the scale which the Herr Baron outlined.

"You don't believe this," he said quickly, and before I could protest my faith in anything he said, he went on: "I tell you that this hotel is filled with English spies. They probably saw you come into this room, and it is fairly certain they followed you from London and will go back with you. That is why I asked you my telegram to come down and have a friendly argument on the question of trade after the war, as outlined in your letter to the Post Herald. That telegram was read and re-read before it reached you. Have no doubt of that, Heine. In England they know I am a German. They hope I am loyal. They do not trust me any more than they trust you."

"But surely, Herr Baron," I smiled, "this does not mean that your Excellency will not be able to serve the Fatherland in moments of emergency?"

He shook his head.

"If by that you mean wireless, my answer is no,'" he said, "my wireless apparatus is dust and ashes. I have burnt it and destroyed every single code. I have one more piece of work to do for Deutschland and if I succeed, or if somebody else succeeds, I am finished, and leave well alone. I cannot advise you to do the same, because it is your business to take risks just as it is my business not to take risks. Now I have called you down partly to warn you, and partly to give you certain information. Whether you act on that information or not is also your business. You have heard of Lord Leatham?"

I nodded.

"He has an estate in Shropshire. He is not a rich man, and some years he used to let his estate to a tenant. He is a friend of a friend of mine and I have learnt that it is the intention of the Government to take over his property as a prison camp for German officers. Now it may be necessary — this is merely a conjecture, and I am only looking ahead — to communicate with gentlemen who will be in that camp. Leatham Priory is a very old house," he spoke slowly and impressively, "at one time it was in the possession of a persecuted Catholic family, and there is a legend that beneath the grounds runs a secret subterranean passage. That it was something more than a legend Lord Leatham discover twenty years ago, for a portion of this tunnel was unearthed, but it seemed lead to nowhere. What his Lordship does not know, is that that tunnel virtually intact and that the passage which was discovered was not the real one but was merely a branch which was never completed and which was intended to lead to the crypt of the village church. Remember that this is all I can tell you. I know no more, and I merely pass on the information to you for what it worth."

I went back to London that night, a little puzzled as to why the good Baron had, brought me all the way to Brighton to give me information of this kind. It was not a certainty that any well-placed person would be accommodated on Lord Leatham's property, and it was less certain that I could be of any assistance to such a prisoner, unless I was prepared to take down a gang of workmen (which was obviously impossible) to open up the hidden passage.

The whole scheme was impracticable and I could only put it down as an excess of zeal for the Fatherland on the part of his Excellency.

At parting the Baron had given me a little plan showing the direction of the tunnel, the entrance of which he said would be found in a tiny ravine through which flowed a small river, and had also advised me to look up particulars of Leatham Priory.

The first discovery I made when I began my investigations was that Leatham Priory was not in Shropshire at all. It was in fact in Buckinghamshire, midway between Maidenhead and the small town of Beaconsfield. I sent a good friend down into Buckingham (or Bucks as they call it) to discover what was happening and he brought back the news that Lord Leatham's house, the Priory, was being extensively decorated and refurnished.

Now, I know that the English, because of their fear of Germany, treat German officer prisoners with the greatest kindness, but I could not believe, in view of certain outcries in the public press to which I contributed my share, that they would spend large sums of money to furnish magnificently a country house for Germans, and I saw that even as the Herr Baron bad been inaccurate in one particular, so was it likely that be had been wilfully "misinformed" in another.

I bided my time, for I knew that the significance of the Baron's communication would be revealed. In the meanwhile, I myself had paid a visit to the ground and had discovered, not without a great deal of difficulty, the end of the subterranean passage. It needed some furtive digging, for the end had fallen in and was entirely covered up, before I could make sure that I had discovered the entrance.

The day, or rather the very early morning, I wriggled through the debris and found myself in a small paved tunnel, smelling terribly musty, was the day on which I understood the purport of the Baron's communication. On that day the papers announced that there was to be a great War Council in London. There had arrived military representatives of all the Powers, and I, standing in Whitehall, had seen these officers enter the War Office, where they remained for two or three hours, when they were escorted by British officers to Downing Street, where again they remained some time.

At half-past four in the afternoon six great motor-cars drew up in Whitehall and the members of the Council entered the cars and were driven off. From the end of Downing Street I saw they turned into St. James's Park and, hiring a taxi I followed, giving the driver instructions to keep the cars in sight as long as he could. They passed through the park, up St. James's Street, and I though they were going to their hotel, but instead of this they went straight along Piccadilly to Hyde Park Corner, where they turned into the park. Realizing that I could not follow with my taxi, I put my head out of the window and ordered my driver to go up Park Lane. At the Marble Arch I picked them up again. They passed along the Bayswater Road and in a flash their destination was revealed to me. It was in order to entertain this Council that Lord Leatham's house had been decorated! It was here that the real conference was to be held!

It was a breathless, tremendous problem which the Herr Baron had set me about I am not a man easily baffed. There is something in our German nature rises superior to difficulties and which enables us to meet the most tremendous problems in a calm spirit of transcendent perception.

I flew back to my office as fast as my taxi could carry me, and for an hour my phone was busy. Understand that whatever risk I ran was more justified. For there were men in that Council whose names were household words, whose faces were familiar even to the child of the cottager; there were names to conjure with, reputations and records that would have dazzled and frightened a man of a smaller calibre than myself.

By twelve o'clock that night two desperate and well-armed men were exploring the tunnel. They were men who were prepared at the call of the Fatherland to lay down their lives, yea, even on an enemy's soil.

I was not one of them. I was sorely tempted to go, but common prudence dictated that the brain of the movement should be far removed from the scene of danger.

Apparently the party met with no opposition and traversed the tunnel, which had collapsed in places, until they reached the ruins of a flight of circular stone stairs, which led up to a sort of shaft and terminated abruptly at a circular stone flag.

In preparation for such an emergency they bad brought collapsible ladders and one of our friends mounted to the top. He could hear footsteps above him, and I judge that he was in the old baronial banqueting ball which is celebrated throughout England as the most perfect type of Norman architecture extant in country.

Its stone-flagged floor, its vaulted roof, its grim stone fireplace, great mullioned windows, have been so often described in guide-books that it is necessary for me to attempt to rival our good friend Karl Baedeker.

But every attempt which was made to raise the flagged trap-door, which undoubtedly existed, was frustrated. I employed in this task one Hermann Swartz, or, to give him his English name, Herbert Black, a very skilled member of my staff who was also, curiously enough, a stone mason. Finding their efforts unavailing, the party made their way back to London and reported to me.

"I can tell you this, Herr Heine," said Swartz, with that profound earnestness which is the charm of the German working man who has no peer in the world, "that if you let me bring my tools I will guarantee to open that trap to-night. I feel in this that I cannot assume responsibility unless I am directed by a superior officer, and I suggest that you should come with us."

"My dear good Swartz," said I testily, "why should I go with you? You understand that it is very necessary that I should not he identified with such enterprise as this, that I am the brains of a great movement and that upon my safety depends, perhaps, the ever-to-be-desired safety of the Fatherland."

Whereupon Swartz (and I regret to have to report this, and have already notified Berlin of the occurrence) refused to go except under my leadership.

Having made a most exhaustive inquiry of all the circumstances, and having discovered that there was very little danger of my detection, I agreed, and at three o'clock in the morning, behold me crawling stealthily through a square in the banqueting hall of Leatham Priory. One dim electric light burned in the roof, giving the gaunt apartment an air of size and mystery. Save along the centre, it was uncarpeted. The smouldering ashes of a fire still burnt in the grate and from somewhere a great clock ticked solemnly. The room was almost innocent of furniture. There was a long, an interminably long, table set upon the parallelogram of carpet and against this were pushed about twenty chairs. There were three or four suits of armour, two big pieces of tapestry covering the principal walls, a black oak buffet or sideboard, half a dozen easy chairs about the fire-place and, so far as I could see, nothing else.

There were four doors leading from the room, two at each end, and I gathered that those flanking the sideboard would lead to the kitchens and servants' quarters, and that the two doors facing them, which were beautifully' carved, and one which was half hidden by a portiere, would lead to the wing in which Leatham and his guests were asleep.

I had pulled on felt-slippers over my boots and made my quiet way to door which was covered by the portiere. My objective you may easily guess. These high nobilities who were visiting Lord Leatham were members of the Conference, that Conference would be held possibly in one of the great saloons and the portfolios containing the notes of the meeting would be found in the high-born lord's study or office.

I proceeded very stealthily, because I knew that in view of the presence of such important people, watchers and sentries would be placed about the house, and in this I was not mistaken, for looking through one of the long window there were half a dozen in the hall — I could see two policemen walking slowly along a path which ran parallel with the house. The only danger was that they would also post watchers inside the house. As a matter of fact there were two, but these men were posted on the next floor, one at each end of a passage leading to the apartments where the distinguished guests were sleeping. The study I found after a tiresome search. It was situated in an annexe and reached by another passage which ran at right angles to the main corridor.

Tho door was fastened by a patent lock which, however, presented no difficulties to Heinrich Falkenburg, one of my assistants, whose services I am pleased acknowledge. I made a very careful examination of the door with my pocket lamp and there appeared to be no wires and no alarm signal.

You may wonder how I came to distinguish the study from the other rooms. I will tell you. It was the only room that was locked. I opened the door cautiously and listened for the sound of a bell. We stood for nearly five minutes before we ventured into the room, and when we did, we were rewarded. There was only one window and across that heavy purple velvet curtains had been drawn. There was a large library-table in the middle on which were several ash trays filled with cigar ash. There was no need for me to make this discovery for the room was heavy with the scent of cigar smoke and cedar wood.

So, thought I, the excellent plenipotentiaries have met here and not in the saloon. I looked about and found some scraps of paper in the waste-paper basket. Some were covered with figures, a few were just fantastically scrawl designs such as men make when their minds are occupied and their hands idle. There were one or two blue books relating to food supply, but nothing any great moment, though I very carefully pocketed all the written matter. The search was necessarily slow since we depended upon our flash lamp though we might have switched on the lights with impunity. In one corner the room was a large and an old-fashioned safe. It stood about two metres high and a metre broad and had two narrow doors. Upon this Heinrich got to work and in half an hour I had the satisfaction of seeing the doors swing open.

What a tribute to my perspicacity! What a triumphant vindication of a "Hun's" foresight! Call us "Boches," call us by every vile name that your kultural deficiencies may suggest, but bear ungrudging witness to the everything foreseeing perfections of German organization!

For there, stacked neatly, one on top of the other, were six black portfolios, bulky and bulging. There was no need to ask whose properties were these. The golden "R.F." on one, the arms of Savoy and another, the crowned eagle on a third, advertised their ownership. Very carefully I removed them, handed them to my assistants.

The safe contained nothing else except a battered tin cash-box. I lifted with difficulty, for it was heavy.

"No," thought I, "we are not burglars. We do not require this haughty Lord's treasure. We Germans are not pot-house thieves, horse-holders and cut throat hang-dogs, to steal from a house like burglars! Let my Lordship keep gold. I have something better!"

I gave the signal and we crept forth along the corridor to the trap. We had closed it for fear that somebody passing through the hall should notice the opening and give the alarm.

Hermann knelt down and tried to lift the slab, but without success. He used his pocket-knife and did no more than break off the blade.

I cursed his bungling stupidity so furiously that he cowered before me. "What undependable swine these German working classes are! What brainless idiots, with no other thought than eating and beer-drinking! "Wretched owl," I hissed in his ear, "if we were in Germany I would flay you alive!"

"Herr Heine," he whined, "it is not my fault. I wanted to bring up my tools, but you refused to let me."

I could not waste any time arguing with this scum. In half-an-hour the dawn would be breaking. There was only one way out and that was through the kitchen. We passed through one of the doors behind the buffet and found ourselves in another stone corridor lighted by little stone-framed windows, but heavily barred. At one end of the corridor was another door and Heinrich, after a vain attempt to pick the lock, said it had been bolted from the outside.

"Have you no bolt-removing instrument?" I asked. "No, Herr Heine," he said apologetically, "that requires an apparatus of considerable complication. The only thing to do is to cut a hole through the door, and as the door is sheeted with iron I do not think it is possible."

We went down the corridor to the other portal. This door yielded to the turn of a handle, and we found ourselves in what was evidently a servery. Here there was one window which was also barred and a kitchen door, which, like the one on the farther end of the corridor, was bolted on the other side.

"What!" I said bitterly, "have I trusted my safety and the safety of the empire to a monkey with the brains of a gnat?"

He was silent under my rebuke, for what could he say? There remained only one possible egress and that was a skylight in the servery, and here fortune was with us, for we found a step-ladder which enabled us to reach the ceiling. I insisted upon Heinrich going first because it did not look very safe, and how my heart bounded when the skylight yielded to his touch and he was able to hoist himself, with the assistance of Hermann, through the aperture.

I followed immediately afterwards. We found ourselves on a sloping roof, and edging my way down to the guttering looked down and found that we had a drop of no more than a dozen feet. In three minutes we were on the ground, ad moving stealthily from bush to bush unchallenged by the cordon of policemen, and reached the outside road without mishap.

We were now on the other side of the house, far away from the ravine and my waiting motor-car. The first pale light of dawn was in the sky and I knew that we could not afford to take the risk of searching for the road by which we had come. Yet without the motor-car I was in a quandary. How might I get these portfolios of such world-shaking importance away without detection? I could not carry them myself and I could not trust my companions, for we Germans trust nobody, and by our caution-dictated suspicion we have eliminated half of the dangers which ordinarily threaten a modern state.

We were in a residential road. About Leatham Priory quite a respectable suburb has grown up and this was one of those better-class thoroughfares made of detached houses standing in their own grounds, or, as the English advertisements put it, "Houses with every modern convenience." In a flash I had made my plans. I knew that there was certain to be in such a road as this an empty house, and sure enough the third of the houses we passed bore in the garden a board (or rather two boards) saying it was "To Let."

I beckoned my party to follow me. Heinrich opened the door in a trice—it was child's play to this mechanic—and we entered the house, our footsteps sounding hollowly. It was not wholly furnished, I discovered to my surprise, for on the first floor there was a bedroom containing a few articles of furniture, but apparently the room had not been used some time. The shutters were tightly fastened over the window and I guessed that the room had been used by a caretaker until the owner had tired of paying his wages.

This view was fully confirmed later when I looked at the board outside, for the words "Apply to caretaker" had been painted over and a new address had been given at which the key might be obtained.

In this room there was big cupboard, the key of which was in the lock and into the cupboard I bundled the portfolios, locking the door, and put the key into my pocket.

"Now," I said to my comrades, "each will go his own way but avoid observation as far as possible."

"What about the car and the tools in the passage?" asked Hermann.

"I have told the car not to wait beyond daybreak," I said (German forethought again!) "and as for the tools you may collect them after dark to-night."

I got back safely to my apartment and turned up at ten o'clock at my office very well pleased with my night's work. At the office I found a messenger waiting for me. I recognized the man as the Herr Baron's valet, a trustworthy Bavarian who bad naturalized himself at the same time as my well-born patron. I opened the letter. It was from Baron von Hertz-Missenger. It read:

"By this time you have probably understood the little riddle I set you. Don't forget that it is of the utmost importance that certain things should be secured. I myself am working night and day to obtain results. Leave no stone unturned. If you fail notify me immediately. The Conference will last two more days. If you fail I am in a position to make the attempt myself."

I put the letter down with a smile. With what joy would the good Baron receive my news. If I failed; if I, Heine failed — the idea was amazing! I say here, before I proceed to the end of this incident, and I cannot give to great emphasis to my words, that it would be well if the Department in which I have the honour to serve —which is in other respects conducted with serious cleverness — implicitly trusted the proved genius of their officers and would not allow amateurs, however distinguished, to interfere with the operations of regular departmental officers.

I burnt the latter and sent the good baron's servant on his way rejoicing with half-a-crown. It is always as well to keep the servants of the high-born in good temper and favourably inclined. Then I rang up Messrs. Hedley and Riddle. Yes, I had carefully noted the name of tho house agents, I got them on the 'phone and asked to speak to the proprietor.

"You have a house to let near the village of Leatham Priory," I said.

"Yes, sir," he responded in the servile accent of an English house agent.

"I would like to see the house. May I call today for the key?"

"Which house is it?" he asked.

Here again my forethought served me.

"It is the house called 'Fairlawn'."

"Certainly," said the man, "my assistant has charge of this department. He is at lunch now, but when he comes in I will tell him to meet you at the station."

"Don't trouble," said I; "will you have the key ready for me? You remember, it is 'Fairlawn,' and I want to have the first refusal, so do not let anyone else see the house until I come."

"Certainly not, sir," said the servile hound.

I hung up the receiver and rubbed my hands, and at that moment there came a knock at my door. I walked over to the door and opened it. An officer with the green tabs of the British Intelligence Department stood smiling on the mat and I recognized my treacherous "friend" of other days, Mister Haynes or rather Major Haynes."

"Good morning, Major," I said jovially, "have you come to 'warn' me again?"

"Not a, bit," he said, walking inside and shaking hands, "I have just come to ask you if you know anything about the Baron von Hertz-Missenger."

I pricked up my ears.

"I know the good Baron," I said carelessly, "just as a casual acquaintance."

"How unfortunate you are," said Mister Haynes (I should say Major Haynes) in tones of sadness.

"Why unfortunate, Major?" I asked.

"All your friends seem to get into trouble," sighed the major; "perhaps you don't know that a number of important documents were stolen from Leatham Priory last night."

"Great heavens, you don't mean to say that," I said with well-simulated astonishment.

"Yes, fortunately, the most important, including secret cases, were left behind. They were in a steel cash-box and the thief or thieves did not trouble to examine its contents."

I did not swoon. Nobody seeing me would imagine what thoughts were swimming through my brain.

"The robbery was discovered this morning and naturally suspicion attached to the Baron," the major went on.

"Why to the Baron?" I asked.

"Well, you see," said Haynes, "he has been hanging about the neighbourhood and we discovered some time ago that he had arranged with the clerk of house agent to occupy a room in a house which was ostensibly to let." My flesh went cold and like a goose's.

"From his headquarters," Mister Haynes went on, "he apparently sallied forth from time to time making a very careful reconnaissance of the Priory. He must have known that an important Conference was to be held. We have established the fact that two of Lord Leatham's servants were in his pay, and, naturally, when the portfolios were missing we searched his lodging."

"Oh, naturally," said I weakly.

"And we discovered the stolen property."

"How strange!" I said in a hollow voice.

"And you don't know him," said Mister Haynes, I mean Major Haynes.

"No, sir, I do not," I said with firm determination.

"Well, you are unlucky," said the major, "for if you don't know him now never will know him," and with those ominous words he left me.

There is a moral in these narratives, which were originally written not so much for publication as to convey a true record of an adventurous career to one who was inexpressibly dear to me, the learned and beautiful Miss Kathleen O'Mara, secretary (honorary, for she would not accept payment for performing national service) of the German Gaelic League of Chicago, the most implacable, the most bitter enemy proud Albion ever had.

Reading this narrative over, I think perhaps it would be more consistent if I omitted these preliminary paragraphs in view of the events which are recorded below. Should this story by chance obtain a wider circulation than that which was intended, it would be perhaps necessary to explain my honourable relationships with this sometime belle of Irish freedom.

Miss O'Mara and I met in the halcyon days at a ball. What there was in me that attracted her it is not for me to say. It is sufficient that Miss Kathleen O'Mara believed in me. I wrote to her every week from the day I landed in England. I wrote about my life and about her work and that peculiar bobby of hers that I had many times thought of utilizing for the benefit of the Fatherland. Sometimes she would reply tenderly or in holy rage when she thought of the wrongs of her downtrodden countrymen (i.e., Irishmen) and sometimes she did not answer at all. For three months before this story opened I had not heard from her.

I had posted my letter on the Friday afternoon and sauntered back to office to see if any news had come in. The boy I employed told me there had been a caller, a gentleman who had refused to give his name, but said he would come back later. I do not like callers who refuse to give their names, for though I do not believe there is a British Secret Service, there is always possibility that the regular police may be going outside their province by prying into the lives and habits of "respectable aliens," as they call them.

"Did he leave no message?" I asked.

"No, sir," said the boy, "he merely said that he would call again."

It was not until the following day that my visitor made his reappearance. It was Saturday and I was preparing to go home in the English fashion at one o'clock, when the gentleman was announced. He was a tall, pale man with a dark and heavy moustache, bristling black eyebrows and that look of concentrated fierceness which so often distinguishes the insurance agent.

"Come in," I said, inviting him into my private office, and closing the door.

"What can I do for you?"

"I have a message from Kathleen," he said.

I seized him warmly by the hand and shook it.

"Any friend of Kathleen's is a friend of mine," I said: "sit down."

I looked around uncomfortably and went again to the door and dismissed the boy for the day, paying him his wages.

"You may speak in perfect security," I said.

"Kathleen is coming home," he whispered.

"Coming home?" I could not restrain the joy in my voice. "Do you mean coming to—?"

"To Ireland," he said. "Things are going well over there."

He need not have told me that. Indeed, I could have told him much more than he could possibly have known. I could have explained why things were going well. I could have made his hair stand on end if I had told him the amount of money that bad passed through my hands for distribution to Dublin, I could have told him of stacks of arms landed on the deserted coast by our submarines and of visits which were made by the same vehicle by a certain distinguished Irishman, now unhappily no longer with us.

I could have told him of the organization for which I, Heine, had been responsible, which had provided the patriots of Ireland with ammunition. But why continue the list? I did not tell him anything, and I have reason to believe that he was disappointed. A thought suddenly sobered me.

"Is it safe for Kathleen to come over at this juncture?" I asked. "By the by, I don't know your name."

"I am Theophilus Hagan," he said, and I seemed to remember the name. "You have met me?" he went on.

"Yes, yes, of course," said I, and curiously enough I had a dim recollection of having met him somewhere, but for the life of mc I couldn't remember the circumstances. "Oh, yes, I remember you," I said, for we Germans never admit ignorance on any subject.

"There is something else I want to tell you about myself," he said; "but perhaps this is not the moment to give away secrets."

"Tell me," said I earnestly, "anything you know. It shall not leave these four walls."

I was curious to hear what his secret was, because our people in Berlin were very anxious for news of what was going on in Ireland and they had complained before that they were imperfectly informed.

"No," said the man, "I will tell you later. I am going over to Ireland tomorrow. If we have any luck we shall have a rising on Easter Sunday. Kathleen wants you to be in Dublin when the trouble starts."

I shook my head.

"That would be very unwise indeed," I said; "the more I am kept out of it the better for the cause. When does she arrive?"

"She will be in Dublin a fortnight before the rising starts," said he.

"I will endeavour to be there to see her," I replied. "I shall not be able stay long because naturally I am very busy." I shook hands with him and saw him as far as the office door. After my experience with Mister, or Major, Haynes, I could not deem it advisable to be seen in public with gentlemen who might conceivably fall under the displeasure of the British authorities, and I explained this to him as a reason for my not coming to Euston Station to see him off.

I had spoken nothing but truth when I had said that I was very busy. Extraordinary changes were going on in England and particularly in London, where the constant alterations in the anti-aircraft gun positions, the erratic systems of lighting their streets which the British were adopting, were turning my hair grey. It is said that I sent a new map of London's new defences every week to Germany and that everyone was different, and this was true, but map- making as not my only source of employment.

By this time there were quite a respectable number of German prisoners in England, all of whom were anxious for help to make their escape, and whilst officially, I was not in touch with them, unofficially I had a lot to do with such successes as they achieved. It was I who had provided the motor-car for the four officers who escaped from Dabbington Hall. It was I who provided the tools for digging the underground passage by which three officers escaped from the Marlow camp. It was I who provided the clothing and disguises which enabled four naval officers and a Zeppelin officer to cross England after they had escaped from the Welsh camp. It is true they were all caught again, but that was nothing to do with me. When I had freed them from camp and set them on the road my work was finished and the rest was up to their good German ingenuity and resourcefulness.

On the Sunday following the Saturday I had seen Mr. Theophilus Hagan, I was rung up on the telephone.

"Can you supply three dozen dress-collars for a gentleman from Slough?" said a voice.

"Where does the gentleman live?" I asked calmly.

"Outside the White City. The collars are to be delivered at nine o'clock," was the reply.

"Thank you, I will attend to it," I said, and hung up the receiver.

A curious place to live, you think, outside the principal entrance to an exhibition ground? And is it not strange that a gentleman from Slough required his collars delivered in London? I will make no mystery of the matter. "Three dozen dress-collars" meant "I have escaped and want your help." Slough was the place from which he had escaped. The White City was point at which I must meet him and the hour was nine.

At nine o'clock to the moment my taxi-cab drew up in front of the ornate entrance of the exhibition grounds. The place was of course in darkness, and a man who was walking slowly along the kerb turned to the cab as it stopped and asked: "Have you brought my collars?"

"Step in," I said.

The cabman had his instructions and turned towards the City.

To meet these escaping-prisoner cases I had taken a furnished flat in the Edgware Road. It was on the ground floor and had the advantage of having no porter, so that one could go in and out without being spied upon.

I opened the door of my flat and ushered my visitor in.

"Your name?" I demanded.

"Prinz—" he began.

"Highness," said I quickly, "forgive my peremptory tone and please command me. I am entirely at your disposition. If I have been a little taciturn and quiet on the journey, and if I spoke to you a little sharply, pray pardon an over- tired servant of the Empire."

"With pleasure," he said.

He was a little, short man., who wore glasses.

"My name," he said, "is Prinz, Earl Frederick Prinz. I am a Lieutenant of the 34th Selician Regiment."

"Indeed," I said a little coldly "you led me to believe you were highly-born. Now what the devil do you mean by doing that?"

"It is not my fault, Mr. Heine, that you were deceived," he said humbly.

"What do you expect me to do?" I asked angrily, for one cannot waste time on a reserve lieutenant and such-like cattle.

"You ought not to have called me up at all," I said, raising my voice; "it is abominable. Have I nothing better to do?"

He stopped me with a gesture.

"Pray do not excite yourself unduly, Mr. Heine," he said; "for any trouble you may take, my father, the Colonial Secretary, will repay you."

"The illustrious Doctor Prinz?" I said. "Are you his son?" I stretched out my band and gripped his.

"Welcome, a thousand welcomes! I know your Councillor of State father and his Excellency has frequently spoken to me of his son. Come, come," said jovially, "help yourself to the good Rhine wine, for it is not often that are honoured by a visitor of your calibre, Herr Lieutenant."

We drank a bottle together, and then he told me his plans. The difficulty getting out of England is, briefly, to get out of England. To secure a place on board a ship is well-nigh impossible, unless you are vouched for by Foreign Office officials, whilst the punishment for stowing away is so heavy that few the neutral captains care to take the risk of allowing their ships to go out of port without conducting an independent search.

Herr Prinz, however, had received a message from his father by same secret cipher to the effect that four times each month a submarine would come in-shore off the Scottish coast. He was to reach a deserted part of the foreshore, flash a signal from an electric lamp and a boat would be put off to pick him up. The system would be put into operation the moment the Herr Doctor Councillor of State, Prinz, learnt from me that he was free.

"Content yourself, my dear lieutenant," I said, "you are as good as in the Fatherland. I will notify your august parent, to whom I trust you will remember me forthwith."

"I have already notified him, and I desire that you should not communicate," he said, so I took no further steps. There was no difficulty in getting the young man to Scotland, and I ventured to take a little holiday and accompany him. After all, one should show a little attention the men who have fought and bled for one's country, especially when they are nearly related to councillors of State who, if not noble, are exalted personages on the way to nobility.

I supplied the young man with passports and various documents to identify him, and left him with £50 (which I advanced out of my private purse) at an hotel in a small town not many miles from the coast of Scotland in the care of a good German Head-waiter who promised to look after the lad. And there I thought I had heard the last of him, and he had gone out of my mind, until I received an urgent message from Scotland saying that the submarine had not come and asking me for another £50.

I went straight up to Scotland and found the Herr Lieutenant living at the hotel and very weary.

"It is very strange, Heine, I have been at the appointed place every night, on the 7th, 14th, 21st and 28th. I have flashed my lamp and nothing has happened."

He told me he had waited on one occasion for four hours on the beach; on another he waited till daybreak.

"It is very extraordinary," I said. "When you fixed this scheme with His Excellency the Councillor of State, Doctor Prinz, was it by writing?"

"By secret cipher, and what is more, the message was written in secret ink."

"Did it reach you without having been opened?"

"Yes," replied the Herr Lieutenant; "I have one of the letters in my pocket now."

He took the letter and opened it. Apparently it was an innocent letter such as an affectionate father might write to his prisoner son.

"Now wait," said the young officer. He sent for a glass of milk and immersed the letter, then held it before the fire to dry. There instantly appeared string after string of words which were meaningless to me, apparently written in brown ink.

"I carry the code in my head," he said. I looked at the envelope, carrying it to the light. I noticed that the stamp and the postmark had been torn off and inwardly I praised the young man for his discretion. The flap was stuck down, though it had of course been cut at the top where the letter was taken out, and to all intents it had not been tampered with.

I examined it with a magnifying glass, however, and saw that suspicious gum line which can always be sect in a letter that has been opened and surreptitiously closed.

"This envelope has been steamed," I said, "the letter has been read, replaced, and fastened down by a kind of spirit gum which the censors use, and smoothed with a hot iron."

"How do you know?" he asked in alarm.

"I have opened too many myself," I said, with a smile, "not to recognize the signs."

"But supposing they had brought up the secret writing," he said, "they could not understand the code."

I thought for a moment and presently I said: "There is only one person in the world who can read that code and that person is a woman. More than that, Herr Lieutenant," I added proudly, "that woman is the dearest friend I have in the world, Miss Kathleen O'Hara, of Chicago, U.S.A."

And I told him something of this delightful girl's history, of how her father had been a Fenian and how she was bitterly anti-English. She had taken up codes and ciphers as a hobby, and she had come to be so expert that you were always reading in the Chicago papers articles either written by her or about her. There was not a cryptograph that ever appeared in the agony column of a London newspaper that she couldn't discover.

"You said her name was O'Mara," said the Herr Lieutenant thoughtfully; "is she a tall slim girl, with dark hair and blue eyes?"

It was my turn to be amazed.

"Herr Lieutenant," I said, "even your illustrious father could not have described her more accurately."

"And is her husband a tallish man with bristling black eyebrows and fierce black moustache?"

I drew myself up stiffly.

"The lady's husband, Herr Lieutenant, you see before you in prospect. She is unmarried."

He looked at me and shook his head.

"Well, then, it is not the same lady. This was a Mrs. Hagan, the wife of Captain, Hagan of the United States Secret Service."

I stepped back and clasped my brows. Now I remembered the man! Hagan from Washington! And she had married him. By heavens! When I think of the depth of woman's duplicity I could despise the race. She, the Irish patriot, the strafer of England, to send that man to me in the hope that I should commit myself! Thou perfidious betrayer of one who entertained for you naught but the tenderest, holiest feelings! Oh, what a low woman!

"I see it all now, Herr Lieutenant," I said, "this woman was brought down to your camp to unravel your cipher. When did you receive it?"

He thought a moment.

"The night she left."

" Now you understand,'" I cried passionately. "No wonder you have waited in vain upon the beach! No wonder the four submarines disappeared! No wonder you were allowed to remain at liberty! These cursed, treacherous British! Was there ever a nation that more deserved to be obliterated?"

I made my plans quickly, as is my wont. Before leaving that night I gave the Herr Lieutenant another £50, making £100 he had received since his escape. I myself was in considerable danger and if Hagan suspected me, the traitorous Kathleen knew me. I sent a man specially to Dublin and discovered that they were staying at an hotel in Sackville Street and that so far from Hagan having arrived recently, both he and his wife had been in Dublin for six months and they were undoubtedly in the pay of the British Government.

Of the events which occurred or Easter Monday in Dublin, I do not propose to speak. I sent very full reports to the Government, which may be read with profit by any who have the entree to the archives in Wilhelmstrasse.

Two days after the rebellion started I saw Hagan and his wife in Regent Street, they were looking in the widow of a jeweller's shop. With me to think is to act. I stepped up to her and offered her my hand.

"Congratulations, Mrs. Hagan," I said.

"Sure, 'tis the little Dutchman, Mr. Heine," she smiled. "You know my husband?"

"I have that pleasure." I bowed stiffly and hid my emotion behind an inscrutable face.

"And what are you doing in an enemy's country?" asked Kathleen innocently.

"Enemy!" I laughed bitterly. "There was a time, madam, when there was only one enemy for the honorary secretary of a German-Gaelic club and that was — England!"

"There is only one enemy for me now," she said, gripping her husband's arm foolishly, "and that is Theo's enemy. Sure, a wild young girl never knows her own mind, Mr Heine, and she runs this way and that with the divil an idea what she is seeking. I guess I was seeking Theo, and now I've found him I've stopped hustling."

We exchanged a few words. I strolled with them to Piccadilly Circus and they accepted an invitation to lunch at Prince's.

"By the way," I said in the midst of the meal," Do you still keep up your cryptograph investigations?"

I thought I saw a little look pass between her and her husband and then she smiled.

"Oh, yes," she said, she may have said "sure" (I will not swear as to the exact words of any dialogue which I report), "oh yes, faith, it's highly amusing."

"And profitable too, I suppose," I said carelessly, helping myself to some celery.

"Faith, it is that," she said; "many is the laugh I have had going through silly ciphers coming from Germany — bad cess on the place, and from Scotland too," she said.

You observe she was shameless! There was no blush of guilt, no faltering, no lowering of eyes. She stood detected, blatantly confessed, an agent of the English!

"When Theo came over to look after the American crooks in London. I came with him," she said. "that is how I got to know those boys at Scotland Yard, and I sort of drifted into the work and took to it like a duck to water!"

My hand was trembling, I could not help it. Righteous indignation shook me from head to foot. I could have boxed her ears, but for my German chivalry and the presence of her husband, who might have been distressed at such a display of emotion, though I am sure he would have agreed with me had he only known the amount of money I had spent on that frail creature in flowers and theatre tickets and candy, to say nothing of postage stamps.

"They would amuse you, Heine," she went on, "especially the queer things they say about you. There was a fellow the other day got a letter, phwat was the boy's name, Theo?"

"Prinz," said her husband, who hitherto had not spoken a word.

"Sure that was his name," said the girl, "'twas from his old dub of a father and written in a very simple cipher."

"A child could have read it," agreed her husband, "and it was all about you," he nodded to me.

"It said go and see Heine," said the girl. "Tell him your father's a prince, and if you haven't got the pluck to do that, say you are the son of Colonial Officer Prinz, and he will do anything for you. There was a long bit about the lie he had to tell you. About submarines going up to Scotland to fetch him. When we told the commandant he let the boy go, he was safe. He was arrested yesterday and his father has been interned."

"His father interned?" I gasped

"Who was his father?"

Kathleen looked at her husband and Hagan spoke. "He was the head-waiter at the hotel where the boy was staying," he said, "'twas his way of getting the lad a vacation."

When I came to England I took charge, as I think I have explained before, of the hundred and one departments which were in some way or other associated with Intelligence. My task was to co-ordinate the whole of the common service of Deutschstrum, to gather up all the strings in my own fingers and to pull them, each to serve the higher purpose. One of the most important branches of our work had been inaugurated ten years before I came to England, and I think if you spent the whole of those ten years guessing you would not divine how the business which had been established was to serve Germany in her hour of need.

Perhaps you have noticed, you who have been to London, a modest yet substantial building in Jermyn Street, which is known as the Jermyn Credit Bank. It is, or was, a very unpretentious and serious building with a modest facia and a small but imposing interior. If you had not seen the place you would not fail to have seen the advertisements of the bank which ran consistently in most of the English papers.

The advertisement was as follows:

Gentlemen of position, officers of both services and officials of the British or Indian Civil Service may arrange loans on note of hand with the Jermyn Credit Bank. No security required. Interest 7 per cent. per annum. Apply by letter, which will be treated in the strictest confidence, to the Secretary, Jermyn Credit Bank, 642, Jermyn Street, St. James's.

There was nothing flamboyant about the advertisement any more than there was about the building. The advertisement occupied a space of two inches in most of the newspapers, but generally in the more respectable and conservative of newspapers. Those who called by appointment were treated with the greatest courtesy. They were ushered into the luxurious room of the manager, the needs of the client were discussed, the question of security delicately touched upon — there is always some security to be had even though the advertisement made a point that none was required — and loans were arranged, very often for considerable amounts.

The bank was very popular with officers of the army and navy. Men who found themselves in a tight corner blessed the name of the Jermyn Credit Bank. If, when their bills came due, there was any difficulty about payment there was certainly no difficulty about renewing the document on a very reasonable basis.

Sometimes, of course, it happened that the bank manager, a polite and charming gentleman who was, alas! killed on tho western front by the treacherous English could not, with all the best will in the world oblige the client. Needy professional men, doctors, lawyers and unimportant journalists would learn what even with their security the golden coffers of the Credit Bank remained tightly closed. But to any officer, especially to an officer who had the magic letters P.S.C. after his name, or any head of a civil department or any naval gentleman, who had won the slightest distinction and promotion m his profession, might be assured that if not the whole, at least part of his necessities were met.

The business grew to an extraordinary extent. One officer would introduce another. Mr. Rosenberg the manager, would occasionally give little dinner parties, to which he invite one of. his more exalted clients, on the understanding that he would bring two or three friends. I cannot say that the business was particularly prosperous from our point of view, but there were singularly few bad debts, and I do not suppose it cost the Fatherland more than £10,000 a year to secure an intimate financial history of every officer serving in the army plus a pull over such of the bank's clients as were in its debt. For men who borrow money are very grateful and a grateful man is talkative, especially if conversation is assisted by a little Veuve Clicquot and a chic dinner, and what is more natural than a man should talk about his brother officers and their financial positions?

The bank had the reputation — so valuable — that it never dunned its clients or brought an action against even the most backward and unfaithful amongst them, and such a reputation helped considerably when war broke out and Mr, Rosenberg was called upon by his directors to resign immediately owing to his German origin and his place was taken by Mr. Mathew Ritten, a neutral gentleman of great integrity.

As the English army increased so increased the business of the bank, for young officers are impecunious all the world over. I am not going to say what steps were taken to secure information. This, however I am willing to confess, that much news came to me which otherwise, I should not have heard, for Mr, Ritten gave little dinners and went to clubs and met many men who were glad to talk to one who was so enthusiastically an anti-German, and I, Heine, sitting in my little Fleet Street office would receive short notes in the code and would learn that the 10th Blankshires and the division to which the 10th Blankshires were attached were being withdrawn to General Reserve, and the 19th Wessex were training for attack behind the lines and being taught by means of models the topography of the country to the east of Lens.

For myself, I never went to the bank. If you had told me of its existence I should have expressed surprise and wonder. I saw the advertisements as everybody else saw them, but to me, Mr. Ritten was a name and nothing more. We Germans have the reputation of devoting too much attention to insignificant details, but let me tell you, my friends, that the might of Germany was built upon details, expanded on details, and came to its highest and most world- defying decision in August, 1914 upon the faith which we bad in the detailed plan.

Though I despised. the English Secret Service, though I could shrug my shoulders and snap my fingers at these amateurs, I was too much of a German to rush bull-headed into danger. Realizing that Mister, or Major, Haynes, was a man of duplicity and low cunning, I purposely avoided associating myself in the slightest degree with the Jermyn Credit Bank, though it was originally the idea of those who sent me to England that I should appear in London in the capacity of manager of that bank.

One afternoon I had returned from the country, where I had been superintending the erection of a temporary wireless plant when my office-boy informed, me that a man was waiting to see me. I found him sitting on the edge of the table, smoking the stump of a cigar. He was a tall man, rather broad, and by the fact that he was wearing his hat in my office, and that the room was filled with the rank smell of tobacco, I gathered that he was an American of the lowest class. He was dressed expensively but loudly. He wore a great bunch of seals which dangled from a broad silk ribbon, and had two diamond rings upon the little finger of his right hand. He nodded as I came in, but did not attempt either to take off his hat or to stand on his feet. For the moment I did not recognize him.

"May I ask to what I owe the honour of this visit?" I demanded politely.

"Cut all that out, Heine," he said coarsely, "Why, don't you recognize our old friend, Big Jim?"

"Don't call me Heine," I said hastily. I recognized the man at once. As one of the private detective staff of the Hamburg-America line, it bad been my duty to keep an eye upon undesirable characters, and Big Jim Riley was well known to New York as he was to London as a "con" man. He used to work the boats of the Hamburg-America line in the days before the war, and for some time was one of a gang of crooks that spent their lives crossing and re-crossing the Atlantic. Though we had many complaints about the man, he had too big a pull in New York for us to interfere with him. I had lived with Big Jim and his gang in a spirit of camaraderie and tolerance which typifies the attitude of a shrewd German detective to the criminal classes.

"Why, so it is," I said heartily, "but you must not call me Heine, Jim."

"Ain't you a Dutchman?" he said.

"I never was a German!" I doubt whether he saw the subtle correction. "I am a Chilean and I am happy to say that I hate the Germans and all their work."

Big Jim's eyes opened wide. "Well, now, if that don't beat the band," he said, "so that's your name, is it?"

He pointed to the name that was painted on the glass panel of the door and I nodded.

"Well," he said, "I guess those people in New York have made some mistake. Pretzl told me I was to come along and report to you and that you might put some good work in my way. I don't care what it is," he said, swinging his legs and puffing away at his cigar, "anything short of a business that will send me to the Chair is good enough for me."

"My dear Jim," I said mildly. "I am afraid Herr Pretzl is under altogether a wrong impression."

How I cursed that interfering swine von Pretzl who had placed my life and freedom in the hands of a common confidence man! I have frequently warned von Papen that Pretzl was an old woman and a fool. How much was I justified!

"See here, Heine," said Jim, speaking with great earnestness, "I want some kinder job. There ain't any suckers left in the world — I guess they're all gone to war. There's nothing crossing the Atlantic now but Dago acrobats on their way to join up with the Alpinis, and they're wrapped up so in life-savin' suits that they couldn't get at their wad even. if they wanted to give it to you. Them and feeble-minded old men and women are all the passengers there are — and women as you know are meaner than hell when it comes to a show- down of real money. I've been across three times dodging submarines and mines and all I could raise was a game of auction bridge at two cents a hundred. Now you know the ropes here. Put me wise to a few."

I thought rapidly. He might be a useful man. Then again he might be a source of grave danger. A man of that character would not come to England without the British police force being informed and probably he was shadowed. In the circumstances I rejected any offer of personal help, but I gave him the address of two or three gambling clubs and promised to call on the 'phone a good friend of mine who was the proprietor of the largest. He cheered up when I told him this.

"If there is money to be made," he said, "I am after it. Some of these young officers have got plenty of money, you say."

"Some of them are worth millions," I said solemnly.

He shook hands heartily and I was glad to see the back of him. I watched through the window his departure. There was a man standing on the other side of the road, apparently watching the traffic, but as soon as Jim made appearance and turned westward the idler turned too. Of course he was watched. The imbecility of sending such a man to me with all the interests I represented!

I was in despair, but pulling myself together I put on my hat and going out into the street hailed a cab and was driven off to my club, where I told an amusing story to a few of the members who were loafing in the smoke-room about the confidence man who had come to me with a letter of introduction. I felt sure that somebody would repeat the story, and in this I was not mistaken.

I heard no more of Big Jim, though I saw him one night at dinner at the Ritz- Carlton, and from his prosperous appearance I gathered that he was not in any immediate want. My friend, to whom I had given him an introduction told me that Jim had cleaned up a lot of money one night at the gaming club, that he was friendly with a number of officers, and that he had become persona grata at a certain Bohemian club, the members of which are mostly of the theatrical profession.

I remembered, when this was told me, that Big Jim, before he began his nefarious career, had been an actor, if you can dignify with such name one who travelled one-night stands with a third-rate burlesque company and he was alternately comedian and baggage man.

What I expected, and what did not occur, was a visit from the police in regard to Big Jim. For this I was prepared, but apparently the story I told at the club must have been reported in the proper quarters, as I intended it should be, and nobody questioned me as to my acquaintance with this undesirable American.

Whatever place Big Jim may have occupied in my mind was dispelled by a piece of news which came to me one morning whilst I was in my bath — it was Friday, that being the day I invariably bathe — which was of so remarkable a character, and its possibilities so far-reaching, that nothing else occupied my thoughts.

My servant knocked at the door and told me that there was an urgent message awaiting me from "Mr Thompson". Now, "Mr Thompson" was the telephone name for Mr Ritten, and dressing myself hastily in my bath-wrap I hurried to the room I used as a study, knowing that Ritten would not call at this unearthly hour unless something important was afoot or unless he had secured some information of an unusual character."

"It is I, Thompson," said the voice, "can I see you? It is most important."

"My dear Thompson," I said testily, "you know very well that it is impossible that we should meet."

"But I must see you," be said, "it is a matter of the first importance. I cannot communicate over the telephone."

"Come then at once," I said, "bringing some documents which would excuse your presence."

"In ten minutes the bell of my flat rang, and Mr. Ritten was ushered in. He was a suave, gentlemanly man, who was, I believe, well born in his own country. With a preliminary apology for troubling me, which I coldly dismissed, he laid before me the object of his visit.

"I have had a request for a loan of £20,000 for seven days," he said.

"Twenty thousand pounds!" I was surprised at the largeness of the sum. "That is an enormous amount. Who asks for it?"

"General Sir Stanley Magward!"

I whistled.

"Sir Stanley Magward!"

This was indeed a remarkable request. This general as everybody knows, commands one of the English Armies. He is a famous strategist, and marked for further promotion.

"Here is the letter. It arrived this morning," said Ritten, and passed me across a sheet of note-paper, which bore at the top the inscription "Headquarters of the 9th Army."

The letter was brief and peremptory:

Dear Sirs:

I am in need of £20,000 to pay off a mortgage which falls due on my Somerset property this week. My brother-in-law, Mr. Hiram S. Carter, the well-known railroad magnate of America, is on the ocean homeward-bound, and I cannot, therefore, get in touch with him. Upon his arrival the debt will be liquidated. I agree to pay a sum equivalent to 10 per cent. per annum for the accommodation. I apply to you because I have no desire to let my banker into the secret of my embarrassment. I shall be in London the day after to-morrow, on short leave. A note delivered to the Senior Army Club will find me.

"Well?" said Ritten, when I pushed the letter back to him.

"By all means let him have the money," I said.

"You authorize it?"

"Certainly," I replied.

"I have made inquiries," said Ritten, "his brother-in-law is on the homeward trip, but the date of his arrival is rather uncertain. The mortgaged property is Penton Close, and the mortgagees are the London and Manchester Bank."

I nodded.

"That explains why he does not wish to bother his bankers," I said. "Send to the Senior Army Club and have the money ready for the General — this may mean a lot to us. It is the kind of connection that would be very useful."

Well might I feel elated. That an army commander should place himself in the hands of money-lenders, and such money-lenders, was distinctly a feather in my cap. It would not be well for my Lord Magward that the mighty War Office should know one of their trusted generals was borrowing money. On the other and, it might be well for the Jermyn Credit Bank, if any questions rose as to its bona fides, that it had amongst its clients so august a personage. Whichever I looked it was all to the good.

The letter was despatched, and on the Monday Mr Ritten called me up to say that the General was in his private office, and had signed the necessary documents.

"Come round and meet him," suggested Ritten.

"Am I a fool?" I replied sarcastically.

"He is very interesting," said Ritten. "I have much to tell you when I have time. He has invited me to go to France to his headquarters, and to bring any friends I wish."

I could have hugged myself with delight.

"Accept the invitation," I said quickly, "also discover where the headquarters the 9th Army are. Find out why he is on leave for such a short time, and whether his army had many casualties in the last offensive."

Ritten acknowledged my instructions and hung up the receiver, and I sat down at my desk to formulate a plan for the forthcoming visit which I intended to pay an important headquarters of the British Army in the field.

I suppose I must have been working away for two hours when I heard a commotion in the outer office, the door was flung violently open and a tall broad officer dashed in, slamming the door behind him. He was breathless and could not speak, He was perhaps no more breathless than I, for he wore cross batons and stars of a superior general, and across his broad chest were three rows of medals, ribbons and decorations. He tore off his gold-laced hat and wiped his brow.

"Pardon me, general," I began.

"Shut up, Heine," he gasped. "Forget that general stuff and help me out this."

It was my turn to gasp.

"Jim," I said, "what is the meaning of it?"

He sank down into a chair.

"I have got away with £20,000 from a bank," he said rapidly. "Gee, it was easy money, Heine. A bit of notepaper that I borrowed from a kid on leave from one of these army headquarters, a suit of clothes, and it was like taking money from a child. But they're after me; one of those darned English officers spotted me and asked me in the street who I was. I just had time to jump in a cab and bolt."

The dreadful truth was slowly dawning upon me.

"Twenty thousand pounds," I said, "you have got £20,000 from a bank—from the Jermyn Credit Bank, Jim?"

"Sure thing," he said, "do you know them?"

I passed my trembling hand across my brow.

"Leave the money here in my desk, Jim," I said. " I will take care of it; then, when the coast is clear, you can come back for it."

"Give nothing," he said brutally. He walked across the room and took a cautious glance from the window.

"I am going," he said, "they didn't pick me up."

"Don't go with that money," I cried in alarm, "it will be bad if they catch you with the goods. Be a good boy and leave it here," but before I could finish he had thrown open the door,

"Hell! " said Jim, as Major Haynes walked in.

"Friend of yours, Heine?" said Major Haynes; "dear me, what excellent company you are keeping. I hardly know what to expect next. I shan't surprised to find the Minister of War here one of these fine days. How do you do, general?"

"Quit kidding," growled Jim.

"What horrible language for the commander of the 9th Army," said Mr Haynes, and then—I suppose you know it is an offence to wear a uniform to which you are not entitled?"

It was now my turn to speak.

"This man," I broke in, "is a thief. He has robbed a certain bank of a great amount of money."

"As to that I know nothing," said Major Haynes, "all that I am concerned with is the fact that your friend is wearing a uniform to which he is not entitled.

"He is a robber," I cried excitedly, "he has obtained by trickery and fraud great amount of money."

"From the Jermyn Credit Bank?" asked Major Haynes in a tone of interest, "the officers' friend, the help-one-another association? How perfectly shocking! " He beckoned with his finger and Jim and he left the room. I saw them drive away in a cab together, and sat in an agony of apprehension, not only that day but for the rest of the week. Then, one afternoon, Major Haynes strolled into my office.

"Your friend, the general, has sailed," he said, "and you will be pleased learn that I took from him everything to which he was not entitled."

"The money?" I said eagerly.

"The uniform," said Major Haynes; "I think he was entitled to the money, don't you? As a matter of fact," he went on, "I will ease your mind about the money. That also was taken from him, and is now with the rest of the bank's credits — in the hands of a British official."

I turned sick and faint.

"You are thinking of your friend von Ritten," smiled Haynes, "He also in the hands of a British official!"

9 — MR. COLLINGREY, MP — PACIFIST!

I have often said that there is something grossly immoral about the profession of journalism. These men who live on the woes of others, who batten on the miseries of the world, must of necessity be dead to all kindly impulse and to the gentler emotions. They must be sceptical of all that is good, and have immeasurable faith in the wickedness of human nature. They must have neither reverence for the great ones of the earth nor charity for the sins of the weak.

My experience of journalists and of English journalists particularly, had been with a Mister Haynes, who behaved with the greatest treachery toward me, insinuated himself into my office under false colours, for was he not an officer of the English Intelligence Department and has he not, as I have reason to believe, the blood of two high-spirited German youths upon his gory hands?

In the Autumn of 1916, I learnt that Berlin was sending to me a Swedish gentleman named Heigl, and I was ordered to follow his instructions and to give him all the assistance which lay in my power. I have a constitutional objection to the intrusion of outsiders and more especially to amateur intelligence officers who, in my experience, have never failed to bungle any task to which they set their hands, so I cannot say that I viewed with any enthusiasm the coming of Mr. Heigl, fraught as it would be, and as I knew, with additional risks for myself — and possibly the disorganization of the perfect system which I had, with such labour established.

Mr. Heigl proved to be a very pleasant gentleman, a merchant of Stockholm, a short man with an untidy grey beard, well dressed and having the appearance of prosperity. In fact, as I learnt, he was a gentleman of considerable wealth, and though not well born, even in a Swedish sense, he was a persona grata with the leaders of the Conservative Party in Sweden and was frequently consulted by his Government on all matters affecting trade.

Amongst other things he was the proprietor of a weekly newspaper published in Stockholm. All this he told me within the first hour of our meeting; in fact, on the way up from an East Coast port to whither I had gone to meet him.

"You must understand, sir," he said with great affability, which I need hardly tell you I returned, since be was the trusted agent of my beloved country and was, moreover, a man who might be able to put a few things in my way. One never knows when one requires the help of a man of this description or, as we say in Germany, "Don't refuse the carter the tyre, one day the wheel may be yours."

To resume the record of our conversation.

'You understand, sir," he said, "that I am a citizen of a neutral state and therefore, I can take no active part in any propaganda designed to assist Germany."

"That is understood, excellent sir," I replied, "and, believe me, I will not embarrass you to the smallest extent by requesting your assistance."

He inclined his bead graciously.

"There are certain people in Berlin whom I have recently had the pleasure of meeting. They are anxious that in this great world war the German view shall not be entirely lost sight of."

It was my turn to nod.

"The English press is not exactly friendly or inclined even to print the German point of view, save to ridicule it."

"The English or British press, my dear sir," I said warmly, "is a Government press. Every evening as is well known, the Government send every newspaper the outlines of the leading article which they will write. So cunningly contrived are those leaders, that in some of them they criticize the Government, and nobody outside the office would realize that all those articles are written by a special band of writers who work day and night in Downing Street."

He seemed interested at this news which was well known to me and to many of my friends.

"But I interrupted you," I said, "pray forgive me."

"In Berlin," Mr. Heigl went on, "it is thought that an excellent opportunity exists either for founding or for purchasing a newspaper. It is understood that the Post-Herald is for sale."

"That is so," I said, nodding. I did not know it before, but I took his word for it. We Germans can never be caught napping. "The price that is asked," Mr. Heigl went on, consulting a little note-book which he drew from his waistcoat pocket, "is £100,000 that is to say, two million marks. It is a paper which has had a great deal of influence in the past but seems to have fallen away gradually until it has got into very low water indeed. We believe that if we found the right man and spent a little money the paper could be revived to its former prestige."

"Of that I am convinced," I said, "and it is a view which I have often thought of advancing to Berlin. Believe me, Mr. Heigl, I have not neglected the press. There is scarcely a newspaper man in Fleet Street whom I do not know. I can tell you their circulations, the family history of their editors, the names and records of their principal correspondents."

He interrupted me with a little gesture.

"I am delighted to hear this," he said, "I had no idea that you had taken the matter up. In fact, they thought that you were unacquainted with the personnel of the newspapers."

I smiled a little bitterly. "Wilhelmstrasse is sometimes a little unjust," I said, quietly and sadly.

"Now, what would you say the circulation of the Post-Herald was?" asked Mr. Heigl.

It was an unfortunate and tactless question to ask at the moment, but I replied with readiness.

"I cannot tell you until I have consulted my books. There are so many newspapers in London and one cannot possibly keep their circulations in one's head."

I could see he was a little impressed, and later he asked: "Can you suggest a man to act as go-between? Neither you nor I can buy the paper, but if we could only get hold of a good substantial fellow, a bit of a crank preferably, we could easily hide ourselves behind a bank and a lawyer and complete the sale."

I knitted my brow and compre4ssed my lips. "For the moment I cannot" I said, "This is much too important a matter to be settled off-hand."

I then proceeded like a good general, to examine the ground. The Post-Herald is an old-fashioned Whig newspaper which has fallen on evil times, due to the fact that it was owned by a family all of whom took something out of its coffers, and none of them put any brains in to its management. With true German thoroughness, I discovered that it was deeply in debt to paper manufacturers and to a syndicate of printing machine makers.

This poverty-stricken rag, without two penny pieces to rub against one another, had the temerity to attack "unscrupulous Germany." I confess when I opened the sheet and read the scathing and vulgar abuse of our truly great kulturland, I was filled with righteous anger. But business is business. The Fatherland has need of thee, Post-Herald. Thy columns shall yet scintillate with sarcasm, not directed toward the genius of Germany, but toward the vile and frivolous men who have dared the wrath of Michael! Thy readers from these dull pages shall imbibe the principles which have made Prussia feared, aye, and hated the world over. Deutschland shall be vindicated in triumphant and very clever articles written by professors of learning and translated by English hack writers.

My spirits rose and my heart glowed within me at the thought that I, Heine, should pull the strings and direct in the heart of this great and sinister city a policy which should still further enhance my beloved land.

Deutschland über Alles! Also, I thought there might be some commission on the purchase, for these things can be arranged. The first thing to do was to find a go-between, a man who could be implicitly trusted, and I began to ransack my mind for a likely person. To put one of the known English pacifists in control would be to give the show away, and to upset the apple-cart, to employ two English idioms.

Collingrey was the man! It came to me in a flash of inspiration. He was a member of Parliament and hard up, having an extravagant wife and other obligations which my good German modesty prevents my describing. He had been a failure as a barrister, and a failure as a member of Parliament. He might have held a position in the Government but for certain disclosures which came to light in the matrimonial suit in which he became involved.

During the war most of his questions and speeches in Parliament had been directed against Italy — our perfidious ally! There never was a man who so hated the Italian Government as he, and with good reason, for Mr. Collingrey, a year before the war started, had invested all his fortune in the purchase of two pictures by that master, Leonardo da Vinci. The Italian Government had prohibited the export of the pictures and when on top of this a lawsuit was started, which involved the ownership of these works of art, Collingrey got neither the pictures he had bought nor the money he had spent.

He had stood to make a fortune, having resold these gems to the American millionaire, Tilzer. The lawsuit dragged on, and Collingrey had declared that the Italian Government was putting every obstacle in the way of a settlement, and as the English Government refused to give him any assistance, he was doubly incensed.

He was, therefore, a bitter man, and never lost an opportunity of embarrassing the Government. His articles appeared regularly in those journals which we had subsidized — very few, alas! — in this country. He had a reputation for honesty, was a brilliant writer and a clever debater. The thing was to secure his co-operation, and to convey to him, with as much delicacy as possible, the policy which he would be called upon to support. I have before me the draft of instructions which I received from Berlin at a subsequent date, and I cannot do better than print these:

1. The editor will adopt a conciliatory attitude toward Germany and German War Aims. It is not necessary that the German point of view should be urged, since this would defeat the object aimed at. The Germans may even be attacked, though no uncomplimentary reference to the Great General Staff to the Kaiser, or to any member of the German royal family must be permitted.

2. It is permissible to condemn air-raids or U-boat sinkings in a decorous and serious manner, but at the same time a note should be appended to the effect that whilst these things are unfortunate, the English have largely themselves to blame for failing at the beginning of the war to observe the distinction between open and defended towns, and also for not observing the Treaty of London.

3. At all times the editor must urge the necessity for arriving at an understanding with Germany. The cost of the war, the loss of life, must be deplored, and the possibility of avoiding further losses by meeting the Germans at a peace council must be insisted upon.

4. References to the taxation which will follow the war, and how hardly it will fall upon the working classes as well as upon the moneyed classes must be made frequently.

5. Whenever possible it should be hinted that the British have no reason for continuing the war, and that they are being bled white to support the insensate ambitions of France. French military actions should in consequence, be criticized as far as possible.

6. Stories dealing with the humanity of the German soldier, which will be supplied from time to time, should be given prominence and references to German strikes may be made the most of, especially at moments of industrial unrest in England.

These were only a few of the instructions. I cannot help thinking that Wilhelmstrasse made a great mistake in its moderation. If it had been left to me I would have instructed the editor to lose no opportunity of attacking every other newspaper which spoke slightingly of our great country — but then I am a patriot!

I had no difficulty in getting an introduction to Collingrey, and he invited me to dine at the British House of Commons. In a few words over a post-prandial cigar I explained the object of my visit. The good friend whose letter of introduction had procured the interview had smoothed my path by representing me to be an agent of a South American rancher (name unknown) who desired to break into London society, and in tones of gentle but amused tolerance hinted at my client's vanity. Mr. Collingrey readily undertook to act as go-between. He entered into the spirit of the matter with great enthusiasm, and when I met him two or three days later he produced two manuscripts dealing with the Italian Government which he read to me in the lobby of the House of Commons. When the purchase was completed and the Post-Herald had passed into the possession of a certain syndicate, which it is not advisable to name, he had manuscript on Italy in every pocket.

Having done my part of the work and taken the small commission which was my right, and having seen Mr. Heigl safely on his journey back to Stockholm, I had little time to bother about the newspaper, the more so since Berlin in its folly had decided that I was not to interfere in its management.

I bowed respectfully to the high authorities and to the well-born gentlemen who directed Germany's policy, but I submit in all humility that had Heine been at the helm much that subsequently happened might have been avoided.

Mr Collingrey carried out his instructions faithfully, and when they were explained with more elaborate detail he accepted his orders (to my surprise) without demur or question. His vivid leading articles on the Italian Government attracted a great deal of attention and led to a strict application of the censorship, but this only gave him a new interest in life, namely, in so couching his words that he could do the maximum amount of damage to his enemies without incurring censure. He was gentle with Germany, restrained in his reference to the U-boats, never spoke of the Kaiser except as the Emperor William, and his references to labour were invariably quoted in the extreme organs of the masses. He was indeed a most satisfactory person, and I have in my possession a letter addressed to me by the noble-born Count von Mazberg, the head of our propaganda department, congratulating me upon my most excellent choice. This I can show to any interested person who doubts my word, and especially to those, evil-minded un-German journalists who have so often attacked me and my work.

I was out of London a great deal, being concerned in consultation with certain labouring men who desired to bring the war to an end by an understanding with Germany. These English patriots were organizing a strike, and, naturally, I rendered them all the assistance that lay in my power. This meant that I had to travel with a great deal of money and could not afford to allow my attention to be distracted from the business at hand.

I arrived in London one evening and on reaching my flat discovered an urgent telegram from Mr. Collingrey asking me to dine with him at the Carltonia Hotel, as he had news of the greatest importance. I immediately changed into my evening dress and drove down to the hotel where the editor was waiting impatiently. He was happier than I have ever seen him. His thin, cadaverous face was wreathed in smiles, as he heartily shook my band, brushing aside the compliments on his conduct of the paper which I had prepared.

"Come and have dinner, my boy," he said. "I have got great news."

"I am delighted to learn this," I replied. "Have you got one in the eye for Italy, if you will pardon the expression?"

"Oh, much better."

Grasping my arm he led me into the dining-room.

"After all," he said as we sat down at the table, "perhaps I have been rather unkind about Italy — my articles have borne fruit."

"What do you mean?" I asked in surprise.

He chuckled as he unfolded his serviette.

"They have released my pictures, my dear fellow," he said, "you have no idea of the weight there is off my mind. It means a tremendous lot to me — my fortune and my wife's was invested in those infernal daubs. Look here," he took a piece of paper from his pocket and passed it across to me. It was a cablegram which had been handed in at New York that morning:

Agree to your price, hundred and fifty thousand dollars for da Vinci pictures. Ship them by first mail boat in charge of reliable man — Titzer.

"We will have a bottle of champagne on this."

"But what induced the Government to take this step?"

"The lawsuit is ended," said Mr. Collingrey, "and ended in my favour. I tell you it has taken ten years off my age."

He babbled on like a boy, but presently he grew calmer and we discussed the policy of the paper, and I was glad to see that be still retained those honest convictions about Germania which had ever distinguished his writings.

It was just about this time that America was trembling on the verge of war, when, the unscrupulous Wilson. was making his preparations to commit the great crime against civilization of plunging his country into the horrors of strife, for me it was a time of the greatest stress and anxiety. Cablegrams from certain neutral countries reached me every hour. Secret and confidential wireless messages from the supreme political chiefs reached me through the usual channels.

The excuse the Americans made was the initiation by our Admiralty of an unrestricted U-boat campaign against the munition ships of the Allies and it was still hoped by the superlatively clever men who guide the helm of the German state that war might be avoided. On a night I shall never forget I received a message from Amsterdam which I decoded. It ran:

VERY URGENT.— To Chief S.S, Agents, London, Madrid, Paris, New York, Stockholm, Amsterdam.

Editors and directors of friendly and subsidized papers must be instructed to deal sympathetically with U-boat campaign. Point out iniquity blockade which is starving German women and children, and suggest a compromise between Germany and her enemies. Endeavour counteract enemy propaganda which will be unusually virulent. Prepare articles and comments in this vein. Acknowledge to chief of staff.

I wrote a brief note embodying these instructions to Mr. Collingrey, telling him that the South American, the mythical proprietor of the Post-Herald was a big shipowner, and desired to save the shipping of the Allies. This I despatched by special messenger and immediately dismissed the matter from my thoughts for, as I say, I had not only the organization of a great strike but also I bad to condense the very heavy reports which wore coming through from our agents in the various shipping centres. I worked till three o'clock in the morning and then snatched a few hours' sleep.

At seven I was at my task again with all the newspapers ready for perusal. Naturally I turned to the Post-Herald first. Here I knew I had material for a good report and with my code book open in front of me, I was preparing to translate the leading article into language which would pass the censor for transmission to Holland.

I opened the paper. There was the leading article, but to my amazement it was headed:

GERMAN MURDERERS AT THEIR FOUL WORK.

I gasped. From the very first word to the very last the article was the bitterest, the most vehement, the most unscrupulous attack upon Germany that had ever appeared. I grew red and white as I read it. It called the Germans assassins of the sea, barbarians, Huns, Boches, pirates, blackguards, thieves — I shudder as I recall the language which was used by Mr. Collingrey.

I was in a maze, bewildered. I read on like a man in a bad dream, conscious of the awful avalanche of fury which would sweep down upon me when Berlin read this dreadful and disloyal article. It was not till nearly the end of the leader that I began to understand Mr. Collingrey's attitude. The final paragraph ran:

"If any doubt existed that this nation of Hun marauders is lacking in the elements of kultur, that doubt is removed by the wanton sinking of the Italian steamship San Salvadoro. It was an open secret that that ill-fated vessel was carrying to England two great masterpieces of Italian art, two priceless examples of Leonardo's genius. Did that fact stay the barbarian's hand? Nay! Rather it lent zest to tbe lustful and bestial representative of a savage and uncultured people.

"Those two masterpieces, unfortunately uninsured by their owner, lie at the bottom of the Bay of Biscay.

"Let the British Government make instant reprisals. Intern the aliens in our midst! Imprison and shoot secret agents whose evil activity seducing the allegiance of our people, whose hands are discernible even in the press itself."

I laid down the paper and wiped the perspiration from my brow. I took up a pen to indite the traitor's dismissal, but on second tboughts I put it down again. After all, it was not my idea. Let Berlin do its own dirty work.

10 — THE GREY ENVELOPE

It was in 1917, in the early part of the year, that, as a result of communications which had passed between myself and our agent in Amsterdam, we decided upon opening the most elaborate, and though I myself say it, one of the best planned campaigns against the morale of the British that had ever been undertaken. The occasion was the arrival amongst the enemies of the Fatherland of the United States of America. The U.S.A., as everybody knows, came into the war owing to the fact that the munitions makers of America, who had spent millions of pound on plant, had found themselves faced with ruin. For this they had to thank the perfidious behaviour of the British, who cancelled their orders, well knowing that to keep all the American munition factories running the American government would be compelled to declare war.

I had this information from a dear friend of mine who is in the secrets of Washington and was on terms of personal friendship with many Senators and Congressmen, one at least of whom had openly exposed the perfidious Wilson — such balderdash as his speeches has never been uttered by serious statesmen! — and his nefarious plan.

I had not lived in America for nothing. I knew how deep-rooted was the detestation felt in America against the English. I remember before leaving New York I dined with two true-born patriotic Americans, the Mr. Shaun O'Gorman and Mr. Adolph Dinklewurtt, who assured me solemnly, that any movement of the President towards assisting the English would result in revolution from one end of the country to the other.

I felt, therefore, that although the die had been cast, and Wilson had committed the unforgivable and diabolical crime of plunging America into war for chauvinistic aims — a responsibility from which the unfrivolous mind reels in gasping horror — there was still an opportunity for a man who could think quickly and act instantly, providing always be had that genius for organization which so few of my rivals possess.

It made it easier for me that America was intensely unpopular with the English people. How they sneered at that expression of his "Too haughty for war!" How they gibed at his notes and derided his chauvinistic speeches! They refused to accept this impertinent man, this ex-colonel of cowboy rough-riders, at his own valuation, or to take his "big stick" speech in any but a frivolous spirit.

Knowing this uncompromising hatred of the American, it did not take me very long to set my agents working. Within a week the country was ringing with stories of the behaviour of American soldiers in Lancashire. You, yourself, must have heard of the quarrel between the English and Americans which resulted in the American being thrown into a river and drowned? It has probably reached your cars that certain American soldiers, refused liquor at a saloon, set fire to the house and decamped carrying with them the hotel keeper's young daughter.

You may also have heard how all American soldiers spoke despisingly of England and boast that they have come in to finish the war. Some of these stories were more widely spread than others, but all of them fulfilled one excellent purpose — they brought annoyance to that ridiculous person, Major Haynes — the so- called Intelligence Officer, under whose nose the despised Heine worked so brazenly!

I do not pretend to know intimately the mentality of such men as Major Haynes. I confess it is difficult for a plain-thinking German, blunt and honest, to understand deceit for deceit's sake (I justly absolve myself of all acts of deception performed on behalf of the Fatherland), or to lower his moral vision to the gutter wherein much slimy kultur flows.

To me, it is abhorrent that men. should be so frivolous that they should engage themselves in despicable undertakings for wholly despicable reasons. That such a stigma applies to Major, or Mister Haynes, I can prove by his own words.

Sometime after my last encounter with him, we met in a cafe in Fleet Street. I had gone in to drink a cup of coffee and smoke a cigar when the swing doors opened and I saw the somewhat drab and insignificant figure of Haynes enter. He walked in furtively, almost apologetically. How different, thought, would have been the bearing of one of our German officers! He would have flung the door open with a crash and have stood erect with flashing eyes and haughty mien surveying the room ere he strode forward, his sword clanking with every movement of his big earth-trembling German feet.

Major Haynes came in timorously and seeing me came towards me. My throat went dry with hate, my hands shook with righteous anger and I felt myself go pale at the thought of his perfidy.

But there was nothing to be afraid of, as his first words assured me. "Good evening, Heine," be said, "may I sit down with you?" Here again, what a contrast to a major of the Highest German Staff. He would have ordered me to rise and go to the devil, and probably honoured me with a good German cuff on the ear!

"Certainly, Major Haynes," I said, "this is indeed a pleasure I did not anticipate. May I order you some coffee?"

He nodded and I summoned the waiter.

"It is such a long time since we met," I went on, "that I have almost despaired of seeing you again. I began to fear that you had been sent to the front."

"I am afraid that must have given you some sleepless nights," he said foolishly. Why should this confounded hound imagine that his departure for the front would disturb my rest? Such arrogance!

"You may think I exaggerate," I said earnestly, "but believe me, I have been much impressed by your personality —"

"It is curious that you should have said that," said Major Haynes, "for I was just on the point of remarking how much I bad been impressed by your personality. You see, Heine," he went on, noting, I trust, my modest surprise, "I have been watching you pretty closely (my blood ran cold) and I realize how utterly trustworthy you are and bow different from other of the South American neutrals one meets. I always have an admiration for the Latin races and it is such a joy to meet a thorough-going South American with a German name, and especially one so whole-heartedly in favour of the Allies as yourself."

"Major Haynes," I said solemnly, "I have no interests but the interests of the Allies. If I could shoulder a musket to-morrow—"

"You would look very silly," said Major Haynes crudely, ignorant of the fact that I was speaking in a figurative sense, because muskets are no longer carried, even by the German-trained native troops of West Africa.

"Yes I am certain you would fight, Heine, and I am certain it is only the fact that you have a wife and family, that you are the sole support of your ancient mother, and that you suffer from a weak heart, which prevents your flinging yourself joyously into the battle."

I inclined my head with a certain quiet dignity.

"You are pleased to jest, Major Haynes, for being an Englishman you will have your joke, but I assure you in all seriousness that if ever I could render a service to the Allies you have but to command me."

Major Haynes looked at me for a long time. It would be true to say that he stared very rudely before he spoke, but when he did speak his words shocked me.

"That is exactly what I want you to do," be said slowly. I was all attention, curious, and at the same time apprehensive. If he had dared asked me to commit any action which would have injured my beloved land I should have first smacked his face and then shot myself, if I still lived.

"Command me," I said coldly.

Major Haynes looked around, then he lowered his voice.

"The matter I am going to discuss," he said, "is a delicate one, I want you to upset one of the cleverest gangs of spies we have had in this country, headed by a man who is without doubt the biggest genius in the German Intelligence Department."

I blushed with gratification, even though those words of praise were from an enemy, can you blame me? If my pleasure overcame my fears, can you wonder?

"There is a man in England," Major Haynes went on, "who is directing the real world of espionage. I am not referring to the hacks that Germany employs to send her weather news and reports on the effect of air-raids and movements of troops, but to the big gang, the men who work in the dark, who go after the big coups."

I nodded again, not I trust with any evidence of self-complacence, but certainly in a spirit of pride, for I seemed to realize more of my importance to the State when I heard my work recounted in the cold and passionless language of a man whom I regarded at that moment as one of the most intelligent English- men I had ever met.

"They are the people we are anxious to get," said Major Haynes, "and, I might add," he said, "to shoot."

I shivered, but hid my shiver in a laugh.

"Go on, dear Major Haynes," I said, "you interest me."

"I know the man I am after," said Haynes. (I clutched at the table-cloth.) "But I have not been able to catch him. He has a dozen aliases, but his real name is Professor Zollernborn."

"Zollernborn?" I said in astonishment.

I think it was at that moment that my quick German brain grasped the situation. Professor Zollernborn was in Berlin. The clever Major Haynes did not know that only that morning I had received instructions from the Herr Professor. I saw the trap plainly, but from my impassive face Major Haynes would never have known the rapid, lightning-like thoughts which were flashing and crackling in my brain.

It was a trap for Heine! Beware and walk warily, thou faithful servant of government! Match thy wits against this dull Englishman and put him in the soup!

"Indeed," I said.

"I have reason to believe," this so-called Intelligence Officer went on, "that a document of a very important character, which in some mysterious way recently disappeared for twenty-four hours from the papers of the Director-General of Recruiting, will be transmitted to Berlin — or rather a copy of that document - which is in such a code that it cannot be forwarded by wireless."

"In what way can I help you?" I asked, playing my part in the farce with admirable sang-froid.

Major Haynes leant back and thrust his hands in an ungentlemanly manner in his trousers' pockets.

"I am going to put all my cards on the table, Heine, all except the ace," he said. "It cannot have escaped your notice that you have been associated with people who have been very naturally the objects of suspicion. Two or three gentlemen with whom you have had dealings — in a perfectly innocent manner, I am sure — have paid the penalty for espionage. I know what you are going to say," he said, checking my indignant protest with a shake of his head, "that you know nothing about their nefarious work? Quite right, I can believe it. But for some reason or other, Heine, they think, these enemies of the government, that you are favourably disposed to help them."

"Then they make a very great mistake," I said firmly, "and if they ask me to assist them I shall be extremely annoyed."

He nodded.

"So I think. And yet they will ask you to assist them. The document in question will pass from hand to hand. Sooner or later it will fall into your possession and on the envelope will be the address of another agent to whom you will deliver it. It will probably be thrust into your pocket when you are walking along the street and somebody will whisper in your ear 'Frieburg,' which means, 'you have something which must be passed on without delay.'"

As he proceeded the perspiration was pouring from me—indeed that night when I came to change my undervest (it being Friday) I found it quite damp. "Frieburg" was the password which we used in the sense that Major Haynes had stated. What traitor betrayed his Fatherland and placed this stupid officer in possession of our code will perhaps one day be known and his name will be execrated from one end of Germany to the other.

"But," I said, calming myself, "how should I know what 'Frieburg' meant if you had not told me?"

"You would probably be notified by letter," said the Major suavely, "at any rate, you will know."

"What am I to do?" I asked. The scheme was now to me as plain as daylight. I was suspect, and this was a trap for me. How was the trap to be sprung?

"The moment you find yourself in possession of that letter you will bring it to me," said Major Haynes.

"Of course, I could have you watched all the time but I could not be searching you every five minutes, and I could never know, unless you assisted me, when you were in possession of this interesting document. I could even have you arrested now," he shrugged his shoulders cold-bloodedly, "but that would not help, because another agent would be found."

"You want me to bring you the latter as soon as I receive it?" I said.

"That is all I ask," said Major Haynes.

I offered him my hand and smiled.

"On the word of a sportsman and a gentleman," I said, "I will bring it to you."

I walked down Fleet Street whistling a tune. Even in that moment of danger Heine's well-balanced mind was not seriously perturbed.

"I shall know no danger until I am blind," said Schiller, and so might I say, for with my eyes open to the plot which was being laid against me half the danger vanished. The cleverness of it, the cunning underhandedness of it! I was suspect. They had no evidence against me and they wanted to secure proof that I was a dirty devil of a German. A police agent would hand me the envelope. I should probably find the name of a comrade inscribed. I would be watched all the time and if I attempted to escape with the spurious document I should be arrested.

I have a much better plan, dear Mister, or Major, Haynes! Into thy guilty hands will I deliver this fake or dud, document, and shall stand with quiet, smiling contempt, watching thy confusion, when thou discoverest that Heine, with bland innocence, has carried out thy wishes!

Two days later I was called up to the telephone and a strange voice speaking with a German accent said: "Be prepared for 'Frieburg' to-day," and immediately rang off.

I chuckled my amusement. So this was the day for the plot to materialize. I went about my work in the usual manner. I lunched at a fashionable restaurant in the Strand, returned to my office, finished up my work at 5:30, and strolled, as is my wont, westward.

It was whilst making the purchase of a paper at the bookstall at Piccadilly Tube Station that the thing happened. Somebody pressed close to me. I heard the word "Frieburg" whispered in my ear, and when I had disengaged myself from the crowd and carelessly put my hand in my pocket I found a somewhat bulky envelope which, as I felt with my fingertips, was heavily sealed.

I walked down Piccadilly and turned into the park, and presently found my way to a quiet spot. Making sure that I was free from observation, I pulled the envelope from my pocket, pretending to take out a handkerchief which I had previously pocketed, and examined the letter.

It was enclosed in a big grey envelope and was addressed in English:

"Deliver without delay to out agent in Southampton."

I put the envelope and handkerchief back. The solution of Major Haynes' plot became ridiculously simple. It was not only a test for me, but it was an attempt to discover who was the agent of the Government at Southampton. Could you not imagine me driving off to Waterloo followed by Secret Service men, and shadowed until I met and betrayed the brave fellow who overlooked the interests of Deutschland in Southampton?

Five minutes later I was out of the park, hailing a taxi cab.

"Drive me to the War Office," I said in a loud voice, for the benefit of a skulking loafer who was nearby, and who was probably a detective in disguise.

Immediately on my arrival, I sent up my card and was ushered into Major Haynes' office. He jumped up as I entered.

"Have you got it?" he said eagerly. For answer I handed him the grey envelope, and he seized it.

"Sit down, Heine. Excuse my agitation," he said, "but I had a feeling that they would try you."

I looked at him in wonder for, for the first time in his life, the major was agitated. He pressed a bell and a soldier came in.

"Will you ask General Brackenhurst if he can come," he said. If Major Haynes's excitement was astonishing, what shall I say of a staid and veteran staff general, who tore the wrappings from the envelope, eagerly scanned the unfolded pages and gave a loud and vulgar cry of joy.

"It is the original, Haynes!" he said. "Thank God we've got it!"

"They haven't taken a copy, you think?"

"It was the copy they sent back," said the general, wiping his forehead, "it is impossible to make a copy of this. That is how we detected the theft. This is the original. In this code a pin-point's difference in the position of the letters would have made all the difference. That is why they are trying to send it to Germany, because they couldn't translate it here."

He turned and looked at me.

"Is this the gentleman who assisted us? " he asked, and shook me warmly by the hand.

"We owe you a great debt of gratitude, sir," he said. "As Major Haynes has told you, this document, if it fell into the hands of the enemy, would have been of inestimable value to the Germans."

If it was acting it was good acting. My German instinct told me that it was not acting at all. I knew by the trembling of my knees that I had misjudged the position, and I left the War Office like a man in a dream. Only one thing remained to be done. I left that evening for Southampton, and was fortunate enough to see our agent in the vestibule of a theatre; I whispered "Frieburg" in his ear, and put my band in his pocket, but I did not leave any letter. Let him explain it if he can!

11 — THE MURDERERS

In the latter days of March, 1915, I had received a communication from headquarters which was contained in a box of Dutch cigars forwarded to me from Rotterdam. It was written to me on the usual grey paper and was neatly sandwiched between the two thin pieces of wood which formed the bottom of the box. You would never think of splitting the bottom of a cigar-box into two shavings in order to discover a message from the Political Intelligence Department would you? Such was German ingenuity. The communication may be given in full:

Kriegsministerium,

Berlin.

March 12, 1915

By order of Section 10, Politik, Great General Staff.

There go to England, on March 16, two men

(1) Carl Jan Kattz

(2) Rudolph Kister

convicts from the Imperial Prison at Dresden under sentence for (1) Murder and robbery, (2) Dangerous wounding and burglary. These two men speak English and are acquainted with English life and conditions. They are released on condition that they place themselves at the disposal of the Chief of the Intelligence Bureau in London. These men may be depended upon to perform the most desperate acts. They will be placed on the pay-list of the C. of I., London, at 10 marks each per diem and 20 marks each per diem for normal expenses. The C. of I., London will not hesitate to shoot either man in the event of his failure to carry out orders.

I confess that my first care was to keep this precious pair of rascals as far away from me as possible. I could not have such hang-dog cut-throats haunting my office, and I sent Wilhelm Peters to meet them and install them in lodgings in Coventry — which was one of the towns I was not likely to visit.

Wilhelm informed me that they preferred to go to Wednesbury, as they were both acquainted with glass-working and there were two or three glass factories in that town at which they could work. I made arrangements for them to receive their weekly stipends, registered their addresses, and sent them the card code (which was ingeniously got up in the form of a time-table) and dismissed them. from my thoughts with the earnest hope that it would never be necessary to utilize their services.

For we Germans abhor deeds of darkness and violence. Who has looked through the spectacles of a serious German boy and has seen his clear and honest blue eyes shining thoughtfully, could ever question either the gentleness of his disposition or the transparency of his motives. We hate deceit and cruelty, we shrink from the infliction of needless pain and exalt the fulfilment of the law to a worship.

So I shuddered and passed from my mind all thought of Carl Jan Kattz and Rudolph Kister. And yet, despite this innate tenderness of ours, we Germans are all granite and iron. When we set ourselves to the accomplishment of a task we are not to be arrested by parsnip-buttering words or even the allurement of the most indecorous siren, as you shall see. I have referred to the assistance I offered to our gallant Zeppelins by tho triangle of lights.

One of these Light stations was arranged in the stable-yard of a good Polish friend named Jabowski. The yard was a small one shut in on three sides by very high walls, and on the fourth by the stable. (Jabowski was a tailor in a large way of business, and employed to carts for the collection and distribution of goods). He hated the English, who had treated him very scurvily and had prosecuted him for some small breaches of the Factory Act, and he was, in consequence of his tyranny-hatred, and for a very handsome sum I paid him, willing to show the light — a motor head-lamp coloured green.

One night after a raid was expected Jabowski came to see me. I had just got back from an over-night trip to Bristol and I was eager for news. He seemed puzzled and troubled.

"Was there a raid?" I asked.

"Well, Herr Heine," he said, "there was — but it was the most curious raid we have had. I came to tell you about it."

"Proceed, Jabowski," said I graciously, although be was a man of the lowest social order.

"At eleven o'clock last night my son and I were standing in the yard, watching the lamp and listening for the footfall of a policeman outside, when we heard distinctly the noise of an airship it grew nearer and nearer until the sound was terrific and I could hear the people in the street scurrying away to their houses. I looked up, as did my son, but I could see nothing. Whatever it was passed overhead and when immediately over something fell with a thud — right in the centre of the yard!"

"A bomb?"

"No, gracious Herr — it was a big paper bag which was evidently filled with a sort of yellow vere. Thinking it was a new kind of poison or some diabolical—"

"Ingenious's the word, Jabowski," I interrupted.

"Exactly, gracious sir, some dangerous form of explosive. I did not attempt to remove it until this morning. I gathered most of it up but it was impossible to remove the stain from the stones."

"There were no bombs?"

"None," replied Jabowski with emphasis, "the raider was heard by many people and, according to a policeman who came to see me this morning, these yellow bags have been dumped all over the neighbourhood."

I was thoughtful. What did these bags portend? Obviously there was a message of some kind, thought I, intended for me. That green light showed the raider that there was a friend in the neighbourhood and yet—

Whilst I was talking, there was a knock at the hall-door of my flat, and my servant (an excellent Swiss youth who had the good fortune to be born in Breslau, of German parents) announced that the two Mr. Giesslers wished to see me. I was amazed at the coincidence, for these two brothers were in charge of the two other lamps which completed the triangle.

"Show them into my bedroom, and I will come and see them, Adolph," said I.

The Messrs Geisslers were bakers, and good friends of their Fatherland. One had a shop near Albany Park, and the other a bakehouse south of the Thames.

"Victor came over to see me this morning, Herr Heine," explained Kurt Geissler, the elder of the two, "and as he has had the same curious experience that I had in last night's raid, I thought we had better come along and see you."

Briefly his narrative was on all four-legs with the story which Jabowski had told. They had heard the whirr of airship engines, and a bag of yellow dust bad fallen, in Victor's case upon the roof of the bakehouse, and in Kurt's case on a chicken house in his back garden.

"The police say that these bags have fallen over the South of London," said Kurt.

"They've been dropped on north-west London too," said Victor, and produced an envelope full of the stuff. I looked at it without touching the powder. It was as fine as flour.

"You must leave me to think this matter out," I said at last, and sent them on their way.

I was engaged in intensive cogitation half an hour later, when Major Haynes, of the British Intelligence Department, called. While I at first resented his calling, I had now overcome my repugnance to meeting one who was engaged in such underhanded and sneaking work as the Military Intelligence Department condescend to do. We Germans have a delicate gorge, I told you, and there were times when, remembering that his sly cunning had probably sent many, and had certainly sent two brave Germans to their death, I could scarcely bring myself to flatter him.

"Good morning, Mr. Major," said I with a readily-adopted smile, "you are looking inside the pink this morning."

"Good morning, Heine," he said. He had called me "Heine" many times lately, and somehow I never had the nerve the correct him. "Were you in the raid last night?"

"The raid?" I said in innocence — amazed. "I saw nothing about it in the papers — was there a raid?"

He laughed. "So some people think," he said, and then turning suddenly from the subject he asked, "What size gloves do you take?"

It was an extraordinary question. All my wits were working at top pressure. I was at my alertest, my mind reviewing all the circumstances which had attended my doings of the past week. Had I left a finger-print in my visit to the Chetwell Munition Works, or dropped a glove on my recent conference with the executive of the Workers for World Peace?

"I take an eight or nine size," I said deliberately.

"That would be much too large — show me your hands." I extended my hands. Why did a cold and sickly feeling come into a certain digestive organ? Why did the beads of perspiration stand out on my brow? Why, in spite of a mental effort of the strongest, did my face blanch and my hand tremble? Did I expect to hear the click of steel, and feel chill bands about my wrists, and hear the jangle of the link that holds handcuffs together? Yet none of these thing happened. Mr. or Major Haynes just took my hands in his and turned them over with the same delicacy of touch that I have observed in the German haus-frau when she is buying fish, and turns over the soles on the stall to find the biggest.

"Yes — a seven," said the major, and I thought there was a note of disappointment in his tone.

We chatted about the war for a while and then be said good-bye and left me with two puzzles to solve instead of one. Fortunately the rest of the day was so fully occupied with sheer routine work that I had not time to speculate upon the mystery of the Yellow Raid, as I called it.

I had started two new societies, The Brotherhood of Humanity and the Thinkers of Britain League, and these entailed an enormous amount of correspondence. The former society had as its motive the elimination of all wars; the latter was intended to bring together under one aegis that considerable body of students and tractarians who regarded frontier lines as artificial limitations set up to divide the many for the benefit of the few. They were promising plants, and though I hoped that Germany would never need to seek a peace but would triumph in the field that she would be able to dictate her terms to greedy England, bare-legged Scotland, libertine France, and barbarian Russia, yet we Germans are habitually cautious.

That night I learned from the usual quarter that the weather was propitious for a Zeppelin raid, and warned the "leaders" (the car drivers whose powerful headlamps guided the Zeppelins to their destinations) and my signal friends, before I left town by the 8:30 train for Bath. I got on the 'phone to London that night and discovered that no raid had occurred, and returned by the early morning train which reaches Paddington at 8:30. My new assistant, Mr. Wilhelm Peters, was waiting for me at the flat.

"Bad news, Herr Heine," he said.

"Tell me," I replied.

"Jabowski and the two Geisslers were arrested last night in the act of signalling."

That was bad news indeed. I learnt that they had been raided practically at the same hour by three parties of police, and had been taken to Scotland Yard.

"I have been all night at work making inquires," said Peters, "and I have discovered how they were detected."

"Betrayed, of course," said I, but to my surprise Wilhelm shook his head.

"They betrayed themselves," he said, "the raid of the previous night was no a raid at all. The noise they heard was that of an English dirigible balloon flying at a very low altitude. It was up looking for signal lights, and detected Jabowski's light first. It flew over the yard and dropped a bag of yellow ochre as near the light as possible, and on the following morning the police went round the neighbourhood with a story of a mysterious airship which had been throwing such things. When they said that the airship had dropped many they lied. There were only three bags dropped — on Jabowski and the two Geisslers. Once the stain of the ochre was discovered, the police had only to wait a favourable opportunity. The rumour of a coming raid was circulated all over London for the purpose of deceiving us."

I saw the thing clearly now. So that was why Mr or Major Haynes had come to my office. He thought that some of the yellow stuff would be brought to me for my inspection, and that I would handle it! So you are interested in the size of my gloves, my officer! So you would inspect my hands, thou artful man of low cunning!

But Heine had been too clever — too wide-awakened! I could not deny myself so much exhilaration of feeling, yet the position was a serious one. The Geisslers I could trust. But Jabowski ! Here was a man without a country — a cringer, a born traitor, one who under pressure to save his own miserable skin would not hesitate to betray me and the sacred cause for which I worked.

Whatever doubts I had about the loyalty of Jabowski were removed when his son came to see me that afternoon. This young Jabowski was about twenty-five years of age, very dark, with a curly head of hair and a long yellow face. He was dressed fashionably (and a little above his class) in a check suit and a yellow tie, and wore the diamond ring and scarf-pin that one would rather have expected on a German gentleman than on a Polish tailor!

I was annoyed to see him.

"Why do you come here?" I asked, when he was shown into my room."How dare you come to my apartments?"

"It's all right, Heine, I wasn't watched," he said. "I came by Tube and what's more, I waited till it was dark. I suppose you know that the old man's pinched?"

"The old man pinched?" I said in astonishment-simulation, "What old man — and what pinch?"

"Oh, come off it," he said coarsely, "you know what I'm talking about — my father, Mr. Jabowski."

"For Mr. Jabowski I have the highest respect," I said, "and I have had many dealings with him, strictly in the way of business. Do I understand he has been arrested? Dear, dear — I trust he has not been doing anything very naughty?"

The young man scowled at me. "Look here! " he said with violence, "you know why be was pinched — for giving Zepp signals at your instructions."

I sprang up, "Shameless, lying Jew!" I cried in a great voice, "traducer of innocent truly-neutrals! How dare you — how dare you make so infamous an accusation! By heavens! I've a mind to grip you by the neck and your coat- tails, and hurl you from the window!" I saw a look of fear creep into his eyes, but he did not budge from his contention.

"Have sense, Heine," he pleaded, "can I allow my old man to be shot? It's a terrible position for me, and I was getting married to a widow-lady with money too. The disgrace will kill me!"

"Your father can prove nothing against me," I said, and the miserable fellow smirked.

"That's where you're wrong," he said, "the old man was too wide for you. 'Jacob,' says he to me, 'this Prussian is so careful that he won't put anything in writing. If I get into trouble, he'll pretend he doesn't know me, so when he comes this afternoon to talk things over in the stable yard, get your camera and take a snap of us together,' and," said the despicable young man in unmistakable tones of pleasure, "I've got that photograph to show the police unless you do something to get my father out of trouble."

"Have you the photograph with you, my dear young man?" I asked with mildness.

"Am I nutty?" replied Jabowski junior

I promised to give him an answer that night. What could I do? To whom could I turn to secure the release of this misguided and fearfully threatening Pole? That he would betray me I did not doubt, and the horror of the thought stunned me. I had escaped the graver perils. I had incurred the suspicion of the highest authorities and had yet won through. It was because I had tricked them with the bluff of the experienced player that I had escaped detection. Even Major Haynes believed that I was no more than a dupish fool — but would he believe as much on such an accusation supported by visible evidence of hob- nobbing with the dubious alien of Polish origin?

So they would trap me — me, Heine, who would not tread on a turning worm, unless it turned against the Fatherland. My gentle nature is notorious amongst my friends. The song of the skylark rising to the dawn, the mist of bluebells in the shadowy aisles of woods have made me cry like a child, and this dirty dog of a Jabowski would send such a man as Heine to the execution chair.

I sent a telegram to friends Kister and Kattz, at Wednesbury, telling them to report to me in my apartments, by the first train. If there were any burnt- offerings required, it were better for the Fatherland that the sacrifices should be Polish.

Let me describe Kattz and Kister as I saw them when they came walking into my sitting-room. Kattz was a thin man of about thirty-five. He was slightly bald, and he wore a pair of steel-rimmed pince-nez. His face was thin and studious, with deep furrows and wrinkles. He reminded me of a bust I once saw of Dante. He was quietly and respectably dressed, and his attitude and manner were subdued and respectful. His companion, Kister, was of stouter build, and he bore a facial resemblance to the English King Henry VIII. He was broad- featured, had a small moustache and trim beard, and a rosy complexion. Like his companion he was quiet in speech and deportment.

"Sit down, gentlemen," said I, greatly relieved by the uncriminal appearance of my agents. "I will open a bottle of good wine — in the meantime, help yourselves to the cigars."

They seated themselves, and when they had been made comfortable, I briefly outlined the nature of my difficulty. "So you see, gentlemen, my position," I concluded, "these two men have the fate of our service in their hands."

"They must be put out of the way," said the jovial-faced Kister, "you agree, my dear Kattz?"

Mr. Kattz nodded.

"We can settle the younger man very easily," he said, "you have his address, of course?"

I inclined my head. "You will probably find that he has the photograph in his pocket, in spite of his protest," he went on. "I can get on to him to- night."

He felt in his pocket and drew out a short length of cord, to the ends of which were fastened two small wooden handles. He unrolled the cord which was wound about the sticks and re-rolling it, returned the instrument to his pocket. The jovial Mr. Kister frowned and shook his head.

"You know, my dear Kattz, I would not hurt your feelings, but I feel compelled to demur at that method of yours. I believe in this." With a dexterity which hardly seemed possible, he slipped a long-bladed knife from the inside of his waistcoat. I pushed my chair back a little.

"The knife or nothing, I say," said he, "it is noiseless, it is instantly effective it can be used in a crowd, and the victim will not utter a sound. Why?" he said, looking at me, "I once killed a friend of mine in the Wintergarten in Berlin, surrounded by policemen, and they thought be had fainted."

"A friend?" I said.

"When I say a friend," said Mr Kister apologetically, "I mean one who had been a friend. We fell out over a lady — you remember, Kattz."

"A tight-rope walker," said Kattz.

"Exactly. She was not worthy of the quarrel I have often regretted my haste in the matter, for poor Joseph was a good fellow, and played skat like a master."

"I don't think you should speak against the cord, Rudolph," said Kattz, "you have probably only seen it used by a bungler. There are three men — there are two now, for Friederich Mullenheim laid down his life for the Fatherland at the Battle of Roye — who can use it. It is as silent as the knife, and I remember—"

My blood went cold as I listened to the exchanges of experience which went on between the two, and when Kister was using my waistcoat to illustrate what he called "the complete-silence stroke," and Kattz was showing on my neck the exact spot where the carotid artery nearest approaches the cervical vertebrae. I thought matters had gone far enough.

"Make your own arrangements about young Jabowski," I said hastily, "but how are you going to deal with the old man — he is safely in prison?"

"That I think is simple," said Kattz, "we have been studying the prison system in England — naturally that interests us more than anything else, an we know the procedure. A prisoner on remand is allowed to have his meal sent in. I think there will be no difficulty in sending our friend something more than he will digest."

"I will leave the matter entirely in your hands," I said.

I gave them £10 and bade them report to me by telephone when their dread task was accomplished. I confess I spent a wretched night. How frail and thin is life! The snap of a thread and the veil is rent — a puff of wind and the serene flame goes out — a crack of a rifle and the accumulated genius and experience of forty years, a million memories and a million hopes, are dissipated to nothingness. How dreadful is that visitation. I shuddered. I did not want to die. As for these two traitors, death would rid the world of much corporate infamy. The day came slowly, and I was up long before my servant.

There was nothing in the morning newspaper to tell of any happening such as I expected, but I could hardly expect to have news so soon. I resolved to stay in my apartment till the afternoon, and it was ten o'clock when I heard a ring at the bell, and went hot and cold. I heard my servant go along the passage and open the door and presently came a knock.

"Come in," I said, and to my surprise in walked young Jabowski. His face was pale, his eyes wore wild, and as for myself, I could frame no question.

"Oh, Mr. Heine, Mr. Heine," he said imploringly, and I thought he was going to kneel at my feet, "Give me another chance, give me another chance. Here is the photograph."

His trembling hands searched for a pocket-book, which presently he produced. The book shook in his palsied fingers, but presently be mastered himself sufficiently to extract a small photograph which he handed to me. It was the photograph of myself and the ill-fated Jabowski.

"There, there is the evidence," he gasped, "now do be a good friend and save me!"

"I hardly know what you mean," I said coldly, " all that I know is that you came here yesterday and accused me of a crime from which my very soul revolts, disloyalty to the British Government, for the members of which I have the highest respect."

"The old man will take his punishment without bleating," he said, eagerly ignoring my reference to his wild conduct. "The lawyer say he will only get about twelve months' imprisonment, and if he opens his mouth about you, he will probably get more. But if they convicted me — why, I'd get five years."

I was silent. This talk still held a mystery for me, and I waited for him to reveal that which, even in my curiosity, I did not dare ask.

"I ought to have known, Mr, Heine," he said mopping his forehead with an ungentlemanly handkerchief of many colours, "I ought to have known that with all the spies you've got, you would be wise about me."

"I am indeed wise about you," I said very severely.

"Don't think," he said eagerly, "that I am a regular burglar, because I'm not. The old man never allowed me more than eighteen shillings a week, and a man can't live in a gentlemanly way on that, can he? I got in bad with a crooked lot of people, and one job led to another and that is how it happened."

"I know exactly how it happened," I said coldly.

"When I got home last night," the young man went on, "it struck me that you might know that I was in the Regent Street burglary and it gave me the shivers, but I wasn't sure until I found myself being shadowed by the two detectives you put on to follow me."

I could have laughed out loud. Kattz and Kister — detectives!

"How did you know I had put them on to you?"

"I gave them the slip," said young Jabowski, "and presently I spotted them getting into a cab. It was about one o'clock in the morning, and I got another cab and followed them and, they came back here."

"Came back here?" This was indeed news for me.

"Well, they didn't come up," said Jabowski, "they stood outside the flat , talking, and one of them pointed up to your window, and then I knew that you had put them on to me."

I readily supplied an explanation. My friends Kister and Kattz had come back to tell me of some difficulty they had met with, and I am rather glad they took this step. What Jabowski told me greatly relieved me, If the old man would remain silent and take his punishment, with the photograph in my possession, and burnt, and Jabowski in terror of my betraying him, a load was removed from my mind. There was no need for any drastic measures, and I could only hope that my two friends, with characteristic thoroughness, had not already despatched a deadly draught to the man in the cells.

I was anxious to get rid of Jabowski before they turned up or telephoned, as I had asked them to, and after lecturing him on his evil life and on the necessity for dealing honestly by his fellow creatures and abandoning his course of wickedness, I allowed him to depart with the promise that I should take no further action against him.

"Honesty and straight dealing with your fellow creatures is the surest road to happiness and success," I said. "How beautiful is the life of the virtuous man - who can look the whole world in the face, as the poet says, and owe not any man!"

He thanked me very humbly and went his way. Neither Kister nor Kattz put in an appearance, and I began to worry whether they had got into some trouble, or whether, in some spirit of friendly rivalry, they had gone outside my instructions and in good-hearted competition had been practising their science upon some unfortunate pig-headed Englishman or Englishmen.

When they had not turned up by the afternoon I am afraid I became very angry. Was I to be kept waiting in my flat all day by two despicable jail-birds? However, a diversion arrived in the shape of my assistant, Mr. Wilhelm Peters, that amiable young man arriving after lunch with my letters.

"I am sorry I am so late, Herr Heine," he said, "but I had no idea that you were not at the office."

"Of course, of course," I said genially, "you have been out of London. Now tell me your news."

He chatted away about various matters. He gave me a memorandum of the amount of T.N.T. which was being made at —, the big new English factory, and told me of the trouble that had arisen because Woolwich had rejected so many flawed shell-cases which were made in a certain factory in the North of England. He also placed in my hand the memorandum compiled by our agent in Liverpool of the cotton shipments and furnishing me with particulars of certain petroleum boats which were due to arrive in the Jersey.

"I saw Herr von Friedlander at Birmingham," he said. "He has not been able to find an agent in the small-arm factory, but he hopes—"

"He hopes!" I said irritably, "that infernal man may live on hopes, but I can't! I shall pack him straight back to America. Does he imagine because he is well-born that I must endure these harrowing disappointments? I cannot find excuses for him any longer. You have done very well my dear Wilhelm Peters, and I shall report in terms of favour."

"I thank you for your gracious words, Herr Heine," he said, going red under my approbation. "I also took the liberty of calling at Wednesbury and seeing how our convicts are progressing."

"And how are they?" I asked innocently.

"They are behaving themselves," said Wilhelm Peters, "and seeming to like the life. The red-headed one, Kattz, is quite amusing."

"Red-headed one?" I said.

"Yes, the little one who has red hair. Don't you remember I describe them, after I had met them on the steamer, Herr Heine?"

"And what is the other man like — Kister?" I asked.

"He is a man with a long black beard and rather consumptive looking," said Wilhelm.

"Are you sure?"

My hair almost stood on end.

"Quite sure. The only thing that worried them was a visit which was paid to them by two secret service officers last week — at least I gathered they were officers of the English secret service by the questions they asked."

"Do you know what they looked like, the secret service officers?" I said, endeavouring to control my voice.

Wilhelm Peters smiled like a fool.

"Don't grin, stupid owl," I said angrily.

"Pardon, Herr Heine," said Wilhelm Peters, "but I was smiling because I asked them that very question. One was a thin-faced man with lines in his cheeks and the other was rather a stoutish man with a rosy face and a little beard."

"Secret service officers!" I breathed."

"Do you know them," asked Wilhelm Peters.

"I have met them," I said, and somehow at that moment I knew my stay in England was nearly up.

12 — THE PASSING OF HEINE

The British people, in their boastful, arrogant, and frivolous way, have a saying that the British do not know when they are beaten. This betrays their folly, their short-sightedness, and their inability to grasp the obvious. We Germans, on the contrary, recognize facts. I had enjoyed a great innings. I had done useful work. I had served the Fatherland with a loyalty and unselfishness which I trust will be held as a shining example to the unborn generations of secret service officers who will follow in my steps.

To continue in England would be folly. There were many reasons why I should determine my residence. It was growing more and more difficult to get into communication with the Fatherland. Trading steamers, ostensibly engaged in peaceable commerce, but in reality maintained to keep the communications open between England and Germany, were constantly disappearing in the most ominous fashion. The wireless stations which we had established with so much thought were being eliminated and, worst of all, since the conviction was forced upon me against my will, I had to confess to myself that there really existed in Britain a secret service of a peculiarly deceitful kind.

I had been constantly coming into contact with its members, constantly foiled by its machinations. Its officers were to be found in all ranks and departments of public life; they included members of Parliament, and little shopkeepers, newspaper reporters and doctors, railway officials of all grades, ship's stewards and parson. It was unbelievable, and it took me nearly two years to be convinced.

And now I had the feeling that a well-prepared net had been stretched and was gradually encircling me. I had a sense that I was being played with as a mouse is played by a cat. I notified Headquarters that I was retiring gracefully, and one night I sat down and worked out the details of my escape.

I had four passports, and my first move was to obtain the endorsement of all these. That in itself was a difficult business, but the original owners of the passports were well chosen. It was an American, a

Swede, a Chilean, and a Canadian, and had you seen the four photographs attached to those four documents, you would have observed that there was not a great dissimilarity in appearance between any of the four.

I was due to leave England on May 15th, 1916. I actually left on May 14th. On the morning of that day, I took one of those bold steps which the most daring spies invariably find profitable. I called at the War Office and asked to see Major Haynes, of the Intelligence Department. I sent in my name, that is to say, my Chilean name, and in a very short time I was ushered into a very large, bare office, where the gallant major sat at a table which was covered with documents of all kinds.

He rose and greeted me heartily.

"How are you, Heine?" he asked, , pulling up a chair for me to sit on. "and how are our friends Kattz and Kister?"

"Kattz and Kister?" I repeated, my face a blank.

"The scientific murderers," said the major with a cheerful laugh. "The bow- string expert and the stiletto specialist."

"I do not understand you, dear major," I said.

"I didn't think you would," said he, and pulling out a drawer, removed a box.

"Have a poisoned cigar," he said, "one of our Kattz-Kister Perfectos."

He simply roared with laughter. Such vulgarity!

"I certainly remember the two names now you mention them. They called upon. me with a hoity-toity plan which I was much too busy to discuss with them. As a matter of fact, they had not been there long," said I with a cunning smile, "before I realized that they were members of the great " (I emphasized the word "great" with a little sneer) "English secret service, and I had an amusing evening pulling their several legs."

Major Haynes winked (he was not well born).

"What I like about you, Heine," he said (again that objectionable word, which I passed in silence), "is that you have a sense of humour. So few of your fellow countrymen possess that sense."

I laughed politely because I felt that it was what be expected me to do.

"Why have you come now?" he asked. I shrugged my shoulders.

"Mister Haynes," I began.

"Major Haynes," said he, "but go on."

"Major Haynes," I said, "it seems to me that my most innocent actions are misconstrued, and as I am going to-morrow to Brighton to spend a week-end, I thought it advisable to notify you, so that you may know where you can find me."

"So you are going to Brighton, are you?" he said after a pause. "What an eccentric fellow you are!"

"Eccentric, Major Haynes?" I repeated.

"To go to Brighton an hour's journey from London to an ordinary man, by such a roundabout route."

"Which way do you think I am going!" I smiled.

"I am not sure be said, "but, judging from the fact that most of your boxes went up yesterday to Liverpool under the name of Heigl, I gathered that you were making a round trip of it. Still," he said, rising and offering his hand, "I will wish you bon voyage. You have entertained me vastly, Keep clear of the mine-fields and 'ware submarines. They are dangerous little devils."

Oh! Had he seen my mind? Had he known the embittered thoughts that flocked through my brain like a flight of wild geese? Could he have detected the harsh and cynical expressions which trembled on my tongue, I do not think this fatheaded Englishman would have seen me to the door with such awkward grace.

I saw his idea. For his own purpose he desired to keep m e in England until the moment came to strike, but my friend, thought I, as I walked along Whitehall, in Heine there are four people and Liverpool is not the only gate to the "dark sea flood."

Another man might have taken a long time to consider his plans. Mine wee already made. He expected me to go back to my office, or to my flat perhaps, under the supervision of his detectives. I walked to Westminster Bridge Underground station, took a train to Charing Cross, descended the moving escalator to the Tube, and rode as far as Oxford Circus, where I changed for a city train which carried me to the Bank. Here I changed again and rode to Waterloo, came up to the surface in an elevator and caught a train on the elevated electric to Clapham Junction.

From Clapham Junction I journeyed to Willesden, from Willesden by a slow train to Rugby. Here I changed, leaving the North-Western station and joining the Central Line, found myself at half-past ten at night at Sheffield. I walked across to the station hotel, taking a packed trunk which was waiting for me at tho cloak-room, registered myself, filling up the necessary form, and was conducted to Room 43.

I was no sooner in the room and was unbuckling the straps of my trunk, when there was a knock at the door. Thinking it was the chambermaid, I said "Come in," and the door opened — and admitted Major Haynes in civilian dress.

"What time would you like your breakfast in the morning, Heine?" he asked, with such savoir faire that you might have thought he had accompanied me and had only parted from me a few minutes before he came into the room.

Not to be outdone in coolness, I replied: "At nine o'clock."

"You look tired," he said, "I think the rest at Brighton is going to do you a lot of good. When they told me you had got out at Clapham Junction I really thought and hoped that you had decided upon taking the short route. I expect it is the underground journeys that make you look so weary. Have you a headache?"

"The only thing that gives me a headache, Major Haynes, is boorish and unkultured conversation." I felt it was the moment to assert myself, even though it cost me my life.

"Then avoid soliloquies," he said, and with a nod he shut the door. There was nothing to do the next morning but to go back to London, which I did, taking my suitcase with me.

Major Haynes was on the same train, nearer the engine than I. I saw him step into a motor-car that was waiting and drive off, and I went into the buffet and had some breakfast.

My difficulty was going to be to arrive at the port of embarkation rather than the actual getting on board the steamer, and I knew that I should have to abandon both the Liverpool and the Fishguard routes and go by way of Glasgow and Greenock.

The thing was to shake off the men who by this time were watching me, and Fortune favoured me to an extraordinary extent. That night there descended on London one of those thick white mists which sometimes occur in the late spring. I packed a grip with a special kind of disguise, put the necessary documents in my pocket, and sent for a cab.

I came to the door of the front entrance of the flats, walked out bareheaded to the driver and told him that I should want him to take me to St. Pancras station to catch the 10:30 Scottish mail. I asked him how long it would take me to get to the depot, then I walked back into the vestibule, picked up my hat, coat, and portmanteau, that were waiting in a dark corner, slipped through the back door across the yard by which the tradesmen enter to deliver their goods, through a mews, and in a few minutes I was swallowed up in the darkness. I stood at the end of the mews and listened. There was no sound of footfall. Rapidly threading the narrow streets which lay at the back of the apartment house in which I lived, I gained a second road, hailed a taxi and instructed the man to drive me to Langley, which is a wayside station fifteen miles out of London, and lies between Slough and West Drayton. He promptly refused the fare, but I slipped a couple of notes into his band and his views on the shortage of his petrol underwent a remarkable change. So much for the veracity and honesty of English cabmen!

On the way down I changed my mind. My appearance at so insignificant a station might excite comment, and as we cleared the patch of mist, the cabman offered no objection to taking me on to Reading. At this station a slow train from London to Plymouth leaves shortly after midnight. I reached Bristol at 3.30 in the morning, and by 5 o'clock I was on my way northward, journeying by workman's train part of the way, until I changed on to a main line train at Worcester.

Had you stood that same afternoon on Carlisle station, you would have seen a clean-shaven clergyman with a white collar and a black soft felt hat, immaculate black garments, and the various other insignia of his holy office. You would have observed that he was drinking tea, and that under his arm was a large and serious book, and that his gold-mounted spectacles would occasionally be turned benevolently left and right looking for Major Haynes.

In this guise I reached Glasgow, a comfortable English parson. I passed the inspection of the alien officer, my passport was stamped officially and I crossed the gangway of the ship with a feeling of malicious joy.

"Here," thought I, "is an object-lesson which Major Haynes himself might take to heart as an example of German objectivity."

We Germans never falter in our purpose. We set our minds upon a goal and to that goal we attain. I stepped down the crowded gangway to the purser's office to present my ticket. The purser looked at it and nodded.

"Take this gentleman to stateroom 64," he said to a steward, and the man gathered up my trunk and my coat, led the way to the stateroom I had booked, opened the door and. I walked in — and there was Major Haynes sitting on the settee smoking a cigar and looking bored.

"Close the door, Heine," he said, and shook his head, reprovingly. "I have not had the opportunity of telling you before," he said gravely, "but I think it is only right that you should know that a clergyman of the Church of England does not wear gaiters, unless he is a bishop, and I feel sure, Heine, that whatever you are, you are not a bishop."

I felt I could not bandy words with him. I sat heavily down upon the settee.

"You have been getting your ideas of the clergyman," he said, "from Simplicissimus. For example, that apron you are wearing, and which I have no doubt was supplied to you by a theatrical costumier who thought you were cast for the good clergyman in 'The Silver King,' is the apron that rural deans dream about, and countless vicars regard as being half-way to a halo. I wonder you didn't bring a shepherd's crook," he said bitterly.

"So I understand that I am forbidden to travel on this boat?" I asked.

"Certainly. It would be no less than a scandal to allow you to misrepresent the Church of England to our good friends in America," said Major Haynes. "Now get into some sensible clothes like a good fellow."

"Very well," I said. I took up my trunk, watery at heart, walked up the companion-way and crossed the gangway on the wharf.

Oh, that journey back to London, how long, how dreary, how full of conflicting emotions! With what soul weariness did I recall every incident of the northward journey! With what respect had I been greeted in my Episcopalian character by the common people!

Major Haynes was not on the train, I am happy to say. I was too depressed to make any other attempt to escape, too weary even to formulate some alternative plan I did not even have the energy to speculate upon the reason I was being detained, for I had not been charged, as I might have been charged with using false passports, nor was I charged, with any of the other offences which might have been alleged against me. I was just simply let loose and given another chance of escape.

I made no pretence of going back to my flat, but drove to an hotel where I knew I should be constantly under observation. I was eating my dinner in an unhappy fashion, when I heard my name breathed, and, looking up, I recognized in the waiter a man who had given us a great deal of information, and was a worker for The Day. While he was bending over me with the menu in his hand, and apparently taking my orders, he was speaking rapidly.

"You are watched, Herr Heine," he said under his breath.

"I know," I replied in the same tone. "I am trying to get away from London."

He said no more, but when he came back with the soup he whispered: "I think I can help you."

When the fish arrived, he added a little more information.

"When you get back to your room to-night," he said, "ring for the sommelier. I will come up."

I told him briefly that I had made two attempts and failed, and he nodded. I waited till fairly late before I rang the bell, and my friend — his name deserves mention in these records, it was Gustav Stheil, a worthy fellow who, I understand, has since fallen into the hands of our hateful enemy — responded very quickly.

"In half an hour," he said, "come out of your room and go down the service stairs. You will find them on the left. At three o'clock to-morrow morning the chimney-sweeps are coming to clean the kitchen flues. I will get an old suit of clothes for you and with a bag of soot and your face blacked you can get out of the hotel without anybody being the wiser."

"And after that," I said.

"I think I can get you a horse and cart. Drive to this address. It is my brother-in-law's — he is in the country — and lie low there for a day or two and I will come and see you."

He gave me a key and the address. It was in a place called Palmer's Green. The plan worked admirably. I descended without interruption or observation, made a change of clothes and so covered my face with soot that no person would have recognized me. Gustav let me out through the service entrance and I found a light cart and a horse waiting, with a boy sitting in the seat.

"He is my son. You can trust him. Good luck, Herr Heine."

I took a £5 note, it was somewhat dirty, I am afraid, for I had to rub it to make sure there were not two, a mistake which I had once made — and slipping it into the honest fellow's hands, I drove off.

Picton Street, Palmer's Green, is a street of small houses, and that house to which I went was poorly furnished but was good enough for my purpose. I washed the disguising soot from my face and lay down on the bed to finish my sleep.

It was not a comfortable day by any means, because there was no food in the house, and I was ravenously hungry that night when Gustav came bringing me provisions and busying himself at the kitchen fire preparing me coffee.

"There is a cattle-ship leaving Avonmouth in two days' time," he said. "A friend of mine will smuggle you on board and look after you on the voyage over."

"How am I to get to Avonmouth?" I demanded.

"By train," said he, but I shook my head. "All the trains will be watched. Can you get me a motor-bicycle?"

He promised to do his best and, late as the hour was, he went out to inquire. He came back with a push-bicycle, and told me I should have to do the best I could with that for one stage of the journey, and that he would arrange to have me met on the Reading-Newbury road by a good patriot with a motor-car, but that it would be necessary for me to lie in the bottom of the car and allow myself to be covered by rags.

I will not describe the frights and apprehensions of that journey. I cycled through the night and just before day-break I reached the Reading-Newbury road and came within sight of the tail lights of a motor-car drawn up at the roadside.

The journey was not an uncomfortable one. I descended from the car on the outskirts of Bristol and made my way to the place where friend Gustav told me I should meet the sailor. It was a little bar and from the description which Gustav had given me I was able to recognize my friend, a stalwart patriot of Finland, which despised the British even as he hated the barbarous and tyrannical Russian.

To recall even that night's adventures and to place on record all the events which occurred between my leaving my friend's lodgings and my arrival in the hold of the soon-leaving ship would occupy a volume. How I climbed two walls, how I ensconced myself in a railway truck which was slowly shunted to the side of the ship with the most uncomfortable bumpings, how I stole up the slippery side of a coal chute and lay for two hours amongst the pots and pans of the cook's galley how I eventually swarmed down an interminable ladder into the depths of the ship, an adequate account of these happenings might be written by a Zola, but my poor pen can neither describe the agonies of mind and body which marked my reaching the ship, nor the miseries of soul which followed when the vessel drew clear from the wharf and began to sway and heave, to jump and sink in the open seas.

I was hungry until I went on board ship, but the moment the vessel started on its voyage I felt I would never eat again. I almost wished I had not left England. For a day and a night, it seemed like two months, or even two years, I endured the agonies of sea-sickness beyond description. At the end of the second night my friend made his way to the hold and brought me up to the galley, for I should explain he was the ship's cook. Here I was able to take the little nourishment which he gave me. Just before daybreak and when I was preparing to return to my submarine dungeon, the thud of the screws ceased.

"Are we stopping?" I asked my friend, the cook. He went out on to the deck and presently returned.

"Yes," he said, "you had better stay here. There is an English patrol coming alongside."

I could hear nothing but the whine of the wind and the ceaseless roar of the sea, and the first thing I heard was the sound of voices on the deck just outside the galley. He was an English naval officer speaking.

"You have a stowaway on board, a German agent," said the voice; "oh, yes, I know you are not aware of the fact, but he is here. You can either search the ship and bring him up or we will save you the trouble."

I looked at the cook, and the cook looked at me.

"Herr Heine," he said sadly, "there is only one thing to do. They will find you — they are certain to find you. This is a small ship."

I drew myself up and straightened my shoulders. Pushing open the door I stepped out to the deck in the light of the dawn.

"I am the man you seek," I said proudly. I had to climb down the rope ladder on to a bobbing little motor-launch, to the well of which I was conducted. We were very near land and I supposed (and here I was right) that the land was Ireland, that down-trodden nation, the sport and mock of the misgoverning English.

The motor-launch ran into a little harbour and came up by the side of the jetty A man in a long military overcoat was pacing up and down, but stopped when the boat reached the landing stage. I sprang on to the steps and mounted to the quay.

"Had a good time?" said the voice I hated more than all voices.

"Major Haynes," I said with dignity, "I have not had a good time."

"I am sorry to hear it. Anyway you have got the soot off your face, I am happy to see. You are looking quite white, Heine. Come and have breakfast."

I accompanied him mutely to a little one-storeyed hotel which faced the landing stage.

"You had better go up and tidy yourself," he said, "I have engaged a room for you."

I bowed and followed the hall-porter, who was the only servant up at this hour of the morning. He opened the door and showed me into a room, and to my amazement I found all my trunks on the bed. One had been opened and my razors and shaving apparatus was neatly laid out. Over the rail of a chair hung my best suit, and my patent boots, nicely polished, stood neatly against the wall. I shaved, washed, and changed, and in half an hour I presented myself in the dining-room where to my surprise, a good breakfast was waiting, Major Hayes being already at the table engaged in reading what appeared to be a volume of poetry.

"Well, Heine," he said, "your travels are nearly over, and I think that some explanation is due to you."

I bowed again, though it was a difficult performance, since I was at that moment balancing a piece of fried egg upon my knife.

"Try the fork," said Major Haynes. Really this man's inquisitive eyes saw everything.

"The fact is, Heine, we knew all about you before you arrived in England. We knew you were at the head of the organization, we knew your ways, your habits, your abnormal conceit — you don't mind my speaking frankly, do you?"

"Not at all," I said stiffly. "I am in your power."

"And we knew that wherever the corpse was there would the vultures be gathered, or, to put it better, wherever was the magnet there would be the iron filings. If we kept you going and left you alone, we always knew where to look for your workers, who were ever so much more dangerous than you. We thought once or twice of taking you," he said reflectively, "but I persuaded the powers that it would pay in the long run to leave you alone. And it has paid," he said, "all the satellites that revolve about you have been taken and destroyed. New suns will arise and attract new planets, and in course of time will be dealt with, but the period of danger has passed."

"And now, I suppose," said I miserably, "having no further use for me you are going to finish me off?"

"Exactly," said Major Haynes, with great cheerfulness, "you shall go back to America, Heine, as an awful example to all spies. In that capacity you will still be useful to me. You will at least be able to tell them something of the difficulties that await a man who tried to get out of England even with a forged passport. Believe me, it is just as difficult to get in, unless we want you in."

"You are going to let me go free?"

He nodded.

"The outward-bound Cremantic calls here by arrangement in two hour's time. You will be taken out in a motor-launch and. put on board. Your cabin is 143 and you will find it quite comfortable."

He put his hand in his pocket and took out a flat case which be opened. "Here is your passport," he said.

I took the passport in my hand and read the description of myself, even my photograph was pasted on. "I was described as "Heine", "Occupation: German Spy." "Reason for travel: By Special Deportation Order 64731, the British Government having no further need of his services."

To my mind the cruellest thing was the photograph which showed me in that infernal clergyman's garb. Underneath was written, "Religion: Church of England."

I looked at Major Haynes.

"You have spared me no humiliation," I said, and there were tears in my eyes, for remember what position I had held in the service.

"Oh, yes, I have," said Major Haynes, "I might have taken a flashlight photograph of you as a sweep. You've no idea how funny you looked."

Two hours later I stood upon the first-class passenger deck of the Cremantic watching with folded arms the land sinking slowly astern.

Farewell! False Albion! Thy doom is assured! The ever-victorious German U- boat — I stopped suddenly and thought, then turning to a sailor I asked: "Is there any danger of being torpedoed?"

"They gets a ship sometimes, sir," he said with callous indifference. "But, when we sees 'em we shoots at 'em and that generally frightens 'em off. If every passenger keeps his eye skinned there ain't much danger."

I spent the rest of the voyage with my eyes skinned.

As I stood on the broad deck of the English steamer and shook my fist at perfidious Ireland, I realized in a flash what my beloved Fatherland was losing by my departure from a land in which I had rendered Germany so many signal services.

"Keep your eye skinned for submarines," said a kindly meaning mariner, and these words brought me to the alert. My situation was serious. It could not be known in Berlin that I had sailed, and the stupid fools of U-boat commanders would be ignorant of my presence on the British ship. At the thought a cold shiver of horror percolated through my spinal column. What tragedy if such be the end of a splendid career.

I skinned my eyes throughout the day and twice by my loud cries saved disaster, once from a floating mine shaped like a wooden barrel (such is the supreme cunning of our race) and once from a U-boat which constantly came up and dived. The stupid English said that the first was only a barrel and that the up-and- down-diving U-boat was a porpoise, but Heine's eyes are sharp.

I did not attempt to make friends for the voyage, and rejected with scorn the suggestion of a frivolous American that I should play poker. Imagine playing poker in the midst of a great war! I asked him if he could play skat, but he knew nothing of that splendid and truly German game. I can give a great deal of information about the methods that are employed to convoy ships through what is called the Danger Zone, and in due course I may write a report on the subject, or rather I should have written a report but for circumstances which I will reveal at a much later stage.

Of how we zig-zagged about, first east and then west, then north and then south, of the balloons and aeroplanes and torpedo boats that watched us there seemed no end. My German heart swelled with pride as I thought that all these precautions were forced by our incomparable U-boats.

I was sitting on the deck waiting for the sound of the dinner-bell thinking out how superior the German race is to all its kind and how it must inevitably, sooner or later, conquer the world, when one of the ship's officers passed by. I took off my hat to him and bowed and he gave me a little jerk of his head and passed on.

Suddenly, however, he stopped.

"You want to keep your eyes skinned," he said with that brutal gruffness which is so characteristic of the English.

"Sir," I said with a little smile, "my eyes are so thoroughly skinned that I can hardly shut them at night."

Instead of laughing at this little jest, he made a grunting, pig-like noise.

"There's a U-boat somewhere about here," he said, "the patrols have lost sight of it. I see you are prepared."

I was wearing an unsinkable waistcoat which I had purchased from the steward, the life-belt which we are compelled to wear, but which I should have worn under any circumstances, a pair of thick waterproof boots, and my pockets were filled with brandy flasks and sandwiches, in case of accident. We Germans are prepared for anything, as I have remarked before.

"Do you mean to say," I said in alarm, "that there is a chance of — of unpleasant happenings?"

"A big chance," he said; "fortunately we have got very few passengers, so I am not disguising the fact to many of them that we are in some danger."

"But," I protested indignantly, "what about the boasted patrol boats? Where are your many vaunted aeroplanes? Why are we not preceded by warships to take the shock, which according to the lying statements in the daily papers, is the custom?"

"Probably they didn't know you were coming on board," he said with true British insolence, and passed on.

The dinner-bell rang, but I remained on deck. I would take no risks. Here I was, and here I would remain until the Danger Zone was passed, even it I had to sit up night after night. All the lights on the deck were extinguished. There was no sound but the steady thud of the screw and the roar of the water running past the hull of the steamer. The night was pitch black, such a night as filled my soul with strangely religious thoughts, and whilst my mind was thus occupied, I heard a shout from the bridge, an excited voice cried something, and I rushed to the side of the vessel and looked left and right, my skinned eyes searching the darkness.

Then something happened! I have never understood what it was. I was conscious of a brilliant flash of light, and a roar in my ears, such as a man feels who may occasionally takes a bath and inadvertently puts his head under the water.

I felt myself leaping through space. I had only time to remember that I had all my money in my pockets, but that I had left several important documents in my cabin, before I received another shock. I was in the water. The life-belt supported me. There was no sign of the ship. I screamed for help with true German thoroughness. I was bobbing up and down like a cork, and I felt dazed and ill.

What had happened? Had the ship sunk? Was I alone in the ocean? I thought of my life. I thought of the Fatherland. I hoped the cursed submarine would sink and all its crew be drowned. I do not know how long I was in the water. They told me it was not more than twenty minutes, but that twenty minutes was an eternity to me. The water was bitterly cold, my hands were numb, but I found my brandy flask and emptied its contents down my throat. I felt a little better after that, but, oh, joy, when suddenly I heard a voice in the darkness shout, almost in my ear it seemed:

"There's somebody," and the words were spoken in German. Almost immediately something big and hard rubbed against me. I can describe it in no other way. A hand gripped my collar and dragged me on to what felt like the top of an egg, if you can imagine the egg laid over on its side.

"Help," I said faintly. "I am a true German."

"A German?" said a surprised voice, "Gott in Himmel! What are you doing here?" I staggered to my feet, assisted by a strong German arm and addressed the presence which was dimly outlined against the starry skies. How godlike is a German officer! How loud and commanding is his voice! What splendid domination there is in his whole bearing.

"Get him below," he said, "there go the searchlights. Is that you, Fritz?"

"Yes, Herr Lieutenant."

"Well, what is she doing?"

"She has just sent an S.O.S. and wirelessed her position," said the other, whom I could not see.

"Be ready to submerge. Come on, my friend."

He gripped me by the arm. I was pushed down a steel ladder and found myself in the confined space of a German submarine. Instantly there was a loud clang as though the lid had closed on a box, a rush of warm air and —

"Hold tight!" said the voice of the commander. His back was to me, but I could tell by his voice that he was a man of noble birth. The deck tilted under me and I had a sinking sensation in the pit of my stomach, and then the horror of the situation dawned upon me. We were going down to the depths of the sea. We would probably be chased by those infernal destroyers and trawlers, and aeroplanes.

It never struck me before what a brutal race the British were. Here were we, boxed up in a frail little vessel, the prey of a hundred bloodthirsty hawks. I felt faint at the thought, and casting aside all restraint, I walked up to the Commander still standing by his directing instruments.

"Pardon, Excellency," I said, and would have taken off my hat, only I remembered that I had left the ship without one.

"Well," he said, without moving round."

"Would it not be wise," I suggested, "if you made for the nearest port and let me land? I feel I am only an encumbrance on your Excellency, and would be eating the food which I feel sure you need."

"Go to the devil," said this arrogant young man, whose name I learnt was von Gwinner. Presently he had finished his work and walked back to me.

"Do you imagine that I would walk into to the nets and risk certain destruction, in order to save you a little discomfort? What is your name, swine?"

"Excellency," I said, "I am known as Heine." I spoke, I think, with dignity, and I hope that the man was impressed. "I am an officer of the Imperial Intelligence Staff."

"How did you come to be on this ship?" he asked.

I explained to him that I was making my escape from England, carrying valuable documents, which were of the highest importance to the German Government. I felt if I said this he would regret his precipitate action in sinking the ship, and it flashed upon me as I was speaking that possibly I could find a way out of my exceedingly uncomfortable position.

"Did the ship sink?" I asked.

"No," he said with a curse, "we probably damaged her bow, but she's still afloat."

"Then," said I eagerly, "why not run me up quite close to her? There are a number of ladders with which I have familiarized myself and I can very easily step from your deck —"

"Don't talk like a fool," he said, "she is probably surrounded by destroyers and trawlers now. If I got near her I should probably have a depth charge on me and never know what struck me."

He looked at me thoughtfully.

"A spy, eh?" he said. "Do you speak English?"

"Perfectly, sir," I said.

"Thunder and lightning," he said, "you are the very man I want."

I cannot say that I was very pleased.

"You want me?" I faltered.

"You are the man I want. By heavens! It's providential. Sit down on that locker."

"May I smoke?" I asked.

"If you want me to kick you in the stomach," he replied viciously; "smoking on a submarine, are you mad? Do you imagine you are on the Kiel Ferry?" He was so angry that I changed the conversation. He then told me that this was one of the super-submarines which had been sent out from Kiel soon after the U-boat warfare had started, and that he hitherto had carried an intelligence officer whose task was to go ashore at unfrequented places, make his way to the nearest seaport and learn something about sailings.

"I have felt the loss of him," he said.

"Have you lost him?" I asked with a quaking heart.

"Yes," he said carelessly. "He was shot dead by a coastguard near Portland. He was an amiable man, and I quite missed him."

"Indeed," I said faintly, "is there any danger of that?"

"Oh, yes, you would have to take that risk! You tell me you haven't incurred the suspicion of the authorities." Like a fool I had told him that in describing my departure from England.

"Very well. You couldn't be better. I remember your name now."

He unlocked a little steel box attached to the wall of the small cabin in which we were speaking, and took out a book which is familiar to me — a list of agents. He looked them down carefully. Presently he stopped.

"What is your code name?" he asked. I told him, and he nodded. "That's right. If you had deceived me, I should have gone up to the surface, put you on deck and submerged again — leaving you without your lifebelt. As it is, I appoint you Intelligence Officer with pay at the rate of six marks a day."

"Thank you," I said, not without sarcasm, though this I did not make evident.

How can I describe my thoughts and feelings during that terrible night? Wild with anxiety as to my fate, the maddening knowledge that I was perhaps thousands of feet under the surface of the sea, and liable at any minute to strike a submerged rock or a sea-mine, facing the prospect of stealing ashore and perhaps being shot by coastguards either coming or going! All these things crowded one upon the other, and robbed me of sleep.

The interior of the submarine was thick and close. The sailors glanced at me disdainfully, and answered any questions I put to them with bluff rudeness.

You cannot conceive, my dear friend, how restricted life is on board a German submarine. It is all whirling engines and projecting brackets that bump your head. There are noises most terrible to hear. The only man who talked to me was a good fellow, whose name I forget, who told me that only one German submarine in three ever gets back to port, and the stories he told me about nets and submarine mines, and how you can be seen from the surface by aeroplanes, and how sometimes the engines go wrong and it is impossible to rise, turned me almost grey.

It is very likely that I slept. My own impression is that I did not, but I am told that it was necessary to kick me because I was snoring. As I never snore this is palpably absurd. But apparently we did come to the surface in the night, but nobody told me this, or I would have gone on to the deck to get some fresh air. The sailor with whom I spoke informed me that if I had, the commander would probably have kicked me into the sea, and that members of the crew were not allowed to come up without special permission.

The agony of the following day beggars description. We were coming up to the surface and our periscope was showing, when suddenly the U-boat gave a violent jerk and I was almost flung off my feet. I thought we had struck a mine, and fell into the arms of the commander, half-fainting. I fell out again with true German alacrity, when I realized that it was not agreeable to him. He afterwards explained to me with a great deal of unnecessary insolence that he had come up close to a destroyer and had had to submerge in a hurry. We were not fortunate that day, and the next time over periscope showed above water it was nearly carried away by shell-fire from a trawler less than a thousand yards away, and I sat and, quaked as I beard the dull throb of the depth charges exploding in our vicinity.

That evening the commander beckoned me to the tiny box which he called a cabin.

"Do you know Devonshire?" he asked.

"Yes, Excellency," I replied.

Of course, I did not know Devonshire but it is very simple to buy a map and discover anything I want to know.

"Do you know Siddicombe Bay?"

"Not very well," I replied.

"It is within easy walking distance of Torcombe Bay," he said. "The coast is not well guarded there. I will land you under cover of the darkness and you will make your way to Quaytown. My information is that there is a convoy of ships there which are sailing either to-morrow or the next day. I want you to make inquiries. Here is the name of the public-house where sailors are to be found. As soon as you have secured information make your way back to the point where I shall land you, flash an electric torch once, and I will come and pick you up."

He opened a case that he took from his desk and extracted two or three documents.

"Your name will be William Smith," he said, "here is an English registration card. You live in Manchester, and you are looking for a ship. Here is your discharge book, which you need not show unless you are questioned."

He told me that these documents had been taken from a sailing ship which he had sunk, and that the owner of them had been killed by shell-fire.

At eight o'clock that night, we came slowly into the deep waters of Siddicombe Bay. It is, I believe, one of the beauty spots of Devonshire, a half-moon of green water surrounded by high red cliffs and sloping fields, chequered red and green.

I did not see this by night, of course, and I am indebted to a local guide book for the description. A tiny collapsible boat was got out and opened, and into this I stepped.

"Remember," said Commander von Gwinner, at parting, "you are to return at ten o'clock. If you are late you will be sorry, my friend."

"Your Excellency," I said quietly, "I am less influenced by your threats, though I recognize that being well-born you mean no harm, than by the knowledge that I am serving our beloved Fatherland, for whose success and victory I ever pray, and on whose behalf I am prepared to make the most monumental sacrifices."

"You talk too much," he said; "get into the boat."

We landed at the beach without mishap. It was deserted, and I made my way along in the direction indicated by the local map, which I had studied with the commander, and presently found the zigzag path that led to the top of the cliffs and to the little village of Siddicombe.

Half an hour's brisk walk brought me to Quaytown, a large, straggling town, which was in times of peace a pleasure resort, but which had been converted in war time to a port of call. The main roads flank the little harbour which, as I could see, contained about six ships, and after inquiring from the policeman, I found my way to the public house to which I had been directed.

It was nine o'clock when I arrived, so I had only half an hour to pursue my inquiries. The common bar was filled with a noisy crowd, mostly sailors and men of the R.N.V.R. I managed to get a drink, and cast my eyes round for a likely informant, and found one in a common sailor of the Naval Reserve, who gladly accepted my invitation to drink, but asked me to bring it to him, because the bar lady had refused to serve him with any more.

"It's a hell of a life," he said, "what with the law and the price of beer. It's a dog's life."

It was providential that I found him. He was a man with a grievance, and a man with a grievance is very voluble.

"Come," I said cheerily, "things are not so bad as you think. We shall soon have these damned Germans beaten."

"Don't you make any mistake about it, my boy," said the common sailor, whose name was Jones, "if we are beating the Germans, why are we keeping our ships in harbour? Look here, mate," he said, speaking with the stupidity of a drunken person, "We've got six ships in this harbour. They've been lying here for a week. Why? Because there are two German submarines outside — or rather one," he corrected himself. "We've looked for them German submarines everywhere. The balloon's been out, the aeroplane's been out, the trawlers and destroyers have been out, but they haven't got 'em — at least they haven't found one," he corrected himself again.

"What's going to happen? Tomorrow afternoon at three o'clock when the convoy goes out—"

"To-morrow at three," I said carelessly, "that's a curious time to leave."

"Never mind if it is curious, or if it isn't," said the man, rudely quarrelsome, "they know their own business better than you do, my lad."

"Naturally," I said hastily. "Well," he went on, "to-morrow afternoon they go out at three o'clock. What happens? Them submarines will get 'em — at least one of 'em will," he said.

So I had my information. Trust Heine to make a discovery of this kind.

At three o'clock on the following afternoon! The excellent von Gwinner should be delighted. He would understand perhaps that he had a different type of man to deal with than what he had expected. Possibly he would send my name in into Headquarters for an Iron Cross — that possibility awakened a thrill of pleasurable anticipation.

"But come, my friend," I said, "you take too pessimistic a view. Now I don't believe that these six ships will be sunk."

"Not all of 'em," said the inebriated sailor gloomily, "but one of 'em will. Them submarines are too artful, or rather," he said, "one of 'em is."

His insistence upon the differentiation piqued my curiosity.

"Tell me, my friend, if it is not betraying any military secret, and speaking as sailor to sailor —"

"You ain't no sailor," said the drunken man commonly.

"Speaking as man to man," I said in haste to get him off the subject, "why do you say first that there are two submarines and then you only refer to one of them."

He was pulling at a short clay pipe, very dark and very stomach-revolting, and he puffed for a long time before he spoke.

"Because," he said at last, "one of 'em's done hisself in."

"Sunk?" I said with the same carelessness. What information to carry to Commander von Gwinner! What a back-slap he would give me, at the same time saying, "Good old boy, you have done very well indeed." I declare to you at that moment that the thought of serving the Fatherland brought tears of joy to my eyes. I would collect all the information I could, for already the hands of the clock were ominously near half-past.

"In what manner has he done himself in? Sunk?" I asked again.

"Well, he ain't sunk," admitted the man, "but he soon will be. He was spotted about an hour ago going into Siddicombe Bay, and all the bloomin' fleet is on its way there with nets and trawlers, and depth charges, and Gawd knows what!"

I held onto the wall for support.

"They'll have him netted in by half-past ten," said my friend. I looked at the clock again. There was time for me to get back to Siddicombe, but the next words of my acquaintance arrested my attention.

'He's bound to spot 'em comin' and make a run for it, and they're bound to ketch 'im," he said with cruel relish. I could get back in half an hour. The boat would be there waiting at ten I could warn von Gwinner, and he would "make a run for it."

What stupidity! What recklessness! Who are these people, these air-giving aristocrats, who risk the lives of the true democracy! What right have they, I thought, to bring men of my intelligence and genius into terrible and spine- shaking danger and perhaps to death?

The clock pointed to 9:30.

"Well, so long," said my acquaintance, "is there anything I can do for you, matey?" I swallowed my drink and looked at the clock again.

" Yes," I said firmly, for with my usual quickness of thought I had made my decision, "Can you recommend me an hotel where I can get a good bed?"

14 — BRETHREN OF THE ORDER

Consider, dear friends, the embarrassing circumstances under which I found myself! Deported from England by a man who I admit is a person of considerable sagacity, though infinitely inferior to the Intelligence officers one finds attached to the German army, both in birth and natural inquisitiveness — a man who had it in his power to drag me straight away to the execution-shed as a spy!

But you, who know Heine, are well aware that he is not a man to be lightly scared.

I woke up that morning in Quaytown without fear, a penniless Ishmael, hunted by the law, the hand of every man against me. Yet I was cheerful. When I say I was penniless, I speak of course in a figurative sense. I had a few pounds in my belt. I had a several thousands in a certain New York bank, and in various places in England there should be men who would help me.

I paid my bill at the little hotel where I had spent the night and caught the nine o'clock train for London. I got off the train at Bath and made my way to a certain large stationer's which accepts advertisements for the leading London dailies. On payment of a little extra money those advertisements are telegraphed to London and appear on the following morning.

The advertisement I inserted was a very simple one. It ran:

"Clerk, over military age, expert book-keeper, with intimate knowledge of the Argentine, Cuba, Batavia and Holland, requires situation. Salary £200."

An innocent advertisement, you may say. Yet, my friend, that was the S.O.S. of a political agent in distress. On the following morning, when I saw that appear, with a certain box number in the Daily Megaphone, I should know that I had to wait for two or three days for one of our industrious agents to answer that advertisement.

The words, "Argentine, Cuba, Batavia, Holland," in that order meant, "I am in urgent need of money." The "£200," which followed was the amount I required. Had I advertised that my experience was in France, Egypt, China, every German agent in England would have known that special intelligence had been received from Germany and that they must gather at an agreed rendezvous to receive their orders. Had I merely written that my experience was in London, Bombay and Buenos Aires, half the agents in England would have made preparations to depart from this country without delay.

I arrived in London by night. That was the object of my getting off at Bath, or rather partly the object, because I had a certain person, a minor agent, to interview. Fortunately, or unfortunately, he was not to be found, and it was not until the train came in and I was preparing to step into my carriage that he made his appearance, rather out of breath, for he had run all the way from the apartment-house he kept.

"I found your note," he said. "Are you alone in this carriage?" I looked around. There were no other passengers.

"Then," said he, "I will take the liberty, Herr Heine, of coming to London with you. I have much to tell you. We thought you had left England."

Briefly I explained to him, as the train moved on, the reason I had returned. I told him how I was carrying important despatches for America, and how the ship was sunk by a submarine, and of how I had reached the submarine and had ordered the captain to take me to the nearest port.

"Sir Haynes," (though I knew he was not noble, I thought it might tickle the fellow's vanity to address him in terms of lordliness), "Here am I like a naughty penny, turning up again under your nose! But quite unwillingly! You have doubtless learnt that the gallant ocean-liner upon which you placed me is no more! She was sunk by a German U-boat! Though I swam about looking for survivors, desiring to rescue as many poor Englishmen as possible from the wicked and mistaken policy of dirty old von Turnips" (may heaven forgive me for this jest at the expense of that great patriot), "I was not successful. I swam about in the water for ten hours and was picked up by a passing steamer! We arrived in London this morning and I am now in a terrible dilemma. I dare not give you my address, for I am in fear of arrest. Guarantee to me by your power- compelling word that I shall not be punished. If you will insert an advertisement in the Daily Megaphone, like this:

"From H. to H, All well,

See me at my office."

I will immediately report myself. In the meantime, dear Sir Haynes, thanking you for your past favours, and hoping by a constant attention to your wishes to merit the continuance of your patronage.

I am,

Yours faithfully,

Heine."

I calculated that it would take two days for this to reach him, another day before the advertisement appeared, and I then had a fourth day before I replied in person — and in four days much service could be rendered to the Fatherland.

I was determined to get as much out of this secret society as I possibly could. All that afternoon I formulated my plans. Through a call office I got into touch with Kriessler, who was one of our subsidiary agents in London, and had rendered me and the Fatherland great services.

We met by appointment that night at the Marble Arch, and almost the first question he asked me was whether I had got into touch with the Sons of Irish Freedom? When I told him I had, he was astonished.

"You don't lose much time, Herr Heine," he said admiringly.

"That is very true, Kriessler," I said gravely, "and I appreciate your compliment."

Kriessler was in a position to pass through any information collected in England. I, of course, had been the supreme medium, but I dare not exercise any of the old machinery of transmission. It was very dangerous. It might be, and probably was, very dangerous for Kriessler, but for the sacred cause of Germany we must take risks, so I let Kriessler take them.

I arranged for him to send to my house on the following morning for a brief report which I told him must be sent to Headquarters with the least delay.

"You see, my dear Kriessler," I said, at parting, 'I know all there is to be known about this secret society. But I am anxious to check my knowledge. You will please tell me all you have heard, and if I do not interrupt you to point out your mistakes, you will understand that it is not desirable that the subordinate officials should know as much as their superiors."

"I quite understand that, Herr Heine," said Kriessler, "but I do not pretend to know a great deal about the Sons of Irish Freedom. One knows that they have meetings and passwords. I also know that the police are actively searching for their lodges, but so far without success. I am told that they are very desperate and dangerous men, and I believe that there is only one lot in London. They hate England—"

"That I know," I smiled.

"I went home and wrote a very full report on the constitution and working of the Sons of Irish Freedom. Blame me not, dear friend, for my innocent deceit, for I had never heard of the Sons of Irish Freedom till I arrived at Bath, nor think harshly of me that I wrote with elaborate detail to Potsdam upon their ritual and objectives. That same night I sent off my letter to Major Haynes, and finished my report on the secret society, which was given to the messenger whom Kriessler sent soon after breakfast. I took my meals alone in my sitting- room and my strange, gaunt friend, whose name was Clarkson, only saw me once and did no more than to smile mysteriously and say:

"At eight o'clock to-night."

I nodded gravely. I did not expect to hear any more about the matter, being well aware that my host would not care to discuss so weighty a secret, and I was surprised in the afternoon to receive a visit from Mr. Clarkson, who was accompanied by a short, stout man, who was also very pale and wore powerful spectacles.

"This, sir," said he, "is my friend, Mr. Moore, who will act as your sponsor to-night."

He turned to Mr. Moore. "This gentleman," said he, "will become one of us."

Mr. Moore bowed. "You realize, of course," he said, a little pompously, I thought, "that you must absolutely surrender your allegiance to the World's Terror, and that from this night forward you may count upon the moral support of a band of brothers, and that you will give yourself heart and soul to our sublime task."

"Have no fear," I said, seizing his hand too, and wringing it, "until the tyrant is crushed I will be a loyal comrade."

"Good," said Mr. Moore, and after a few commonplaces about the weather, they departed.

At seven o'clock that night I dressed myself with care, soberly and unostentatiously. What cared I for the oaths of these fanatical conspirators, with their absurd secrecy, their passwords, their grips and the like?

Mr. Clarkson knocked at my door at a quarter to eight and we sallied forth together. I suggested taking a taxi-cab, but he would not hear of it, and we went by bus to Camden Town.

It was just as we were turning into Baynam Street that we noticed a little crowd gathered about something which lay on the sidewalk. We would have passed on, but Mr. Clarkson, overhearing something that was said by a member of the group, pushed his way through the little knot of people and I followed.

A man lay prone on the sidewalk.

"What is it?" I asked curiously.

Mr. Clarkson made no reply till we were clear of the crowd. "One of our people," he said bitterly, "fallen to the enemy."

"Fallen?" I, said. Mr. Clarkson nodded.

"It happens now and again," he said, "we are fighting a cunning and ruthless foe, my friend."

"But are you leaving him there?"

"For the moment," said Mr. Clarkson, "I will ask one of the brethren to make inquiries as to how it happened, and if it is possible to give any assistance to our unfortunate comrade, it will be given."

This was news indeed. So this mighty British Government was not above striking an assassin blow to rid itself of its enemies.

From Baynam Street leads a smaller thoroughfare, near the Camden Road end of which is a small hall. The night was dark, the painted street-lamps cast tiny pools of dim light upon the pavement as we stole furtively through the door of the hall, and passed through a small ante-room to a smaller room beyond. In this room there was another door, and towards this Mr. Clarkson walked.

"You will wait here," he said in a whisper. He knocked in a peculiar manner on the door, and a sliding panel opened. He whispered something, the door was unlocked, and after he had slipped into the room, closed again.

I waited about three minutes before the door opened, and Mr. Clarkson came out accompanied by Mr. Moore, both of whom wore on their breasts sashes of red. Mr. Moore, scarcely raising his voice above a whisper, asked me a number of questions. They were couched in a curious semi-legal, semi-philosophical vein, and I confess I did not understand very much, nor did I trouble to pay a great deal of attention to what was being said. I knew by their intonation when I had to say "Yes," and when I had to say "No."

When I had finished Mr. Clarkson looked anxiously at his friend.

"I think that is satisfactory, Brother Moore?"

"Eminently satisfactory, Brother Clarkson," said the other. He rapped soberly at the door and again the panel slid back and a voice challenged him.

"Who knocks?"

"Two brethren with a candidate for initiation," said Mr. Moore.

The panel closed and presently it opened again.

"Who vouches for this candidate?" said the voice.

"I," said Mr. Clarkson.

"I," said Mr. Moore.

The door was opened and we passed through, not without a fluttering of heart on my part.

Between my two sponsors I advanced into the hall. At one end of the room on a raised dais sat three men bearing the strange regalia of their order. To left and right at single tables were two other officers, also wearing decorations. I passed from one to the other. Each addressed me in solemn language on the duty of man to man, and presently I came to the raised dais and had to endure yet a further long rigmarole, at the end of which the president confided the password, which was "Fight the Fight," the grip, and the signal knock.

I was led to a seat in the body of the hall, congratulated heartily by Mr. Moore and Mr. Clarkson, and settled myself down to listen to the deliberations of this strange body. They were men of all ages, of all conditions of life, stern, determined-looking men I thought, capable of committing any desperate deed, the kind of men who might be most useful.

There were young and old amongst them, but all bore the same sour disappointed expression, which I had noticed both in Mr. Moore and Mr. Clarkson.

A brother rose and had begun to address the chair when the door was flung open excitedly and a tall, pale-faced man rushed in. As he did so, I heard the shrill sound of police whistles.

"A raid, a raid!" he cried. Instantly the hall was in commotion. I felt myself grow pale and grasped Mr. Moore, who was next to me, by the arm.

"Is there any way out of this?" I asked.

"You had better stay here," he said.

"Stay here and be caught?"

That was not Heine's way. I dashed through the door into the street. There was no sign of policeman, but I heard shrill whistles blowing. I ran up into Baynam Street straight into the arms of a policeman!

"Hello," he said, "you had better take cover. There's an air raid on."

"An air raid?" I gasped. "An air raid!"

"Well, perhaps it isn't one. A mate of mine just told me it's a false alarm, and very likely he's right. There's rather too much wind for a raid to- night."

I could have leant against him. I was so confounded and confused I could collect my thoughts only in fragments and the first memory of that evening which strangely enough came to me was the memory of that stricken form on the pavement.

"Tell me, sir," I said, "did you see a man lying on the ground round the corner?"

It was, I admit, a foolish question to ask, but the memory of that rigid victim had obsessed me.

"Oh, him," said the constable, "yes! He was drunk."

"Drunk?" I said in amazement.

"Yes," said the policeman, "a man named Geary. He used to be a member of that lodge down the road there." He pointed to the building from whence I had come.

"What lodge is that?" I asked.

"The Sons of Temperance," he said, "I thought I saw you come out of there. Ain't you a member? Rum blokes, they are," he went on with a little chuckle, "always talking about drink as the Enemy and Terror and the Oppressor of the World. I wish somebody would oppress me with a pint."

I pressed a shilling into his hard, corrupt fist, and walked back to Bayswater.

I pass to the strangest adventure of my experience, and I tell this story because not only does it reveal the amazing unscrupulousness of the British Government, but I think it will also show the marvellous adaptability of a German agent. I do not suggest that all agents would have acted as I did, but then I do not think there are a great number of German agents who are possessed of my extraordinary capacities.

It will be remembered that after my deportation from England by a certain Major Haynes, of whom more anon, I was submarined and landed again on these inhospitable shores, and by reason of the sentence of deportation, which bad been illegally passed upon me without a trial, I was compelled to lie, as they say in England, doggo.

With most of my friends I dare not communicate, and though I had written to Major Haynes announcing that I was in England, and asking him to give me an opportunity of calling upon him, giving, of course, no address, I did not hear from him immediately. I had, however, inserted an advertisement in the Daily Megaphone, stating that I was a clerk with experience in the Argentine, Cuba, Batavia and Holland, saying that I was willing to work for £200 a year, the combination of those words meaning that I was an agent in distress and that I was requiring £200. I had no doubt in my mind that the call would be responded to. I was officially penniless. I had some money of my own, but why should I spend that when there was so much money to be had for the asking?

I called at the office of the newspaper and received a big batch of letters in response to my advertisement, I took them back to my new lodgings, for I had left the old apartments, owing to the fact that the proprietor was a fanatical teetotaller, and in the privacy of my own room I took the letters from my pocket and turned them over rapidly, looking for one which would have an inky finger-mark on the back flap.

I found and opened the envelope, and discovered, as I had expected, four bank notes for £50 without any reference to the sender. I would have thrown the remaining letters upon the fire, had there been one, but fortunately my time was hanging on my hands. I had arranged to meet Kriessler, the only man in London with whom I could safely communicate, and I had two or three hours to fill in before that appointment. So what was more natural than that I should open those offers of a situation and read them through? Thoroughness is the characteristic of our race. We despise no material, however unpromising. Germany was built up upon by-products, and her wealth extracted from the dust- bins of Europe.

They were letters of a conventional type asking me for recommendations or inviting me to make calls upon the writers. It was the fourth letter which interested me most of all. I read it through carefully, put it aside, skimmed through the remainder of the letters and then returned to this extraordinary missive.

The paper was heavy and rich. There was on the top left-hand corner a coat of arms embossed in gold and blue. The address was 182, Berkeley Square, which is one of the most fashionable residential squares in London. This address, however, had been scratched out and there had been substituted "Stoney Cottage, Hebleigh-on-Avon." The letter was marked "Private and Very Confidential," and ran:

"If the advertiser is a person of discretion, and is willing to act as confidential secretary to a high government personage, and has a knowledge of world politics, a permanent position with a salary of £500 per annum can be offered to him for the duration of the war."

I pondered this letter for some considerable time and before I went out to my appointment with Kriessler, my mind was made up and I had written offering my services, informing the writer that I had acted in a similar capacity to a certain Legation, which I was not at liberty to name, in Holland; that I was the soul of discretion, that I had no friends in England, and that I was not liable for military service. I added that I should be glad if the advertiser could arrange a meeting in town and that in the circumstances I should like it to be as secret as possible, because I was already doing confidential work for a government department and they might not like to lose me.

The next morning came a telegram in reply.

"Meet me to-night at ten o'clock at the corner of Berkeley Street. I shall be wearing a tall hat and light gloves."

Ten o'clock that night found me at the rendezvous and punctually to the minute a taxi-cab drew up and a gentleman alighted answering to the description contained in the telegram. I walked up to him taking off my hat.

"You are the advertiser?" he said sharply.

"Yes, sir," I replied. He looked at me thoughtfully. The light was very dim but I met his gaze without faltering.

"Do you speak French?"

"Yes, sir," I replied.

"Walk along with me," he said, taking my arm. The cabman evidently knew his client and did not expostulate at his departure. Had I been the fare he would have covered me with vile abuse and would have told me that he had no petrol. Such is the unscrupulousness of London cabmen!

We walked down Berkeley Street and turned into the deserted Berkeley Square. He stopped in front of a gloomy house. "I live here," he said, "but I am at present staying in the country."

His voice was sharp. He spoke brusquely and without politeness, and I realized in a flash that he was noble-born. He asked me several questions, more or less irrelevant, and then suddenly he turned about and walked back in the direction of the cab.

"I think you will do," he said, "you will leave tomorrow evening for Hebleigh. I will meet you at the station and drive you to my cottage. I keep no servants in the house when I am at Hebleigh."

This seemed strange, but I was afterwards to discover that the cottage had been specially built for my new employer, with vacuum cleaners, gas and electric stoves, a perfect system of central heating, water on every floor and a bathroom attached to every bedroom. What a comfortable place, thought I, what luxury and how providential for me! Here I could lie quiet for weeks and never be discovered, with nothing to break the monotony of life but an occasional bath.

I had brought down a small hand-bag containing my worldly belongings, and I was ushered into a small bedroom simply but expensively furnished by my host. It was in that room, the first room in which the lights were all switched on, that I had my first good view of him. He was a man of about fifty-five rather thin, very grey, with a pale, aesthetic face and long, nervous hands. It may seem curious to you that I had not asked him his name, but if you imagine I neglected that precaution you do not know your Heine. I had asked him but he had not responded.

"A woman comes every day to make the beds and to prepare our principal meal," he said. "You will not see her because she does her work whilst I am in my study, and the meals are served on a lift which comes straight from the kitchen."

To his study he led the way. It was a large room, one wall of which was covered by a book-shelf filled with large and imposing volumes. A handsome table filled the middle of the room. There were two comfortable arm-chairs and a writing table. Under the window, across which a heavy curtain had been drawn, was a smaller table, and to this my unknown employer pointed.

"That will be yours," he said. "Your duty will be to translate despatches which I shall write, into such languages as I shall tell you. Do you speak German?"

I kept a straight face.

"Perfectly," I replied. He nodded approvingly.

"You wonder probably," he said, as he seated himself at the table and looked at me strangely over the tortoiseshell-rimmed glasses fixed on his nose, "why I require discretion, why I chose you without knowing anything about you or without any kind of reference? I chose you in the first place," he went on, without waiting for me to explain that I could produce references, "because in the first place, I think you are a foreigner. Am I right?"

"In a sense —" I began.

"Very well," he went on.

"Oh, by the way," he looked at me sharply," have you ever heard of Bilbury's Tablets?"

I had indeed heard of Bilbury's Tablets, the advertisements of which covered the hoardings of England all forming the most attractive reading matter in the stupid. British newspapers. I therefore answered in the affirmative.

"Do you know the man Bilbury?" be asked, still looking at me keenly. I was at first tempted to say that I did, but on second consideration I thought it best to tell the truth.

"No, sir. I have never met him."

"Good," he said, nodding again. He leant back in his chair.

"Bilbury," he said — "and this, you will understand, is confidential — is one of the biggest and most dangerous forces working in this country against England. I have reason to believe that, under one name or other, he is supplying most of the German agents with their money. I am satisfied also that his advertisements are code messages to the enemy government — you see, I trust you."

I nodded, a little bewildered, for I had never known of Bilbury, though I had heard that there were in England certain persons of whose identity I was ignorant, who were working with the Fatherland.

"I tell you of Bilbury," he went on, "because in part he explains a great deal of the secrecy both of my habitation and my movements. He also explains why I have chosen, as you might think haphazard, a confidential secretary. You are under no circumstances to communicate with any of Bilbury's agents, and you are at all times to be prepared to counter the machinations of this extraordinary man."

There were two or three letters on the table, and one of these he picked up, slit it open and took out what appeared to me to be a perfectly blank sheet of paper. He held it up to the light and frowned, replacing it upon his desk.

"Your presence here is already known, evidently," be said, "but I don't think we need bother very much about that. Now," he went on more briskly, "you are entitled to know who I am. Do you know Lord Catherton?"

"I have seen Lord Catherton," I replied.

He nodded.

"Do you know the Earl of Seabury?"

I shook my head.

"I have never met Lord Seabury."

"Have you ever seen a photograph of him?" he asked.

"No, sir," I replied, "I have not." Lord Seabury was until recently an English colonial governor, who was now one of the members of the War Cabinet. He is not a man who has figured largely in public life, and not at all in English public life, and as I had never troubled about the colonies he was unfamiliar to me.

He nodded again. "I see you don't know Lord Seabury," he said with a little smile, "for I am he."

My heart gave a great bound. Heine indeed had fallen upon his feet, thought I! To find myself in the confidence of one who was admittedly a most powerful member of the War Council — what fortune, what amazing luck!

"Now you understand why I shall require that you treat everything I say, and everything you witness here, in the strictest confidence."

That practically finished the conversation. His lordship led me to a little dining-room where dinner was already laid, and we ate our meal almost in silence. He told me I could go to bed, that he was an early riser and would require my attendance at six o'clock in the morning.

I scarcely slept that night, turning over and over in my mind how I might use to the best advantage the information which I was certain to gain. I had taken the precaution of buying at Paddington Station a little guide-book of the district, and I carefully studied the roads, the railway stations, and a time- table, with which I had provided myself with my usual forethought, and planned out the course I would take if it became necessary to leave hurriedly. With Kriessler in London, able to forward my despatches to the Highest Quarters, I had no doubt that within a week the name of Heine would be ringing along the corridors of the German Foreign Office.

Punctually at six, I presented myself in the library, and found that his lordship had prepared coffee with his own hands. From six to eight we worked strenuously, his lordship writing, sometimes asking me to translate into Spanish, sometimes into French, occasionally into German, his brief but vital correspondence.

I memorized as best I could all these letters. Some were to the Minister of Foreign Affairs in France, one was to a neutral Legation at Berne, this being marked "Very Confidential and Secret," and sealed heavily with his lordship's own hand. One was to a Spanish Cabinet Minister, and all dealt intimately and frankly with the conduct of the war. I remembered in a vague way that I had heard that Lord Seabury was the virtual dictator of England, but I never realized it until I read those dictatorial, intolerant messages which he sent forth, one being directed to the commander-in-chief of a certain British army, telling him that he was on no account to attack before the fourteenth of the following month.

Breakfast was served in the room where we had taken dinner and once that was dispatched we returned to our labours. For the whole of that day I was kept busy. A draft treaty with the Portuguese Government, dealing with the future of the island of San Thomé, was one of the documents which occupied the greater part of the afternoon in translating.

At dinner his lordship was unusually frank, and under my genial flattery he unbent.

"It is true, Mr. Smith," he said (Smith had been the name I had given him), "that I am dictating the policy of the Cabinet, which reminds me that I must draft a letter to-night to the commander-in-chief of the battle fleet. I am not at all satisfied with—" he stopped short.

"By the way," he asked, "have you had any communication from any mysterious source?"

"No," I replied.

He shook his head a little despondently.

"It seems absurd that one should be dogged by a pill-maker," he mused, half to himself, "but that fellow has got to be dealt with sooner or later."

He left the room to go to his study, leaving me to finish a glass of port, and I was rising from the table when he returned.

"Come this way," he said in a whisper, "I will show you something."

He led me down the corridor into the study in which the lights had been extinguished. We walked across the room and he pulled back the curtain. A bright moon was shining and at the far end of the garden near the road was the figure of a thickset man who was pacing slowly and restlessly up and down the road. He dropped the fold of the curtain and we returned to the dining-room which faces the back of the house.

"That gentleman is M. Tarakanova," he said, "and Tarakanova is the chief of Bilbury's agents."

He pursed his lips thoughtfully. "I shall have to send that infernal dossier to town."

"The dossier, my lord? " I repeated, innocently.

"The dossier," he said.

He made no further explanation until later that night when we were working in the study, a stealthy reconnaissance having revealed to me that M. Tarakanova had disappeared. In the wall of the study was a safe, and just before, or rather immediately after, he had bade me a curt good night, he stopped my departure with a word, walked over to the safe, opened it with a bunch of keys which he took from his pocket, and pulled out a long yellow envelope which was heavily sealed.

He brought it carefully back to the table, switched on the table light which he had extinguished, and placed the envelope under its rays.

"Look at this," he said. I looked. In a firm hand was written on the top of the envelope, with a neat red line ruled underneath:

(1) Statement signed by William II, Emperor of Germany, on July 5th, 1914 expressing his intention of making war.

(2) Letter from Emperor William II, of Germany to Emperor Francis Joseph to the same effect. (Original documents).

I did not speak. I was incapable of speech. Within this envelope lay documents in the very writing of the All-Highest Supreme War Lord! Documents of greatest national interest! Historical documents which, in the enemy's hands, might damage the beloved Fatherland and our Noble and Glorious Kaiser!

I was clear-headed and cool. Those documents should he restored to their Imperial owner. What reward would await the gallant and enterprising agent who delivered these papers into the hands of our Supreme and Noble Master! I grew dizzy with tho thought of the emoluments and the honours which might be showered upon me. No office was too high for the man who could render that magnificent service to the State!

My hand trembled as I touched the secret dossier.

"I must get rid of this at once," said Lord Seabury. "It is too risky to keep it here — put it back in the safe, Smith."

Dare I do it? Half-a-dozen steps separated me from the desk to the steel door in the wall. I half-glanced at his lordship. He was looking at a document which he bad half-finished before dinner. Quick as lightning I slipped the envelope under my coat and under my arm, slammed to the door of the safe, locked it and handed the keys back. He thanked me and put them in his pocket.

"You may go now, Smith," he said.

The perspiration was trickling down my forehead and I walked unsteadily down the passage to my room. I closed and locked the door behind me, took the envelope from my pocket and sat down on the bed.

There was a small writing-table in my room which had been placed there at my request, and a supply of stationery. To enclose this large envelope in one larger was the work of a second, I wrote a brief note to Kriessler telling him that it was a matter of life and death that the enclosed should be sent forward by the safest channels and should be placed in the hands of the All Highest himself. I then began the most important letter I have ever written in my life:

"All-Highest Majesty.

"Your humble and obedient servant has the honour to transmit to Your All- Highest Majesty a document which I have extracted from the safe of the English Cabinet Minister, Lord Seabury, at great risk and with much labour, though I count no labour too great if I am to serve Your All-Highest Majesty. My name, as Your All-Highest Majesty's Minister of Intelligence will tell Your All- Highest Majesty, is Heine."

I added a number of other interesting details about myself, where I could be found, what was my salary, and this paragraph which I regarded as one of my finest efforts.

"Though no decoration blazes upon my humble coat, and no patent of nobility has been granted me, though I am a poor man with no more than my official pay to sustain me, I am nevertheless proud and happy to be of such service to Your All-Highest Majesty as will merit Your All-Highest Majesty's approval. I seek no rewards, no decorations, no monetary grants — I do this for the Fatherland, and for Your All-Highest Majesty, who is the epitome of Germany's greatness."

I placed this and the dossier inside a large envelope, and in the middle of the night I tip-toed back to the study in my stocking feet and found a larger covering in which to enclose the letter which I had addressed to the Emperor.

On the outer envelope I wrote Kriessler's English name and address, and soon after daylight I let myself out of the house and walked in the direction of the village of Hebleigh which was distant about a mile from Stoney Cottage.

I dropped the big envelope into the village post-box, retraced my steps and reached my room without my absence being detected. I had to risk his lordship discovering the disappearance of the letter, but fortunately throughout the next day he showed no intention of going to the safe, and beyond a reference to Bilbury, he scarcely spoke a word.

All day long we were inditing letters to every part of the world, which his lordship sealed with his own hands, and which he packed away in a leather satchel. How he posted them or whether he sent them to London, I did not know, but I presumed that a Foreign Office messenger attended discreetly and performed this duty.

Half-past eight that night, immediately after dinner, his lordship went to his study and suggested, when I attempted to follow him, that I should have a little fresh air.

"You need it, my friend," he said, "you have been playing a part to-day in the government of England, in the direction of affairs of the world. Surely that merits a little recreation." He smiled almost paternally. I walked through the little panelled hall, opened the front door, and stepped out.

A man was standing by the gate. It was Bilbury's man, Tarakanova. To whom he was talking I did not know, but somebody stood in tho shadow and I heard his quiet laughter. I shrugged my shoulders. I had nothing to fear from Bilbury, indeed I was curious to learn what tube agent of this mysterious person had to say to me. So I walked boldly up the garden-path, humming a little tune, and Tarakanova turned to meet me.

He was, as I say, a thickset man, clean-shaven, so far as I could see in the dusk, and not the sort of man you might imagine would engage in espionage work.

"Good evening," he said, as I came up,

"Good evening, sir," I replied politely, "it is fine weather for this time of the year."

"You're a trite devil," said a voice in the half-darkness.

I turned to face the man who had spoken and with whom Tarakanova had been in conversation. I did not faint. I pride myself that I retain my self-possession with remarkable sang-froid.

"Good evening Major Haynes," I said, not to be outdone in cool- collectedness.

"Having a nice time Heine?" he asked.

"Yes, indeed Major Haynes," I replied; "you got my letter?"

"I am sorry I did not reply, but I have been rather busy, and learning you were down here, I thought I would look you up. How is his lordship?"

"Very well indeed," I replied with great politeness.

Tarakanova laughed.

"I presume you know," I said, as the thought struck me, "that this gentleman is an employee of Bilbury."

"I know that very well," said Major Haynes, "though he is not exactly employed by Bilbury, but by the gentlemen who are administering Mr. Bilbury's estate. You see, Heine," Major Haynes went on in his fearfully monotonous voice — how that man irritates me! — "the plutocratic Mr. Bilbury, who is a very rich gentleman, went off his head about four years ago."

"Went mad?" I said.

"Went mad," said Major Haynes, nodding, "not dangerously so, but just enough to be a nuisance. His pet illusion is that he is Lord Seabury."

"Oh, yes," I said faintly.

"He spends all his time," Major Haynes went on, "writing despatches for important personages, and generally in running the war. Mr. Jacobson here, is, if I may put it crudely, his keeper. I suppose he has told you all his secrets?"

"Oh, yes," I said carelessly.

"I wonder if he showed you that dossier of his about the Kaiser. I hope you haven't by any chance pinched it and sent it to his Imperial Majesty," said Major Haynes with coarse brutality, "because it happens that there is nothing more interesting in it than a pamphlet on the remarkable quality of Bilbury's Pills."

"Major Haynes," I said in a husky voice, "I surrender."

"Not at all," said Major Haynes, "look me up any time you are in London, and I will see what I can do for you. Now," said this long, cool devil, with true British wit, "you had better run back to his lordship. He will be wanting you for a new offensive, or may be to send an ultimatum to Sweden."

I made no reply. With dignity I returned to the house, walked up to my room, and packed my bag.

16 — THE SYREN

I have mentioned in an earlier chapter an organization known as the Sons of Irish Freedom. I do not pretend that this is the name of the society which at one time threatened to create the most serious difficulties for the British Government, but which was dissolved owing to the base and ungentlemanly treachery of Major Haynes, an Intelligence Officer, who got himself elected a member of the principal lodge, and by cunning artfulness induced the members to give a grand dinner to celebrate the first anniversary of its foundation.

The members allowed this spurious and treacherous brother to order a dinner which was given at one of the best hotels in London. Everything was of the best, winter strawberries, most rare and wonderful wine, beautiful flowers, and a magnificent entertainment to follow. The dinner, of course, was not announced as one by the Sons of Irish Freedom, but had a much more innocent excuse. When the bill was presented for payment, the cunning Major Haynes, having identified certain prominent Irish personages who were present with the responsibility for the festival, it was found that it absorbed all the funds of the lodge and about £200 in addition.*

[* This tragedy actually happened to a local branch of a certain seditious organization in Ireland— E.W.]

The unfortunate and down-trodden Irish are cursed with that deluded sense of humour which no German can ever understand. Else how could you imagine that so frivolous a reason can bring about the dissolution of a great political organisation. We Germans would have repudiated the bill and, if necessary, have sent secret letters to the hotel proprietor telling him that his premises would be blown up if he did not mend his manners.

I do not profess to understand either the mentality of the Irish or that of such men as Major Haynes. I have tried many times in the silent watches of the night to reduce this officer (and I wish I could add gentleman) to an understandable formula. I have never believed that there was a secret service in England. I never shall believe that anything like the magnificent and forethoughtful department which German genius has organized could come into being in a dull-thinking country like Britain. The man himself was the negation of all good German qualities. He had not the seriousness which distinguishes men of my own department. He lacked that haughty obedience-compelling manner which we look for and expect in the true Prussian officer. His voice was a gentle drawl. He was always laughing with his eyes, full of jokes which gentleman, that is to say a Prussian gentleman, would consider it beneath his dignity to utter.

I have seen him speak to quite common people as though they were his equals, and for this reason I long suspected that he was a Socialist, and that is a view which I still hold, and believe me, Heine makes very few mistakes.

But it would be unknightly in me if I did not pay this tribute to the man; whether he secured his information by luck or by judgment, he knew a disgusting sight too much. I had returned to England, as you know, after being deported by Major Haynes, but I had had the good sense and vision to write to him announcing I was in England.

By the sheerest accident he discovered me and requested that I should call at his office or, as he put it, "look me up." Be assured, Major Haynes, I shall not only look you up, but look you down. You may not see the carefully-veiled insolence in Heine's eye or the sneer behind his teeth. You will not know the bitter and insulting thoughts which crowd one on top of the other in Heine's teeming brain. I will look you up indeed and some day you will look up to me. How dearly I should love to repeat this bon-mot to his face.

Two days after my meeting I decided to call upon him at the War Office. It had not been my first visit, and so I knew the ropes, and having written my name on a slip of paper I was shown up to his office, a very small, unimportant apartment, showing that, whatever Major Haynes might be in his own estimation, he was jolly little thought of by the Army Council, for there was nothing in his room in the way of pictures except a plain map which, incidentally, I glanced at and comprehended as I entered. It was a map of Europe.

"Sit down, Heine," said the Major, who was writing at his desk, "help yourself to the cigarettes — those on the left, the others are poisoned. I keep them for generals."

Such frivolity! Would any major officer in the German army dare speak of the members of the Great General Staff with such disrespect? Would they not stand stiffly to attention and refer to them as "Illustrious General So-and-so," or "The Noble and Illustrious Well-Born General So-and-so?"

He finished writing, laid down his pen, and resting his elbows on the arms of his chair, dropped his chin upon his clasped hands, all the time surveying me with an inscrutable smile, as though — and I believe this to be the truth — recognizing that in me he had a devilish stiff proposition as the English say.

"Well, Heine," he said, at last "how is the Kaiser?" My blood boiled up to my head.

"Don't blush," he said. (Such a cad!)

"How is old von Hindenburg and the shining German sword?"

"Major Haynes," I said coldly, "if you think I am not a German then you are insulting me. If you believe I am a German, then your remarks are both insulting and hurtful to my dignity and my loyalty and my sense of decency."

"Quite right," said Major Haynes; and then after a pause, "I don't know what to do about you, Heine. If I send you to America you will be torpedoed. If you get to America you will probably be executed. If I send you back to Germany you will starve to death."

I made no reply.

"If I leave you here —" Major Haynes went on, helping himself to a cigarette. I noticed it was one of those which he said be used to poison generals, so I presume it was the best kind. The inhospitality of the man and his boorishness appalled me. "If I leave you here," he said, "you will probably be bombed to death. If I put you in an internment camp you will be an expense to the Government. If I have you shot —" He paused.

I turned white with anger.

"I trust you are not going to do anything so stupid owlish as that, Major Haynes," I said, "I have done my best to prove to you that I am a perfectly innocent Swiss."

"Chilean," he corrected, "but it doesn't matter. There are a lot of Swiss- Chileans in London just now, and quite a few Swedish-Turks. No, I don't think I will have you shot, you may be very useful."

"Any service I can render to you, Major Haynes," I said, with my native politeness, "I shall be happy to give. Unfortunately, I am—" I shrugged my shoulders introducing rather cleverly a suggestion of my helplessness.

"Cheer up, Heine," he said with a cynical smile — there's something about that man's smile that I don't like — "I think you can give me the greatest assistance. Let's put all our cards on the table."

"I know that you were for some time the head of German Intelligence Department in London. Take that sad, pained smile off your face, and behave. As I told you before, you weren't dangerous, because your methods were somewhat transparent and I don't think (you will excuse my directness) that you are a very clever man."

"That is a matter of opinion," I said stiffly.

"I think, as a matter of fact," Major Haynes went on, not noticing the interruption, "you have too good a heart to be a spy. Beneath that outrageous waistcoat of yours, and the three or four undershirts which I am sure you are wearing, beats a kindly heart." I am recalling his indelicate words from memory that you may learn what type of "gentleman" an English officer can be. In honest truth he was wide of the mark, for I only had two undershirts on, the weather being warm.

"Now with much of your work," Major Haynes went on, "I am well acquainted. I have your code," he opened the drawer of his desk and took out a very familiar book, and if I changed colour, who shall blame me?

"When I say your code, I mean the code of your kind. I have a list of your sub- agents, such of whom as are still alive," he said, smiling pleasantly. "I know all about your Kriesslers and your Kahns, I know your newspaper advertisement code; in short, I know almost everything about your business" — he paused — "except one thing."

"And what is that, Major Haynes?" I asked innocently.

"It is the one thing I have never been able to discover," said the Major, putting the tips of his fingers together and looking down at them. I pricked up my ears. What was it this clever fellow did not know?

"Many things, I should imagine," I said with a sneer, speaking of course to myself and sneering inwardly.

"It has come to my knowledge," he said, speaking slowly, and raising his eyes to mine in a steady, hypnotizing way, "that the agents of your — what shall I call it? — department have a code whistle which is instantly obeyed. At the sound of that whistle you are ordered, under whatever conditions you are working, whatever you may be doing, however you may endanger yourselves by so acting, to repair instantly to the spot from whence that whistle is blown and report yourself for duty to the man who has given the signal."

I felt my flesh grow rough like a goose's, and my hair almost stood on end. So precious a secret is the danger whistle that I have never referred to it before. It is the last piece of information given to the closely-examined candidate for the service after he has passed to the Executive. Only two men in England had the authority to use that signal, or the means wherewith such a call could be made. Every agent is pledged that, whatever he divulges, that secret at least shall go down to the grave with him.

It was that danger whistle that brought about the rescue of Rosenburg when he was captured on 42nd. Street, New York, when he was carrying despatches from von Papen to the Ambassador. That danger whistle, sounded in the courtyard of Brixton Prison by one of my agents who had himself arrested for debt in order to reach the interior, made Kruhn, waiting trial for espionage, hang himself by his bootlaces.

Major Haynes was watching me keenly.

"Well?" he asked.

"I am surprised you should tell me of this, Major Haynes, I said with splendid self-possession. "I have never heard of this signal or whistle, or call it what you will."

He rose from the table and came over to me.

"Stand up," he said.

I obeyed him.

"Stand against that wall."

I did not think of expostulating. There was something in his voice which dispersed all inclination to argue.

"Put out your arms," he said, "I am going to search you."

He went through all my pockets with extraordinary rapidity — I think he must have been a pickpocket before he joined the Intelligence Department — and of course he found nothing.

"Open your waistcoat," he said. I obeyed. He ran his hand lightly over my shirt.

"Tell me if I tickle you," said he; but I was in no mood for jesting, for under my arm he found the little pocket and the flat gold tube that I dreaded he would find. He laid it on the table curiously.

"So that's the whistle, eh? A peculiar note, I suppose is the code. Four short blasts and a long one?"

I smiled.

"That is merely a little trinket which was given me by a lady friend?" I said.

"Why do you wear it sewn into your shirt?"

"To have it near my heart," I said. "I am surprised at you, Major Haynes."

"I am surprised at you, Heine," he said, "if you keep your heart under your right arm-pit. You are a physical monstrosity — but I suppose you are one of those curious birds that carry their hearts in their sleeves. Come now, Heine, what is the code?"

"Major Haynes," I replied earnestly, "If you were to give me a hundred thousand pounds at this moment—"

"Which I am very unlikely to do," said Major Haynes.

"If you were to give me a million pounds," I said desperately, "I could not tell you, because I don't know."

He walked back to the other side of the table and sat down. For some time he did not speak. He lit another cigarette and looked out of the window, clasping his chin.

"You are a German, Heine, aren't you," he said at last, "and I am an Anglo- Scot, with a touch of American. Generally speaking I am British. Now here is the situation," he said, tapping on the note-pad, "you are a good German patriot" (to my eternal credit, I didn't deny it!), "I am a British patriot. Now, which of us is the more devoted to his Motherland?"

It was one of those kind of stupid questions to which there is no answer. I had quite recovered my notorious sang-froid, and I laughed.

"Now, how can I answer that, my dear Major Haynes," I said humorously. "Supposing I were a German, which of course I am not, and supposing you are a Briton, which of course you are, how can we determine the extent of our various country-loving? Goethe says—"

"Blow Goethe!" said Major Haynes rudely. "Can you answer my question?"

"Major Haynes," I replied, "I cannot."

"Very good," said Major Haynes. He looked at his watch. "You will not tell me the code."

"I know of no code," I replied firmly. He picked up the little gold whistle and put it in his pocket.

"Very good," he said again, "you will report to me here at 1:30 this afternoon. You will be immediately admitted to my presence."

"And then?" I said in trepidation.

"Then I will give you the finest lunch you have had for some time and a bottle of the best liebfraumilch procurable in London."

I went down the marble stairs of the War Office smiling. If this fellow imagined that he could buy my so precious secret for a lunch, or that he could make me so beastly intoxicated on the wine of my country, he was a bigger fool than I had imagined.

No sooner was I ushered into his office at 1:30 than he took his hat and his stick from a peg on the wall and taking me affectionately by the arm he led me out into Whitehall, hailed a taxi, and we were driven to a restaurant in the Strand, where an excellent repast was waiting.

"I have no doubt you think we are lunching luxuriously," he said, as we sat at the table, "but as this is the last meal that either you or I may ever have in this world I think we may risk being considered extravagant."

"These are strange words, Major Haynes," I said, "Very strange," he replied with his foolish smile. "Wine, Heine? Drink hearty or, as they say, 'Eat, drink and be merry, for to-morrow we die.' Cheerio!"

Throughout that amazing meal, I was puzzling my brains. I think I may say without undue conceit that I can grasp a situation as quickly as any man. I am, so to speak, up to the tricks of the game — and then some. That is not low swank. We Germans say no more than we mean, promise no more than we can perform, claim no more than we can substantiate. That is why we are the most respected nation in the world, and why the German sword, once drawn from its sacred scabbard and brandished aloft, strikes terror to the heart of its soon- to-be victims.

But despite my mind ability I could only puzzle over his alarming words and in the end find no solution to the mystery he had propounded. The British are strange people with no sense of decency. They frequently joke upon the most sacred subjects, and I have already described Major Haynes's terrible lack of true gentlemanliness in speaking of our August Sovereign Lord. Possibly, I thought, this joke is British or Scottish idea of humour. What pawkity!

He did not make any further reference to the discussion we had that afternoon. We finished our meal with coffee and liqueurs and cigars, and he paid his bill and we strolled out into the Strand. I offered him my hand when we got outside, and thanked him for his hospitality.

"You are not going, Heine," said the Major, "oh, dear no! You don't suppose I have spent quite a lot of money in entertaining you for the pleasure of your society, though I admit you are infinitely amusing."

"But I don't understand you, Major Haynes," said I in surprise; "if there is anything you want me to do I shall be most happy to do it, as I have told you before."

"It is now three o'clock," he said, "and we have just twenty minutes to get to the station."

"To the station?" I repeated, flabberfounded so to speak.

He made a beckoning gesture, and a car which was at the other side of the Strand drew across.

"Hop in, Heine," he said; and I hopped. He took his place by my side and we were whirled away to Paddington Station. He did not take a ticket. He simply strolled through the first-class booking-hall on to the platform, and a train was waiting, also another officer who, saluting Major Haynes, led us to a carriage which had been reserved.

"Get in, Heine," said the Major, and again I obeyed, still dazed and bewildered by the mysterious proceedings. The second officer got in with us.

"I have telephoned to the factory, sir," he said, "and I have brought the things you wanted."

He put his hands into his overcoat and took out three pairs of handcuffs.

"Thank you," said Major Haynes.

"The other thing, sir, I couldn't get, but I think a gas-mask would do as well, one of the old type. They are not so cumbersome."

From another pocket he drew forth a mask, with mica eyepieces. It had evidently been adapted for a special purpose, for it had been cut off at the bottom.

"Try that on, Heine," said the Major. I took it from his hands and fixed the loops over my ears.

"Look at yourself in the glass," said Major Haynes. One of the panels above the seats was a long strip of mirror. "Your own mother wouldn't recognize you," he said.

A hideous sight I presented. The mask did not cover my face. It left my mouth free. I could not imagine a more horrible spectacle than I presented.

"Fine," said the Major, "put it in your pocket. I think that is all, isn't it, Mr. Samson?"

"That's all, sir," said the officer, saluting. He looked at me with a smile, shook hands with the Major, and left us together. Soon after this the train began to move and, leaning forward, I spoke:

"I am sure you will not consider me unnecessarily inquisitive," I said with gentle sarcasm, "but may I ask why we are taking this journey, why you are carrying manacles, and why you have presented me with this curious mask?"

"You may ask," said the Major, "but I shall not tell you for some time. Here is a copy of Punch. Improve your mind and morals."

The train was an express. It did not stop until we reached a junction called Wellsbury, and here we alighted. It was now half-past one. A closed car was waiting for us and into this we got and proceeded at a rapid pace through the open country. We had been travelling for half an hour, and had reached the top of a hill and were passing over the crest, when the Major tapped the window behind the chauffeur.

"Get out here for a moment, Heine," he said, and obediently I followed, We were on the top of a hill looking down on to a little village, the principal feature of which was a large factory. On the tops of the hills were a number of hutments, and it was clear to me that this was a factory erected for war work.

"This is the Chamborn Shell-Filling Factory," said Major Haynes. "That large building is the mixing house That smaller building behind, which you can just see in spite of its being camouflaged, is the T.N.T store. That long building is the magazine, and that to its right is the live-shell store. There is at this moment in that factory about two hundred tons of T.N.T., and when I tell you that at the Rivertown explosion, which shook up half of England, only fifty tons were touched off, you will understand the nature of the disaster which would follow the blowing up of that establishment."

"But, Major Haynes," I said in desperation, "why do you tell me all this and why do you bring me such a long journey to give me this information?"

"Get into the car," said Major Haynes, "and I will tell you."

We got into the car, but he did not speak and when I suggested he should keep his promise he merely said: "Wait awhile."

We passed through the stone-pillared gates of the factory, along a broad roadway, and came to a set of offices where the car stopped and we alighted. Again the Major looked at his watch.

"Six o'clock," he said, "we have an hour. I want to introduce you to the manager of the works."

He led me into an office which was comfortably furnished, and here I met Mr. Perkins, a well-fed typical Englishman, who hoped I had had a pleasant journey down. A servant brought tea on a silver tray and we chatted generally about various topics, though for my part I had very little to say. After about half an hour the Major again looked at his watch.

"Well, I wish you good-bye, Mr. Perkins," he said, "I hope everything is all right."

A shrill hooter sounded outside.

"I am stopping the women working," said Mr. Perkins, and Major Haynes nodded.

"I think you are wise. You are getting them out of the factory on some excuse, I suppose?"

"Yes," said Mr, Perkins, "I told them we were having a test in the mixing- room and they quite understand."

I stood with Major Haynes at the entrance of the offices watching the ceaseless stream of women passing through the gates. My blood boiled as I thought these women were preparing explosives to destroy my countrymen. How un- feminine, I thought! How degraded! Woman, lovely woman, who should create life, who should be all tenderness and kindness to man, was now engaged in the low occupation of making shells to blow off the heads of the world's chosen people. It sickened me.

"Aha! My fine girls," I said between my teeth, "you are not the only flies in the ointment, for every son of the Fatherland you kill, loyal and death-defying German women are preparing explosives to blow off the heads of your husbands and sweethearts! Beware! Nemesis is on your track!"

I hated this place with its smoke and busy air. Such places should be blown from the face of the earth. I hoped it would not be blown while I was nearby, but I looked forward one day to reading in the paper that Chamborn had gone up to the sky in smoke and fury.

"Now, Heine," said Major Haynes. We walked across the road, down another road, then between two long stone buildings, past a big power-house with two smoking chimneys, and at last we came to a great brick shed painted in fantastic colours.

"This is the T.N.T. store," explained Major Haynes, "Now where are those chairs that Perkins said — Oh, here they are."

Two arm-chairs had been placed against the wall. There was a small iron- topped table with a bottle of whisky, a big syphon of soda and two glasses.

"Sit down and make your miserable life happy, Heine," said the Major, sinking down into one of the chairs and reaching out for the whisky bottle. "Say when."

When he had filled the glass with sizzling soda, he said: "Heine, it is an awful thing to realize that within thirty minutes you and I may be blotted out of life — be dissolved in thin air, leaving no trace of ourselves and never knowing what struck us."

My glass trembled against my teeth and I put down the whisky untasted.

"Explain yourself, Major Haynes," I said hoarsely.

"I will explain to you, Heine," he replied gravely, "I feel it is due to you. You are probably aware that Chamborn is the most important shell-filling factory in England. If you are not so aware I will tell you that it is. If this place went up in smoke the British Army would be seriously inconvenienced, though not crippled. Your friends in Berlin imagine that its destruction would have decisive consequences, and in this, of course they are wrong, for there are other factories, quite a large number of them. They have sent two or three agents from Germany," he went on slowly, "and they are clever men." I did not answer, I looked at the clock above the offices and noted that the gold hands upon the black face stood at twenty minutes to seven.

The Major followed my eyes and smiled.

"We have twenty minutes," he said

"What do you mean by all this?" I asked in an agitated voice, my agitation being of course due to the presence in England of three gentlemen who were probably well-born and my superiors. "What do you mean by three agents?"

"Two or three," corrected Major Haynes, "my information is that there are two; my further information is that they are employed in these works; that they speak English so perfectly that it is impossible to detect them, that they are armed with all sorts of credentials; and— " he paused, "That they intend blowing up this factory at seven o'clock."

I half rose from my seat, but he laid his hand upon my arm and pushed me back. "We have taken the most elaborate precautions — when I say we," he apologized, "I mean the Government. We have weeded out suspicious work-men, but we are still certain that these men have in some way connected up a means of detonation which they will touch off at seven o'clock to-night."

The place swam round. I could feel my knees trembling against the supports of the iron table. My throat and mouth went dry and I could only look round helplessly. Major Haynes was quite cool.

"The only way to save this place from destruction," he said, "is to bring the men who are engaged in this work to our presence before the mischief is done, and you, Heine, are the syren who will call them."

He put his hands in his breast-pocket and took out my little gold whistle and laid it on the table.

"You may not know the code of the danger whistle, but you may guess it," he said. " If you are telling the truth and you don't know the code, then it is very unfortunate for you and most unfortunate for me, because in a little over a quarter of an hour, you and I, my dear Heine, will be continuing our debate in heaven."

"But — but —" I gasped.

"It is no use butting, my dear lad," said the Major, "you will be butting your bead into that wall in less than sixteen minutes unless you can bring your loyal but startled fellow-countrymen to this spot."

I picked up the whistle in my shaking fingers.

"But it would be death to me," I said, "and besides, Major Haynes, I am a loyal man. I cannot betray my friends to their death."

"Spoken like a patriot," said the Major. "It seems to me that you are almost as good a patriot as I am. In which case we shall both die without remorse."

I thought and I thought. Twice I picked up the whistle and twice I put it down. The hands of the clock moved round inexorably. It wanted four minutes to the hour when I turned my perspirationed face towards him.

"They will know I betrayed them," I said; "they will see me."

"You have a mask in your pocket, which I have thoughtfully provided," said the Major. "Put it on, my dear Heine, there are three minutes between you and glory."

With trembling hands I fixed the hideous mask. Better, I thought, that these unfortunate men should be detected and that a great and hideous crime should be prevented than that one whose life was of such service to the Fatherland should be so cruelly extinguished.

I put the whistle to my lips and blew shrilly; short, long and trilling blasts, I repeated it, and scarcely had the echoes died away when two men came blundering round the corner of the building, one in his shirt-sleeves, one in the black coat of a clerk. They stopped dead as they saw Major Haynes, and put up their hands, for his revolver was covering them.

"I am sorry, gentlemen," he said as he snapped the handcuffs upon them, "Fortunes of war." They glared from, him to me, and one said to the other quickly in German: "We're caught. This is Voss's work. We ought to have prevented his leaving us."

"Excellent news," said Major Haynes briefly, "so Voss was the third man. You may comfort yourselves with the knowledge that he was arrested in London — to- day, though your detection was not due to him but to my friend here." I was trembling before the glare of those haughty German eyes.

"If you'd given us another day," one of them growled in English, "we'd have settled your cursed factory."

"So I gather," said Major Haynes. "As for this swine," he made a movement towards me and I stepped back till I realized I was stepping toward the T.N.T. store, when I stepped sideways. But the place was alive with detectives now. They seemed to spring out of the ground and I breathed a sigh of relief as I saw these unfortunate men being led away.

"You can take off your mask now, Heine, they will never see you," said Major Haynes. "Poor devils! We will go up to town by a late train and I'll see what I cm do for you in the morning."

"Major Haynes," I said brokenly, "I don't want to see you to-morrow. I am very ill. The danger I have been through, the strain upon my nerves, how I envy you your coolness—"

"The strain upon your nerves, Heine?" said Major Haynes, with brutal innocence.

"I have not your lack of imagination," I said crossly. "I cannot sit here waiting for a factory to blow up, watching the minutes pass." I wiped my brow with a silk handkerchief, looked up at the clock as it struck seven, and shuddered.

"There was no danger, my dear man," said the Major calmly.

"But you told me that they were going to blow up the factory at seven o'clock."

"Exactly," said Major Haynes, "you heard what the gentleman told you, seven o'clock."

'Well, this is seven o'clock," I said.

"Yes, but I meant seven o'clock to-morrow night," said the Major.

Such a bluffer!

17 — THE COMING OF THE BOLSHEVIKS

If there is one quality which we Germans possess in a superlative quantity it is a sense of justice. We Germans may be proud, we may be too soft-hearted, we may be romantic, but we are just. The idea of injustice is abhorrent to the truly-German. How many quarrels have I seen at the dining tables in the various German pensions in which I have lived, because one good German thought another was getting too large a helping! You see it in every phase of life, and must confess that in my own case, nothing so irritates me, so rouses my deep German wrath, which is a terrible thing in itself, as the knowledge that I am not getting my share.

Understand that I say nothing which may be taken as disparaging to the heads of those departments under whose guidance I have worked and for whose interest I have taken risks — risks which have not been compensated by the meagre salary and the grudging letters of thanks which I have received. We Germans are people of iron will and determination. We are perhaps the best disciplined people in the world. Give a German an order to go into battle or to walk to the cannon's mouth, whether it is loaded or not, and he will obey, marching with parade step and a calm, stern face to what may very easily be considerable personal disfigurement.

I myself have taken orders from my superiors with a sharp "Ja, Herr!" and a stern salute, well knowing that if I carried those orders out I would be going to certain destruction. Many of those orders I have obeyed, having carefully reconnoitred the way and discovered the dangers which might be avoided, for none but a fool would rush bat-eyed into terrible perils if he could avoid them.

I have explained the circumstances under which I came to be under a cloud, not only with the British Government, but, alas! — and my soul weeps at the thought! — with the Government of my beloved Fatherland. I make no complaint. We Germans never whine. We have in the Wilhelmstrasse men without imagination, men without gratitude, men with the brains of she-asses.

After my deportation from England and the torpedoing of the ship which carried me, and my return to these shores on a submarine, I ceased to be what I was, the recognized head and centre of the Intelligence Service of the Fatherland in England. Though I had worked independently, I had worked without success.

Major Haynes, of the British Intelligence Corps, knew I was in England, probably had me watched night and day, and was, as the English saying goes, "fair to my face but bitter to my stomach."

I do not know whether I must hate this man, or whether, in my professional zeal, admire one who must be clever — why should I deny it — since he had got the better of me. He was a suave, calm man with a foolish sense of humour which no German would ever understand, a cynical man who had probably been crossed in love in his earlier life — possibly by some beautiful German girl, who lured the poor fool on and then threw him over with a sneer. I often used to lie in bed picturing the circumstances which brought about his snarling views of Germany, and often I have enacted the scene, in which I was the beautiful young girl.

What bitter things I have said to him! How I have tossed my locks at this proud Englishman or Scotsman, standing pale and dejected before me begging for one rose from my hair!

I had plenty of time to dream. I was out of touch with the organization I had created with so much labour, forethought and genius. I was unattached and officially unrecognized. I suspected that someone else had taken on my work, but I found it difficult to discover who was in my place owing to the embargo which Major Haynes had laid upon me against communicating with certain people, the names of whom in some mysterious way this cunning man knew, who might inform me upon the situation.

I was sitting one day, morose and brooding, in my new lodgings in Bayswater, meditating upon my fallen state and wondering if I had very much farther to fall, I confess there were tears in my eyes when I remembered the power I had wielded, all the wonderful letters of encouragement which had come to me from the well-born and illustrious Captain Baron von Hazfield, the chief of the Military Intelligence Department; and of how I was now without recognition, a fugitive hunted on the face of the earth, doubtless mocked at by men to whom I had extended a helping hand.

It was near coffee-time, that is to say, nearly four o'clock in the afternoon, when a knock came or my bedroom door and my landlady entered with telegram in her hand.

"For you, Mr. Smith," she said. I had given the name of Smith because I thought it was not likely to attract unusual attention. It is a name very commonly used in England by people who wish to remain anonymous.

"For me, my dear madam?" I said, taking the telegram in my hand. "Oh yes, I remember. A friend of mine is coming to London and he promised to wire the hour of his arrival." With this pleasant little fiction I waved her out of the room.

You may wonder why I gave any excuse at all, but we Germans are by nature furtive, and it is part of my business to puzzle and deceive those with whom I am brought into contact. I opened the telegram. My address was only known to two or three people and none of these were compatriots of mine.

Judge then of my surprise when I saw that it was a cable addressed to me from Stockholm, and read:

"Twenty-five kegs of butter consigned to you per The Scandia Export Company."

The telegram was signed "Fredericks." I needed no code-book to understand that message. It was an order from a very powerful and an extremely illustrious member of my profession, a gentleman with whom I had had some correspondence and, indeed, one whom I had met on the occasion to which I have referred in these stories of my purchasing a newspaper.

"Twenty-five kegs" meant "call upon."

The next morning I sallied forth. A glance at a telephone book in one of the telephone boxes told me the address of the Scandia Export Company, which was in Upper Thames Street. You would think, of course, that I made my way direct to my objective. That was not the case. I had seen in the telephone book that the Scandia Company, with whom, by the way, I had never had any previous dealings, was a wholesale provision merchant.

I hired a cab and drove off to Bisbury's, one of the greatest wholesale provision merchants in London, asked to see the manager and demanded from him whether he could supply me with twenty-five firkins of Danish butter at the current price. Butter at this time was getting very scarce and the polite manager informed me that it was impossible for him to supply me.

I drove to another provision merchant's, this time in Long Acre, and repeated my request. Here an offer was made to sell me the amount I required, and I noted the price and said I would call again. From thence my cab took me into the south of London to another butter merchant, who was unable to supply me. And so one after the other I called upon six firms, all of which did business in butter, before I touched the Scandia Export Company.

I am no fool. We Germans are wideawake. I knew, or guessed, that Mr., or Major, Haynes (a more un-military person I have never seen) would have me watched and that probably my shadow was following me now.

How puzzled he would be! What! Was Heine thinking of opening a butter shop that he went to all these great merchants? No, sir. Heine would be no butter- patter, but Heine knew that he had an excuse for calling at the Scandia Company, and that it was no more suspicious to call upon this particular firm than it was to call upon the half a dozen whom he had already visited, or the three or four more that he would visit in the course of the day.

And so I came to the Scandia Company and found its offices on the first floor of a very dark and untidy building. I was met by a clerk in a large and gloomy room which was furnished with a desk, a stool and a copying press, and politely stated my business.

"You wish to see Mr. Brantl, I think," said the clerk. "If you will wait a moment I will find out if he is engaged." He went out of the room through a glass-panelled door and was away for a few minutes. Presently he returned leaving the door open.

"Will you step this way?" he said, and I passed into the room, closing the door behind me. Mr. Brantl was a short, thick-set man with a close-cropped beard who looked at me sharply through his gold-rimmed, spectacles.

"Sit down," he said imperiously, and then without a word of preliminary he plunged into what I can only describe as an impertinent and ill-tongued harangue.

"Now, look here, Heine," he said, and by his simple, direct rudeness I perceived that he was no more of a Swede than a turnip (a play on words which is called a "pun" in English), but a true Prussian and probably very highly connected. "You have made a mess of things."

I stared at the man. "I don't understand you," I said coldly.

"You've made a mess of things, and don't interrupt me," he barked. "Head- quarters are crazy with you. You upset all their arrangements and you have left your work in England in a disgraceful condition. Don't interrupt me! You know me?"

I looked at him closely. "I only know," I said after a pause, and speaking with a hauteur which was quite unmistakable to any sensitive German, "that you are impertinently discussing a matter of which I am perfectly ignorant. I can only say—"

"Now shut up," said Mr. Brantl. "Swine! Pig! Miserable thief! Have you never heard of the Captain Baron von Hazfield?"

I stared at him closely and gasped. Instantly I was on my feet, clicking my heels, my hand raised to my forehead, for this gentleman was the illustrious Chief of the Intelligence Bureau, whom I had had the honour and privilege to see on one occasion through the window.

"Sit down," he growled. "I have had to come to England to clear up the damned mess you've made and I can tell you I am not feeling cheerful about it. Now tell me what happened."

Briefly I explained to him how Major Haynes had detected me and had sent me out of the country. I also described my voyage back in a the submarine and be listened attentively.

"Part of what you tell me is lies," he said, "part of it is true. British Intelligence Department — bah! If you hadn't been a sucking dove, or should I say, a sucking pig—?"

"Whichever pleases you, Herr Baron," I said, with a little smile.

"Don't you grin, you baboon. If you had exercised the slightest caution you would never have been caught. You have simply given yourself into the hands of the Englishman."

"Scotsman," I murmured.

"Don't interrupt," he roared, "you needn't be afraid of Hayes or Haynes, or whatever the man's name is. You have now a chance to rehabilitate yourself in the esteem of the Department. I never agreed to your coming to England, It was against my wishes, thank God I told von Papen that I wanted a man of intelligence who at any rate looked like an English gentleman."

"I flatter myself—" I began.

"You do," said the Herr Baron, "that's the trouble with you, your infernal conceit. Now listen and don't interrupt. In three days' time there will arrive in this country a very large number of forged bank and treasury notes. Every agent in England and Scotland will put those notes into circulation. They are so well done that you can't tell the difference between them and the real thing. They are, in fact," he said, "made—"

"—in Germany," I smiled.

He cursed me for interrupting him.

"You will be in Merson Street, Soho, on Thursday night, standing outside the Petite Dejeuner restaurant. A man will come and give you a large travelling case. It will contain the forged money, and you will spend the rest of your time wandering about England getting rid of it. It will not be an unpleasant experience," he said.

"The forgeries will never be detected until the money comes to the Bank of England. Therefore your job is to get as far away from London as you possibly can."

"But I shall never be able to spend it."

"Give it away, then," said the Herr Baron. "You understand your orders?"

"Perfectly," I replied.

"You won't want any real money. You want buy everything except war bonds."

"I would not think of doing anything so unpatriotic," I cried indignantly.

"It isn't a question of patriotism, you fool. War bond money comes back to the Bank."

He was silent so long that at last I plucked up my courage to say: "Is that all, Herr Baron?"

"No, that is not all," he said slowly, "only I don't know whether I can trust you with the other matter."

I drew myself up.

"I have been entrusted with many delicate duties," I said, not without a certain quiet dignity.

"And you made a mess of 'em. I know all about it," said the Baron, "still I can tell you this because it may not come your way. Have you heard of Loski?"

To another man I should have said "Yes," but to this discerning, thought- reading, truth-compelling German, who was, moreover, of the highest nobility, I replied simply and modestly: "No."

"Loski is the chief of the Lithuanian Soviet. He is a member of the Supreme Council at Petrograd, and is a Bolshevik — hang all Bolsheviks! but they are very useful to us. The mad English Government has given him permission to visit this country on behalf of some industrial corporation at Moscow. I have had a telegram from Stockholm to say that he will be here this week. Now, don't forget, this man is working for us, and if he swims into your orbit you are to do everything you can for him. Render him any assistance that lies in your power. Find out where he is lodging and make his acquaintance. That is all."

I bowed and withdrew. I must confess that on my journey back to my lodgings I was troubled. I did not share this bullying, browbeating, stupid man's views of Major Haynes. We Germans never despise an enemy who is worthy of our steel, and I felt that Major Haynes was not only worthy of my steel, but my carving knife as well. It is hard to jest with a sad heart! So I was not surprised the following morning when my landlady came to tell me that a soldier had come with a message.

He was quite a common soldier, evidently an orderly, and when he was shown into my room I immediately put him into his place by telling him to take his cap off. The fact that he took not the slightest notice of what I said, shows that the English Army is the worst disciplined and the least respectful of all armies in the world.

I read the note. It was from Major Haynes, telling me to come to his office with the least possible delay.

"Tell your master I will be there," I said haughtily,

"Tell who?" said the common soldier.

"Your master, my man."

"Pull yourself together," said the common soldier, "do you mean Major Haynes?" Of course the low fellow called him 'Aynes. I resolved to report him for his insolence, but somehow the idea slipped from my mind on the journey, because I was in some apprehension (why should I conceal the fact?) as to why this officer wanted me.

He was busily writing as I entered and jerked his head to a chair and, since I am a perfect gentleman, I did not interrupt him until he had finished. He blotted his letter and folded it up into an envelope before he turned his attention to me.

"I've got a little honest work for you."

I shivered at the words. I remembered the last time I had assisted him, and he evidently read my thoughts.

"Oh, this is all right," he said with a smile, "no danger, Heine. You are a good German, I believe?"

I shrugged my shoulders. "What is the use of arguing with you, Major Haynes," I said with a smile, "if I were a German I should certainly be a good German."

"And every good German is afraid of the Russian."

"We Germans fear nobody," I said hotly, and then realizing that I had betrayed myself, I went on with scarcely a break, "as a German would say."

"Neatly put," said the Major, "at any rate a well conducted German does not love the Bolshevik, and especially a Bolshevik who is not even — there, I nearly said too much," he smiled, "and that is not like me, is it?"

I could have told him that anything he said to me was too much, but I refrained.

"Foreign as I know it to be to your honest nature," the Major went on, "I am, nevertheless, asking you to do a little professional espionage work for me — oh, yes, I am serious," he said, " you owe me a great deal, Heine. You owe me your life amongst other things, and I am going to give you a chance of paying me back, or rather paying the Government back, without necessarily betraying any of your own fellow countrymen. From such a prospect as that," he said with pious hypocrisy, "my very soul revolts."

And this man who had the brazen effrontery to make a so-canting statement had deliberately forced me to assist him in capturing two of my lamentable fellow- countrymen only a few weeks before! Such is the boasted honour of the British race!

"In reality," said the Major, "the work I want you to do is very simple, very harmless and yet very necessary, and I believe that you, of all the people I know, can best perform the service I require."

I nodded.

"There is a man arriving in this country in the course of this week, named Loski," said the Major. "He may be a Russian patriot. He may be an anarchist, He may be only a simple-minded burglar. On the other hand, he may be engaged by your clever Intelligence Department to carry on propaganda work. There is a man in London named Missovitch who I know is in correspondence with the Loski crowd and is their agent in London. Missovitch lives at 364, Dean Street, Soho. I will write the address for you," he said, suiting the action to the words.

"And what do you expect me to do, Major Haynes?" I asked

"I want you to see Missovitch. He is one of those peculiar Russians who speaks German, the type with which you are well acquainted."

"Probably from the Baltic Provinces?" I said boldly.

"Very likely," said Major Haynes, with a smile. "Pump him. He will confide in you. Nobody would mistake you for an English gentleman. Find out what the game is. No harm can come to our friend Loski. The worst that can happen is that he will be handed his passports and returned to the place from whence he came."

I breathed a sigh of relief and was inwardly chuckling. Somehow I felt in the swing again, an entire master of my confidence.

I found Missovitch without any trouble. He kept a little tobacconist's shop at the address Major Haynes had given me, a pale, unhealthy young man with a slight moustache and a fringe of beard. He was not very communicative. I might say that from the very moment I entered the shop till I left be regarded me with suspicion which he did not attempt to disguise.

I was in a quandary because I could not betray my knowledge of Loski, nor could I tell this unauthorized person that I was an agent of the great German Government that wished him no harm. He grew more and more uneasy at my careless questions, and to my amazement he also grew paler, and beads of perspiration grew upon his brow as I asked one question after another.

"I don't know who you are, sir," he said at last, "but I assure you I have not any knowledge of the Bolsheviks, and I am not interested in anything which is occurring in Russia."

"Come, come," I said jokingly, "that is fine talk from a man with your name. Tell me, who is this Loski I hear so much about?" He looked at me through his half-closed lids.

"Sir," he said, "if you are the police I can give you no information. You may arrest me," he said excitedly, though I tried to calm him, "you may put me in jail, but I can tell you nothing, and Ivanoff's trouble mill be in vain. I am a poor shop-keeper trying to earn my living. I don't know anything about the Bolsheviks, anything about M. Loski. I know nothing, nothing."

This was a bad beginning I thought, as I left the shop, wondering who was Ivanoff, and certainly not a satisfactory one for Major Haynes. And yet in many ways it could not have been better. I had but to tell the truth to Major Haynes and be relieved of a rather embarrassing mission. Strangely enough, when I reported to the Intelligence Officer, he accepted my word without any query, though he was, I could see, rather troubled.

"The man suspected you, that's bad," he said, frowning. "Still, I'm sure, Heine, you did your best. By the way, he didn't mention any other Russian person?"

I suddenly remembered.

"Yes," I said, "he mentioned a man named—"

"Ivanoff?" said the Major quickly.

"That's the name," I said, stupefied by his intelligence.

"H'm," said Major Haynes, "thank you, Heine. I will let you know if I want you again."

I did not hear from the Major, but on the Thursday morning a note was delivered to my lodgings, this time in the well-known writing of Captain Baron von Hazfield. It ran simply:

"Cancel my previous instructions. Meet messenger to-night at 8.30, under the clock at King's Cross Station."

At eight o'clock I was at King's Cross. I gathered that I was to meet the boat train which was coming in from the north. The train itself was about five minutes late, and I composed myself to read the evening newspaper to pass the time. I stood in a little recess and away from observation, and I was immersed in my newspaper when suddenly I heard a smothered cry, and, looking up, I found myself face to face with Missovitch.

He was staring at me with horror. His face was no longer white but green, and as I took a step towards him he put up his hands with a strangled cry, and turning, ran like the wind, dodging between passengers and porters and disappearing through the archway that leads into the station. I was amazed. What was there in my appearance which frightened him. Was he following me with the intention of doing me bodily harm? The thought sent a cold shiver down my spine.

But I had little time to speculate upon this mystery, for a few minutes afterwards the boat train drew into the station, and I took up my position under the clock and waited. The passengers streamed through the narrow barriers, some bailing taxi-cabs, some stopping to pick up other friends who were on the train, some greeting those who were waiting for them.

I had no means of recognizing the man who was to bring me the forged money, but I supposed that he had been well instructed. Do not let it be thought that I was quite free from care, that in a few moments I should be in possession of a vast number of forgeries gave me no pleasure. Suppose anything went wrong! Suppose I was captured! A fine end for a great agent, I don't think, as they say in England.

Presently a man emerged from the crush about the barrier and walked straight across to me, looking at me thoughtfully. He was a tall man with a thin black moustache, and be stopped near me.

"May I take your bag?" I asked softly in German. He smiled, passed the bag to me, and we walked out of the station together.

"Which way do you go?" I asked, still in the same language.

"We shall meet at your place tonight," he said in a low voice. He turned to the left and I turned to the right. My taxi-cab was waiting, and I put the bag in. I turned back and saw two men leap from the shadow upon my late companion. There was a struggle, I heard a shot, and my blood turned to water. Summoning all my reserves I said to the taxi-cab driver, in as calm a voice as I could manage: "Bayswater Square," and in a few seconds I was being whirled away, as I believed, from the greatest possible danger, my mind filled with the most distressing and painful thoughts.

18 — THE GOING OF HEINE

Picture my feelings as I drove away from King's Cross in a cab, with a fat suitcase at my feet. M. Missovich had most mysteriously been struck by terror at the sight of me and bolted. The messenger with the bag had arrived and in answer to my inquiry in German whether I should carry his bag had handed to me and we had separated.

Scarcely had we parted than two mysterious men had leapt upon him. There had been a struggle in the street, a shot had been fired, and here was I driving off in a high condition of perspiration, wondering how much the Government knew, whether they were aware that I, Heine, was burdened with a bag full of forged notes.

I summoned up courage to look back out of the window. I could only see a crowd gathering in the half-darkness, and withdrew my head. Should I throw the bag out of the window? If I did somebody might see me and that would be fatal. Besides, I owed duty to the Fatherland. My chest swelled at the thought.

I did not drive to my lodgings — believe me, I do not live in Bayswater Square — but dismissed the man. and pretended I was going into one of the houses. I waited till he had driven away and descended the steps and walked rapidly to my own humble dwelling which was about two streets away. Here I admitted myself with a key and went straight to my room, locking the door behind me.

I realized that for the safety of the Fatherland and for the honour of the great service, of which I was an unworthy member, my first step must be to prove an alibi. With that forethought which is so characteristically German, I had made myself acquainted with Major Haynes' habits. I knew he spent evenings at Brown's, a well-known club in the West End, and I immediately called him up. To my surprise and delight I found he was there.

"I wish to see you, Major Haynes," I said, "When will it be convenient?"

"Come around to the club if it is important," replied his voice, and having packed away the suitcase under my bed, I drove to Brown's, and was met by the Major in the vestibule.

"Let us pretend you are not an alien enemy," he said, as he signed my name in the book, "if it ever leaked out that I had entertained a German spy I should be hauled before the committee and asked to resign."

"You will have your joke, Major Haynes," I smiled.

"Won't I?" he asked. "Now tell me what is the trouble?"

I had made up my excuse in the car.

"When I reported to you that I had interviewed Missovitch," I said, "you asked me if be had named anybody and I had replied that he had mentioned a person named Ivanoff."

"Quite right," said the Major, "Alexis Ivanoff."

"It has occurred to me," I went on boldly, for I can be a bluffer too and had played many games at poker, "that I know this Ivanoff. Is he not an officer of' the Preobojensky Regiment?"

"To be exact," said the Major, "he is not."

"Oh!" said I, with a well-simulated disappointment, "then my journey has been in vain."

"As a matter of fact, you have never heard of Alexis Ivanoff. You don't believe he is a member of that regiment and you have merely come round to pump me or," he looked at me with cold-devil scrutinizing eyes, "or as an excuse to show yourself at"— he looked up at the clock — "ten-thirty."

"Not at all," I said eagerly, though my marrow shook within me. He did not take his eyes off me.

"There is some reason," he said slowly, "now own up, Heine?"

We Germans are quick thinkers and the idea came to me as an inspiration.

"I will be frank with you," I said, "I have been summoning up my courage to ask you a favour, but my heart descended to my shoes when I saw your official face."

"Go ahead."

"I need permission to leave London," said I. "You were kind enough to tell me that you would facilitate my journey to America, and I have many real genuine, bona-fide businesses to do in England before I depart."

He thought a moment. "I have no objection," he said. "When do you expect to leave?"

"To-morrow," I replied.

"Now look here, Heine," he said. "I don't dislike you. You are quite a decent fellow, but you have to promise me that you will engage yourself in no espionage work, that you will not go into any of the prohibited areas, and that you will report yourself to me on your return to London."

"I promise," I said.

We shook hands and parted. Somehow I knew that this time, at any rate, he was taking me at my word and I was not being followed. Nevertheless, I altered my appearance as best I could, but not until within two hours of my departure did I unlock that suit-case which lay beneath my bed.

You will understand that I had a natural feeling of delicacy about playing the common part of a forgery-distributor. You must remember that I was a student of Heidelberg, that my parents were people of honour, my father being a State district councillor with a fourth-class order of the Red Eagle. Was it honourable, thought I, to distribute forged money? More than that, was it safe?

An examination of the contents of the case satisfied me and filled me with a certain pride in the skill and genius of our German workmen. There the money lay in great thick packets of £5, £10, £50 and £100 notes with innumerable thicker packages of £1 treasury bills. And the cleverness of the forgeries! Not only were they indistinguishable from real money, both in the texture of the paper and in the colour of the printing, but every bank-note bore a different number and the greater proportion of them had the appearance of having been used very frequently.

You would never have suspected that these soiled notes, with the fold marks upon them, were not what they pretended to be. I must confess it gave me greater courage, and filled me with a certain boyish satisfaction to know how many people would be deceived.

I left that night for the North. My destination was Scotland, and I reached Glasgow the following morning. I did not of course put any money into circulation on the train. Heine is not exactly a fool. He had to come back by that railway and a fine flibberty-gibbet he would look if the so-handsomely-tipped guard or the in-excess-paid sleeping-car attendant were to recognize the man who had given him forged notes.

I will not attempt to describe the adventures of that week. I will not tell you how I passed my first £5 note and how I stood in fear and trembling with my heart thumping so that even the shopkeeper thought that an aeroplane was passing overhead; of how I lived in terror for twenty-four hours lest my act be brought home to me. I was soon to discover that I was chewing more than I could bite. My friends, it requires an expert to put forged money into circulation. It must be done note by note, and whenever I offered large sums, like £50, people looked at me askance. In Scotland I found it was almost impossible, because the Scottish people have bank-notes of their own, queer pieces of paper that looked as if they have fallen into the soup and pave been dried in a dustbin. I came south of the line to Newcastle, staying at an hotel not far from the station. My progress was painfully slow. In one week I had only managed to get rid of £100 and most of that was in £1 treasury notes, which were accepted without question.

It was in Newcastle that I got my big fright. I had purchased an £80 motor- bicycle and paid for it in notes, and after ordering the machine to be sent to the hotel, I was leaving the shop when the manager called me back.

"I don't think this £50 note of yours is in order, sir," he said. I felt my knees tremble.

"Not in order?" I blustered. "My good man, are you mad?"

"I've got the number of a note here which is circulated by the police as having been stolen. Will you accompany me to the bank? They have the right numbers there and I may have made a mistake."

To refuse would have been to invite suspicion. I put a bold look upon my pale face and swaggered off in company with the manager with true German insouciance. At the bank my trials and tribulations (internal) can only be imagined by those who have enjoyed a similar experience.

It was not the fear that this note would prove to be one which had been stolen that filled my heart with wild fluttering (as a young girl's when she is first told by a handsome Prussian lover that he adores her), it was the tremblement of apprehension that the bank manager would detect this so perfectly imitated note as a forgery.

We were ushered into the bank manager's room, an evil, sinister-looking man with a close-cut moustache. The shopkeeper explained. For my part I stood a little behind him, having with my usual thoroughness marked the way of retreat and made my plans for a grand bolt. The bank manager took the note in his hand and I set my teeth. He looked at it, turned it over, rustled it, laid it on the desk, examined the number, then, pulling out a drawer, he took a thin black book and opened it. He ran his finger down page after page and at last he stopped.

"This must be the one, Mr. Speddings," he said. "I am afraid, sir," he said, addressing me, "this gentleman has made a mistake. Curiously enough, the number of this note is missing but it is not in this series. Bank-notes, as you know," be explained, "have a number and a series letter, and the stolen note fortunately is not yours."

I bowed my head. Had I spoken my shaking voice would have betrayed me. I shook hands with this benevolent-looking Englishman, left the note in the shopkeeper's hands and, hailing a cab, I drove back to my hotel. The shock quite upset me, and I lay on the bed all that afternoon thinking of some way whereby not only I could get a quicker departure of the money but a method which enabled me to do so in safety.

They brought me up the afternoon newspapers and I turned the pages idly. I have explained before, though the fact needs no explanation, that we Germans leap to an idea as air to a vacuum. It was something in the little smudged space reserved for the latest news which attracted my attention. I rang the bell and the porter came to me. I pretty shrewdly guessed that this man was interested in the subject which I broached. All these porters and common people of England are sport-hunters and race-horse punting men, as they call them. I assumed the air of a bookmaker as he came in, and said with a good imitation of a bettor:

"What's the odds for the three o'clock race!"

"Beg pardon, sir?"

"What's the odds for the three o'clock race, my boy?" I said jovially. "Six to four the field or ten to one bar one? " You see I had got the jargon of the race-course by heart, though I loathed and detested the races. A light dawned in his eyes.

"Oh, you want to know the prices of the three o'clock winner. It's four to one, sir."

"Good," I replied jovially, and putting my hand in my pocket I gave him a £5 note, to his great astonishment.

"Where is the horse-racing to-morrow?" I asked.

"Same place, sir," said the man when he had recovered from his dumb- foundedness.

"Where?" I asked.

"Why, at Newmarket, sir."

"And is there racing on the following day?" I asked.

"Yes, sir," he replied, "it is a three-day meeting. This is the first day."

"Find me the best train for Newmarket, my good fellow," I said; "for I am going down to back the field."

He was mystified by my knowledge of sporting terms. That was easy to see. He went away and came back in about an hour, and told me that the best thing I could do was to go to London on the night train, and take another train from there to Newmarket, and though I did not wish to appear in London, those were the steps I took, arriving at London at seven o'clock in the morning and leaving Liverpool Street Station at half-past eight.

I found on my arrival at that historic centre of gambling and vice, that I was three hours too soon. My pockets were filled with money, and I carried the remainder in my portmanteau. I had some difficulty in finding a room at the hotel, but eventually I was given a small apartment on the second floor of a gloomy inn. I left my bag under the bed and strode out into the town, congratulating myself upon the genius which had inspired me to discover the most rapid way of putting money into circulation.

It was a bright spring morning and the streets were crowded with men who were strolling up and down, and who had evidently spent the night in the town.

I took a brisk walk to what is known as the "Severalls," and then, coming back, turned into the most respectable bar I could find and ordered myself a whisky and soda. I made a great display of my money — (Do you see Heine's plan?) — and several sharp-looking men, who were watching me closely, exchanged glances which I did not fail to see, though I proceeded innocently to swallow my drink as though I were oblivious of their presence.

By-and-by one of them came over to me and asked me if I had seen the morning paper.

"I think I have met you before," he said, "at Ascot."

"It is very likely," I replied politely. "I usually go to Ascot three or four times a year."

"Not for the racing? " he said, taken aback. "Yes," I smiled.

"But," he said, "there's only one meeting at Ascot. A four-day meeting in the summer."

"Exactly," I said, never at a loss for a reply. "I go every day."

"Oh, I see what you mean," he said. Then, after a pause. "Do you think Barleycorn will do it to-day?"

"Do what?" I asked, a little puzzled.

"Do you think Barleycorn will win?"

"Oh, of course," I said hastily, "Is it running? " He looked at me queerly.

"Running? Is Barleycorn running for the Babraham handicap? Why, of course it's running. It will start a hot favourite, too."

"In that case," said I with a simulation of racing intelligence, "in that case it will win. I must have a thousand or so on," I said with careless indifference.

He swallowed hard.

"I know a very good thing for the first race," he said. "It's a pinch."

"What a curious name for a horse," I said, with a gay laugh.

"You're a comical chap," said the man, "What I mean is, this horse is a certainty."

"Oh, I see what you mean," said I. "Forgive me if I am not used to the patois, but you see I am a Chilean planter and I do not speak very well." He nodded, and the puzzled look on his face disappeared, and instead there settled that beautiful look of peace and contentment which a man assumes when he has found an unsuspected gold mine.

"I used to live in Chile myself," he said, "at least my brother did. He is always talking about the Chileans — that's where the chillies come from, isn't it?"

I nodded. I do not know where they come from, and I have only been in Chile once in my life.

"Well, anything I can do for a stranger I am always willing to do," he said. He was a stoutish man with a large gold watch-chain. His face was clean-shaven and very red, and he wore a grey Derby hat on the back of his head and three diamond rings on his right hand. He asked me if I admired the rings and I told him I did. He said they were diamonds and I did not tell him he was a liar, for I know plate-glass when I see it. The end of it was that we all went out to the course together.

On the way up he told me he knew a bookmaker who gave much better odds than anybody else, and that if I cared to let him do my commissions for me he would be happy to put me in the way of making money. It transpired that the pinch was a horse called Implex, and I handed over £150 with a coolness which took his breath away. Implex did not win, and if he had won I should not have got the money, because my new friend, whose name was Mike, did not, so far as I could see, go near a bookmaker. He came back full of apologies, expecting to find me wrathful, but I was smiling and urbane.

He told me he had another pinch and that he could get ten to one to a lot of money. I gave him ten notes of £50, the most difficult notes of all to put into circulation, and he went into the ring and came back and said that I stood to win £5,000. The horse was called Molum. I saw that horse going down. I don't know much about race-horses, but I know a horse when I see one. I watched the race from the stand, but I did not see Molum till after the race was over.

For some time Mike did not come near me, but just before the third race he put in an appearance, full of sorrow and unhappiness and expressed the wish that he would be deprived of his sight if he was not the most disappointed man on the course.

"But you can get all your money back on Barleycorn," he said. "It's a pinch."

I gave the poor fellow £500 and then strolled into the ring. I thought I might as well get rid of the money myself. It was a very simple process. I had merely to go to a bookmaker and say "Barleycorn," and he shouted a lot of figures in my face, whereupon I would hand him money, his assistant writing something in a book and giving me a ticket.

In this way I distributed over £2,000 and Barleycorn was fourth, or he may have been tenth. When you realize that the value of the money I had to distribute was nearly £50,000 — I did not count it, but made a rough calculation — you can appreciate that fact that it went all too slowly. I could not give the book-makers too much money for fear I excited comment. There was only about a quarter of an hour during which they would accept money. Some of them refused to take it.

On the fifth race Mike told me that a horse named Hippo was a stone certainty, and when I went to a bookmaker and said "Hippo" and handed him a lot of money be shook his head and said: "My book's full."

"Get another book," I said pleasantly.

"I can't take your money. I don't want to lay Hippo."

"What will you lay?" I said.

"I'll lay you six to one Jiggling Boy," he said.

"Then make it Jiggling Boy by all means." I handed him my money and took his ticket. I knew that in story-books it would happen that I could not get rid of my money and that the money I put on the horses would be returned to me as winnings, but I found no difficulty in discovering horses that could not win.

To my annoyance, however, I found that I had achieved the result which I was most anxious to avoid. I had attracted attention, and when the last race was over I found myself the cynosure of all eyes. Men nudged one another as I passed through the wicket-gate to the long road which leads to the town and I heard them say:

"That's 'im. That's the mug," and use other admiring phrases. I, Heine, who hated and despised the so-called sport, was already famous as a gambling plunger in this home of rascality. Now, my plan was a two-fold one and all was going well. Why should I travel the country distributing forged money when I could find somebody who would do it for me? I did not know the rascals of England who received and distributed stolen notes, but I knew that they existed, as they do in all countries. I knew that once a bank is robbed, that, with almost lightning speed, the bank-notes stolen are circulated and all traces of the thief are hidden. Here, then, was the machinery for a rapid distribution before the notes began to dribble back into the Bank of England stamped "forgery" upon their faces. I was joined on the way back to the town by Pike and one of his friends.

"You had bad luck, Mister," said Pike. "But, never mind, I can make your fortune to-morrow."

I smiled, inwardly. I could make his fortune that night.

"I don't intend staying for tomorrow's horse-racing," I answered him. "I ought to go back to town. I don't think it is safe for me to carry so much money about with me."

He looked at me.

"It is very dangerous to carry a lot of money about with you, but bless you, this is a very law-abiding country, ain't it, Alf?" addressing his companion.

"Too law-abiding," said the other, a tall, dismal man with a drooping moustache.

"I can speak to you as a friend," I said to Mike, " of course I wouldn't tell anybody else."

"You can trust me," said Mike, "with your life."

"Well, I want to ask your advice," I said. "There is a notice in my bedroom saying that the landlord will not be responsible for any money stolen unless it is deposited with him. Now, do you think I am safe in trusting the proprietor of the Beacon Inn with £30,000?"

There was a long silence. Mike tried to speak twice, and when he did his voice was husky.

"Thirty thousand pounds," he said in a far-away voice; "no, I don't think I would trust the landlord in that. It isn't fair to him. So far as you've got it in a safe place, "under your bed, or somewhere —"

"Exactly," I said, "It is under my bed, speaking as a friend."

"Well, so long as it's there, leave it there," said Mike. "It's the last place anybody would think of looking."

He accompanied me to the door of my lodgings, and I was turning in when Mike said to his friend: "Look here, Alf, why don't you take this gentleman and show him round the town. It's worth seeing. There are some regular old antiquities here."

"With pleasure," I said, "if your friend does not object. And you will accompany us?"

"I've got to see a man in here," he said, pointing to my inn; "but I'll see you later."

For the next hour, under the guidance of the unhappy Alf, I walked about Newmarket listening to my guide. Several times I pretended that I wanted to go back to the hotel, but each time be prevented me on some excuse or other. And all the time I was chuckling. I knew the friend that Mike wanted to see was a certain battered portmanteau under my bed filled with wonderful treasure. By this time he would have caught the train and would be on his way to London where his companion would join him later. When at last I reached the inn, I paused out of curiosity to ask the landlord if anybody had been for me. As I expected, a gentleman had called and had gone upstairs saying that he had come by invitation.

I walked up to my room, smiling broadly. I pulled the bag from under the bed, that bag which had been a source of such bother and worry, and back quivering, I pulled it out. As I expected it was empty save for one thick packet of notes which as they were wrapped in paper had evidently been left behind by the thief under the impression that it was some of my personal belongings.

I cursed him for his carelessness slipped the packet into my pocket, and taking my few belongings I went downstairs gaily, paid the bill, this time with genuine money from my own pocket-book, and drove to the station. I could have sworn I saw Alf in one of the carriages as I passed, but he turned his face away quickly. Be not afraid my poor fellow! Didst thou but know, thou and thy sneak-thief companion are unconscious instruments of vengeance working the will of the Fatherland upon this perfidious and mercenary England.

Fortunately I had the carriage to myself and was able to get rid of the bag through the window choosing the moment when we were crossing a small river for hiding the evidence.

I reached Liverpool Street Station at 9:20 feeling very hungry. There were no taxi-cabs procurable and I went to the station buffet to get a sandwich and a glass of beer. I saw no sign of Alf, or of his thievish companion, and as a matter of fact, I did not have the curiosity to look for them. It was sufficient that I, Heine, had, by my tactics, distributed $60,000 worth of counterfeit coin for the glory of the Fatherland.

What was the object you may ask? Why all this trouble? Cannot you see that whether it were true or merely a rumour, that there was a great amount of forged notes in circulation, that the credit of England at home and abroad would suffer, that people would be loth to accept paper money, and that confidence, which is the basis of exchange, would be destroyed? Truly we Germans are great psychologists and understand the devious arts of making war ruthlessly.

I resolved to call upon the illustrious Captain Baron von Hazfeld on the following morning, and explain to him that my mission had been accomplished. After that I might turn my attention to the Bolsheviks, and try to discover what their little game was. I had had no time to think about them or to puzzle my brains about the mysterious Ivanoff, but now that my mission was accomplished, I could devote more time and attention to that matter.

I stood outside the station waiting for an omnibus or perchance, I thought, I might have the luck to find a taxi, when a poorly dressed man who seemed to know what I was thinking about, came to me and said:

"Are you looking for a taxi, sir?"

"Yes," I replied.

"You will find one round the corner," he said. "I'll show you the way." He led me along the ill-lighted street into a deserted thoroughfare, which led, I believe, into Finsbury Square. There were no lights and there was no sign of a taxi-cab.

"It's round the corner, sir," said the man again. I had opened my mouth to speak when suddenly a sack was thrown over my head. I struggled, but I knew I was in the grip of two or three men. Then I had been detected. Oh! the wild thoughts that coursed through my brain I heard a voice say something, and to my amazement it was in German.

I was lifted bodily from my feet and pushed into what I knew was the interior of a motor-car, I heard the door slammed, and presently the car moved. We had been travelling for twenty minutes when it stopped, the door was again opened and I was bundled out through a doorway down some stone stairs, led and pushed along a passage and through another doorway. I heard the doors closed and locked, and then the sack was removed from my head. I was in a room about twenty feet square, and there were about ten people present, They were foreign- looking men and knew instinctively that the majority of them were Russians. As the sack was whisked from my head a man, whom I recognized as Missovitch, said: "That is the man."

"What is the meaning of this outrage?" I demanded.

"Sit down, Heine," said an imperious voice. Such an evening of surprises, for the man who spoke was none other than the illustrious Captain Baron von Hazfeld!

"Herr Baron," I stammered.

"Are you sure this is the man?" asked the Baron, turning to Missovitch.

"Absolutely certain. I saw him take the bag."

"Then," said the Baron, "there will be no difficulty in recovering the money. There was probably some mistake. Now Heine," he said more kindly than usual, "this gentleman," pointing to a tall man with a red beard who was scowling at me, "is Herr Loski."

I bowed.

"I am delighted to meet you," I said.

"You were instructed by me last Thursday week to wait at a station," said the Baron, "you were told to meet a messenger who was bringing a bag of forged notes — I can speak freely before you, gentlemen. That man arrived," he went on, turning to me, "but you were not there to meet him."

"Pardon me, Herr Baron," I said with a smile, "I not only met him but—"

"Wait," said the Baron, "the man you met was one of M. Loski's companions, who brought £65,000 to this country which had been stolen from the Bank of Petrograd. When I say stolen I should say," he said, with a bow to Herr Loski, "expropriated. Knowing that the English agent of the bank, M. Alexis Ivanoff, had procured a police warrant to arrest M. Loski, should the money be found in his possession, Herr Loski employed another gentleman to take the bag direct to M. Missovitch. Unfortunately he mistook you for M. Missovitch, and the bag containing £65,000 (English) passed into your possession. Where is the money?"

The room was swimming around me. It seemed like a horrible dream. For two weeks I had been engaged in getting rid of that money. I had bought impossible things which I had never handled. I had gambled thousands on horses which could never win, and finally I had deliberately tempted a thief to steal it.

"Where is that money?" said the Baron again. I drew myself erect. "It is spent," I said. When silence fell again, when everybody had stopped talking and crying and waving their hands, the Baron spoke.

"You know Major Haynes?" he asked.

"Yes," I said.

"You went to his club the night before you left London?"

"Yes," I admitted.

"You are accused of having betrayed the secrets of our Department."

"Whoever accuses me of that," I cried indignantly, "is a liar."

"I accuse you," thundered the Baron.

"Then you are a liar," I said. God knows how I mustered up the courage to speak so to one so illustrious, but I did this in my virtuous innocence. The Baron turned to the man called Loski. "My Government will see that you are repaid," he said; "as to this traitor, I think, gentlemen, for your own protection there is only one thing to be done. This man was an agent of ours, but is no longer in our service. He is in communication with the English Intelligence Department, and what that means to us all, you know."

The man called Missovitch bent forward eagerly and spoke in a low tone and the Baron von Hazfeld nodded. Missovitch said something in Russian and I was instantly seized and thrown into a chair, my hands pulled behind and handcuffed. Missovitch took off his coat and took from his pocket a red cord which I watched with a fascinated stare.

I remember it looked like one of those bell-pull you see in old English houses, without the tassel. He stepped behind me and I knew rather than saw, that he was making a slip-knot.

In those few ghastly moments I could not think clearly. I could not pray, I could not scream. I could only sit open-mouthed staring at the sneering face of one who called himself a German, and yet could watch a fellow-countryman at die hands of the barbarian.

"If you have anything to say, Heine, now is your time," said the Baron.

I drew a long breath.

"I hope that Germany is beaten,'" I said, "and that swine like you will black the boots of the Englishmen."

I had hardly finished speaking before the cord was pulled round my neck. I felt the foot of Missovitch on the back of the chair behind me as he prepared to take his grip. From where I sat I could see the door, the key within it, and I could have sworn that I saw the key turning as though some invisible hand on the outside was gripping its end.

The cord tightened with a jerk, strangling the cry in my throat. I felt a tremendous pressure of blood, a horrible, unbearable sense of suffocation, and then:

"Hands up, everybody!"

The cord relaxed. I stared at the doorway and there stood Major Hayes, revolver in hand, and behind him I saw the red caps of the military police.

For a fortnight I lay prostrate in bed and saw nobody but Major Haynes, who visited me occasionally.

He told me he had secured me a passport and a berth to America, and also informed me that the ship was one of a convoy. When I was up and well, and two days before I left, He came to see me.

"You're going back to America, Heine, and. the American police have been informed of your little weakness. But you are going to have a square deal and, unless you misbehave yourself, you will not be interfered with."

"I have had enough, Major Haynes," I said, "I'm through."

He nodded.

"I don't think you know the thing you have been risking, Heine." For the first time he spoke very seriously, without any of the facetiousness which was his peculiar métier. "You think it is an exciting game and a clever game, but I am going to guarantee that you will never engage in espionage work again. I am going to send you back to the United States, cured. I want you to stay the night at an hotel. I am going to get you up very early to-morrow morning. Don't be afraid, I 'm not going to ask you to do anything for me," he smiled. "You are ready for the voyage?"

"Yes, Major Haynes," I said. "The boat train leaves at ten o'clock to-morrow morning," he said, "but I shall want to see you before that; in fact, I shall call at your hotel at five o'clock."

I did not know what he was driving at, but I made no objection. As how could I? With my passport and steamboat ticket in my pocket and my trunk packed, I arrived at the little city hotel which he had chosen, and at five o'clock on the following morning I was awakened and found him standing beside my bed.

I got up and dressed, had a cup of coffee and some biscuits, and leaving my bag behind, I went out with him into the deserted streets. His car was waiting and we drove through the city to a large building, which I recognized, passed under a vaulted archway, and the car stopped in a courtyard.

There was a solemn hush on the world. We heard nothing but the sound of birds singing. The old trees were dressed in the vivid green of spring and in my heart was a greater solemnity than I had ever felt.

Major Haynes looked at his watch and led me to a large bare room. There were eight soldiers there, standing in a line, their rifles at the rest. At the other end of the room was a chair. We took our place behind the soldiers, and a little to the side, and presently we heard steps, and two soldiers entered and between them dressed in his shirt and trousers was Captain Baron von Hazfeld, his face grey, his eyes downcast. They sat him on the chair and strapped his hands, and the eight rifles came up together as if by machinery. I shut my eyes and closed my ears.

Five seconds later I was in the open air again. I had seen the figure in the chair limp and bloody and I wanted to see no more.

The Major drove me back to the hotel and, standing on the pavement, he shook hands with me.

"War," said he sadly, "is a pitiful business, Heine. Do you think you will catch your train?"

"Major Haynes," I said, "if you will be kind enough to drive me to the station now I shall be glad to wait on the platform until it comes in."

www.ingramcontent.com/pod-product-compliance
Lightning Source LLC
Chambersburg PA
CBHW051249170626
46809CB00004B/1564